PRAISE FOR

MW00857243

Advance Praise for *Falls to Pieces*

"*Falls to Pieces* twists and turns at breakneck speed in its exploration of parental devotion, the secrets kept by those we love, and the lengths some people go to in order to escape the past."

—Riley Sager, *New York Times* bestselling author of *Middle of the Night*

Praise for *The Rough Cut*

"A sharply plotted legal drama with a double-barreled climax."

—*Kirkus Reviews*

"Another winner from this accomplished mystery writer."

—*Booklist*

"Clever, witty . . . Corleone offers a thoughtful look at how easily the legal system and the media can be manipulated."

—*Publishers Weekly*

Praise for *Robert Ludlum's The Janson Equation*

"[Corleone] is a perfect choice to pen the latest in the Janson series . . . [he's] a first-class storyteller, and he brings a jolt of energy to this series and a step up to the Ludlum brand."

—*Booklist*

"Corleone keeps the story bouncing along in true Ludlum style, surprising and confounding at every turn, and steering confidently to a satisfying ending."

—*BN Reads*, June's Top Picks in Thrillers

Praise for *Good as Gone*

"[A] heart-wrenching, adrenaline-producing adventure that . . . leaves the reader gasping for breath at the end."

—*Huffington Post*

"Once the story kicks into high gear, which is pretty much at the top of page 2, it doesn't let up, period."

—*Booklist* (starred review)

"A torrid chase . . . *Good as Gone* leaves you with the deep, uncomplicated pleasure of watching a skilled professional kick major ass."

—*Kirkus Reviews*

"An adrenaline rush."

—*Publishers Weekly*

"*Good as Gone* is everything I want in a thriller—an ingenious plot, breathless pace, and one of the coolest new heroes to come along in years. My only question is, when can I read the next Simon Fisk thriller?"

—David Ellis, *New York Times* bestselling author of *Look Closer*

"*Good as Gone* delivers a lightning-fast pace, surprising and heartfelt twists, and action aplenty."

—Jeff Abbott, *New York Times* bestselling author of *An Ambush of Widows*

"*Good as Gone* is as good as it gets. Simon Fisk is a fascinating character, and Douglas Corleone has crafted one hell of a thriller. It is a pleasure to recommend this nonstop novel to my readers."

—Michael Palmer, *New York Times* bestselling author of
A Heartbeat Away

"A terrific international thriller. I expected to be entertained when I picked up a novel by Douglas Corleone and was rewarded handsomely. Highly recommended."

—James Grippando, *New York Times* bestselling author of
Goodbye Girl

"*Good as Gone* goes from zero to sixty in under six seconds and never lets off the gas! If you like your thrillers filled with nonstop action in a race against time through Europe's underbelly, hop in and take a ride."

—Andrew Gross, *New York Times* bestselling author of *15 Seconds*

"*Good as Gone* is the can't-put-it-down thriller of the year that propels Douglas Corleone into Lee Child territory. Yeah, it's that good."

—Jason Starr, international bestselling author of *The Next Time I Die*

Praise for *Payoff*

"A lean, mean pedal-to-the-metal thriller. The novel accelerates to high speed almost immediately and doesn't slow down until the book is finished. Another winner."

—*Booklist*

"If James Bond were in the business of rescuing kidnapped children, he might easily be mistaken for Simon Fisk . . . a character worth rooting for."

—*Publishers Weekly*

Praise for *Gone Cold*

"A heart-pounding third installment . . . In this unstoppable page-turner with its wicked humor, detailed settings, and action-packed scenes, Corleone keeps you on the edge of your seat."

—*Honolulu Star-Advertiser*

"Corleone's prose is lean, his plotting tight, and his characters vividly drawn. [Simon] Fisk is one of the more interesting series leads in the contemporary thriller genre."

—*Booklist*

Praise for *Beyond Gone*

"[A] blend of action and suspense fueled by well-placed surprises."

—*Kirkus Reviews*

Praise for *One Man's Paradise*

"Fans of John Grisham, Lisa Scottoline, and other legal thriller authors will enjoy this for the sheer pleasure of seeing a master defense attorney at work in the courtroom."

—*Library Journal*

"This novel won the Minotaur Books/Mystery Writers of America First Crime Novel Award, and it's no wonder. Former defense lawyer Corleone has created a crafty and memorable character and placed him in a suspenseful and layered story . . . A sequel to this fine debut would seem almost mandatory."

—*Booklist*

Praise for *Night on Fire*

"Douglas Corleone . . . follows his auspicious debut (*One Man's Paradise*) with an equally enjoyable successor."

—*San Diego Union-Tribune*

"Douglas Corleone's second look at the seedy side of life, lawyering, and untimely death on Oahu in the twenty-first century . . . is a page-turner in the best sense of the word."

—*Honolulu Star-Advertiser*

"Kevin [Corvelli] tries a mean case and tells a fine story."

—*Kirkus Reviews*

"The John Grisham–style twists and turns and cinematic courtroom scenes keep the pages turning."

—*Library Journal*

Praise for *Last Lawyer Standing*

"Corvelli is a likable, pill-popping lawyer, and the secondary characters are Elmore Leonard quirky."

—*Booklist*

"More plot twists than you can shake a stick at."

—*Kirkus Reviews*

FALLS
TO
PIECES

OTHER TITLES BY DOUGLAS CORLEONE

FALLS TO PIECES

TO

PIECES

DOUGLAS CORLEONE

THOMAS & MERCER

Text copyright © 2025 by Douglas Corleone
All rights reserved.

Published by Thomas & Mercer, Seattle

www.apub.com

Amazon, the Amazon logo, and Thomas & Mercer are trademarks of Amazon.com, Inc., or its affiliates.

ISBN-13: 9781662522062 (paperback)
ISBN-13: 9781662522079 (digital)

Cover design by Ploy Siripant
Cover image: © Allan Wood Photography / Shutterstock

Printed in the United States of America

For Dotty Baker Morefield,
with love and gratitude.

Paradise is only safe in designated places.

PART I

The Road to Hana

Zoe

Eddie's gone missing and Mom is a mess. I hate knowing she's in such agony. Each minute that passes without news cracks my heart a little more, despite our marathon battles, despite our endless war. She's as terrified and anxious as the day we ran away from home. I'm afraid this time she's going to lose it.

I know it's been months since I last spoke to you but only because I need to keep you hidden. If Mom knew I kept you, she'd kill me. But you're my only true friend. Certainly the only one I can speak to. If I don't get these thoughts out of my head, I'll go as batty and erratic as she has.

Poor Mom. The paranoia, the confusion, the forgetfulness. Still, she flat out refuses to see a therapist. Even Eddie can't talk her into it, and he can talk her into virtually anything.

I miss Eddie already, so I can't imagine what hell Mom's going through. I expected her to finally turn to me, but she's called only once in the past ten hours—just once to tell me Eddie went missing. I've tried calling her every half hour. She keeps sending my calls to voicemail. She's not returning my texts.

I intend to be there for her. She's my mom. Part of me is angry at her—all right, hates her—but another part loves her to death. I wish things could be different. I wish she could be different. But it's almost as if she's embracing her paranoia, as if she's welcoming oblivion. Which, I suppose, shouldn't be too shocking given the past. The past she wants to forget. The past she insists I forget.

Hopefully, Eddie will be found quickly. I think Mom's greatest fear is that he'll never be found at all. I can't say I blame her. If something happened to the love of my life . . .

Shit, it's late AF and getting dark. They're probably suspending the search for the day. Mom could be home any moment.

Time for you to return to your hiding spot.

1

Day One

We're fast losing the light—and with it any hope of finding Eddie alive in the first twenty-four hours of his disappearance.

As the helicopter circles over the southeastern tip of Maui one final time, I feel as though I'm outside myself. My essence, my consciousness, has slipped its shell and now floats thousands of feet above the bamboo forest in search of an existence that was never truly mine.

I've not eaten a bite since my salad last night, yet I feel guilty for even *thinking* about food as we surrender to the creeping darkness and suspend the search for the day. Because if Eddie is still alive, whether on his feet or writhing in the muck with multiple fractures, we've now doomed him to spend the next twelve hours alone, in the ink, without sustenance.

Even if he's fortunate enough to have remained upright and unharmed, he'll have nothing to drink but water from a stream possibly ridden with the bacteria that causes leptospirosis, a fatal infectious disease that culminates with painful bleeding in the lungs. If he's dehydrated, he'll have no choice but to break the first lesson of Hawaii Hiking 101: *Don't drink the water.*

If he's starving—*and damn me for limiting him to lugging a single small bag of flaxseed crackers so as not to spoil his appetite for . . .*

In the distance, a small plane lifting off from Hana Airport fades into the clouds.

And I've lost my train of thought. Something that's been happening frequently over the past several hours. But no, the notion boomerangs back and strikes me squarely between the eyes: If he's missing for days and starving, Eddie will be forced to survive on unidentified and potentially poisonous plants. If he's mobile and in the right area, perhaps he can find wild raspberries and strawberry guavas. However, he's much more likely to be reduced to eating the occasional gecko and however many moths land on him over the dark hours. In my head, I grasp for one of those reality shows Zoe's been watching since we moved to the islands. Shows with names like *Naked and Afraid*, *Man vs. Wild*, and *Dude, You're Screwed* on the Discovery Channel.

". . . landing area, Ms. Dawes?"

The helicopter pilot is speaking to me. I hear his voice through the headphones but can no more decipher his words than those of an adult in a *Peanuts* cartoon.

But it's clear. We're descending. And it's not only us.

The setting sun means the Dolphin copter, too, is calling it a day, returning to the coast guard air station at Barbers Point on the neighboring island of Oahu. The coast guard cutter, the Maui fire department, even the fearless volunteers of Maui Search and Rescue are returning to their respective bases of operation for the night.

One more day like today, maybe two, and then official agencies will begin one by one to bow out of the search, formally calling it off and withdrawing resources. They'll presume my de facto fiancé dead and close the files. At least those files pertaining to the rescue efforts. The criminal investigation, on the other hand, that started with my hysterical 9-1-1 call this morning will continue indefinitely.

The police will presume one of two things: tragic accident or foul play. And if they discover I am not who I say I am, they'll certainly lean toward the latter. Should they learn my true identity, they'll no doubt charge me based solely on the circumstantial evidence already in hand.

But none of that matters right now, does it?

All that matters is Eddie. Finding him alive and ambulatory, with no more than minor injuries treatable by some nurse practitioner at the Hana Health clinic. Eddie is *all* that matters.

At least for the time being.

On the ground, in the gust from the propellers, I'm intercepted by plainclothes special agents Alana Lui and Chris Harris of the Investigative Services Branch of the National Park Service. In other words, feds—park rangers with the same powers as the FBI, DEA, and ATF. They want another statement on record. Now, "while things remain fresh in your head," they say. What they *mean* is now that you're still in shock, now that you've been knocked stupid by exhaustion, now that you're famished, now that you're parched, now that you'll slip up, lie for the sake of lying, say anything just to earn a can of Diet Coke and a KitKat from the vending machine.

On a brief but twisting ride in the agents' four-wheel-drive SUV, we ascend seven thousand feet up Haleakala Crater to the park ranger station at the visitor center. I'm immediately deposited in a small, windowless room, where I sit with a video camera pointed at me. I'm tempted, *so* tempted, to tell them I want my lawyer, but I stop myself. No one has said outright that they suspect me of anything. Requesting a lawyer while a loved one remains missing may be the smart thing to do—but not the *right* thing. Not in the eyes of the investigators, not in the eyes of the local media, and certainly not in the eyes of a concerned public.

I can't allow anyone to snap a photo of me.

My God, has someone taken one already?

I fish my phone out of my pocket. The battery is nearly dead. I can't access the internet sealed in this concrete tomb. I have no way of knowing what news is already out there. Whether some journalist or even a quick-thinking tourist snapped a shot of me and sent it to KITV or KGMB or to some blogger with arthritic fingers and far too much time on her hands.

The door opens. Special Agents Lui and Harris step inside and seal it behind them. I shove my phone back into my shorts pocket and scratch at a rash of mosquito bites on my thigh, catching an unfortunate whiff of myself as I do. *Good.* Hopefully, the agents will speed things up just to get out of the room.

"We'd just like to go over what happened one more time," Lui says, "to make sure we didn't miss anything, that we're searching in all the right areas."

How good of you.

Unfortunately, I've been in this sort of room before. I have waived my rights, believed their lies, blurted things I wished I could repudiate ten minutes later. I know their game, yet I have no choice but to play it. To play it again, that is.

"Let's return to last night," Lui says, brushing back a lock of hair that's far too soft and shiny for this climate. After two years in the islands, my hair looks like I just removed my finger from a light socket. Even Zoe's silky tresses have become a bit lackluster in recent months.

"All right," I say. "Let's."

Harris's frown suggests I just uttered the same gung ho refrain they hear from all their guiltiest suspects. Lui, meanwhile, remains perfectly poker faced. Though petite, she's intimidating with fierce, intelligent eyes, while Harris is pale and tall and lean and looks like a good trade wind would blow him off a cliff. I'd probably like both agents under any other circumstances. But not these.

"Dinner last night," Lui says, "it was just you and Eddie?"

"And my daughter, Zoe."

"She's seventeen?"

"She is."

"Her date of birth?"

Here's where things could get a bit tricky.

An hour later the interview is over. I've recounted my lies which, for the most part, Harris swallowed whole. I couldn't get such a good read on Special Agent Lui.

I can't let them fingerprint me.

Sipping from the lukewarm cup of stale coffee in front of me, I sit alone in the humid, claustrophobic room and wait. They said "just a few minutes," but they're giving me a good sweat now, and what choice do I have but to wait them out? Even if I decided to retain counsel, who would I call? Eddie is my attorney. His partner Noah Walker hardly knows me and may well think I'm responsible for Eddie going missing.

I wouldn't blame him.

I met Eddie eighteen months ago. At that time Zoe and I had been living in Hana for only six months. But they were six *long* months—months spent supervising the construction of our small custom-made home with its unique blend of frontier and futuristic features, including solar panels, a water catchment system, and the much-maligned composting toilet. For six months we remained as isolated as we could, the only faces we'd see belonging to Mac's "official contractor" and his band of not-so-merry men who travel to some of the most remote places on earth to erect sub-rosa structures for professional malefactors, doomsday preppers, and paranoid wives in hiding like myself.

Suffice to say, after six months we *needed* to see other human beings, even if only in a zoo-like setting where we'd be required to keep our distance, content to merely observe. So we ventured for the first time a few miles from our new abode to the only touristy refuge on this side of the island—the Hana Hills resort. Hidey-hole of drying-out CEOs, young actors in trouble with the law, and pop stars on the brink of nervous breakdowns.

There we surrendered to our need for human interaction and mingled with a coterie of locals, including a pair of lawyers who'd just returned from Honolulu after winning a multimillion-dollar verdict against the Lanyon shipping company. Before heading out, Zoe and I agreed not to get too friendly with anyone, not to divulge any information about our current selves, let alone our past lives. But somehow, an attractive Native Hawaiian attorney with broad shoulders and a weatherman's smile captured my full attention. And a half dozen royal mai tais later, took me to his bed, while Zoe got a ride home from his partner Noah.

It was the first time in six months I'd been separated from Zoe for more than a few minutes. Thanks to a hidden Wi-Fi network, she completed her junior year of high school through distance learning. I earned a modest living working from home, writing content for the internet (some of which was fascinating but most of which was leap-from-a-tall-building tedious). The next morning, when I woke in a strange room in an unfamiliar house, I panicked and ran. As far as Eddie Akana knew, my daughter and I were tourists from Providence, Rhode Island, here in Hana for some R & R before Zoe's final year of high school. I never expected to see him again, never mind commence a long-term relationship. But the counselor-at-law proved more resourceful than expected. He tracked me down three weeks later at our supposedly supersecret house on the most secluded road in Hana.

Two nights after that, Zoe and I accepted an invitation to his place for a private dinner. Over the next few weeks, many similar visits followed. While Zoe merrily swam laps in his Olympic-size pool, Eddie and I did what the kids call "Netflix and chill." Before I had even contemplated the idea, I found I'd fallen deeply in love with him. Months later, when Eddie Akana unexpectedly popped the question, I cried out *yes*. Conveniently forgetting the trifling fact that I was—and still am—already married.

Finally, after nearly another hour, the door opens—and *stays* open. Special Agent Harris ushers me through the station, which is small and undoubtedly more cramped than usual given all the activity related to the search. Hana itself is ordinarily a sleepy town. In the two years Zoe and I have lived in East Maui, we've rarely encountered law enforcement at all. The few police on patrol have their hands full with obstinate tourists, mostly full-grown adults behaving like truculent teenagers, flouting the rules of the road and the hundreds of warning signs posted all around. This is private property. Beware of mudslides and flash floods and rock falls. Stay *off* the crags; stones are slippery when wet, and falls *do* result in fatalities. Stay *on* the trail at all times, because wandering off for even a few minutes could turn you around and soon get you lost in the wilderness.

Paradise is only safe in designated places.

Sometimes not even in those.

Outside, Harris wordlessly escorts me to another government vehicle. During the brief ride home, a young uniformed park ranger, who reminds me of our driver Dmitri back east, blathers the entire time.

"Everyone will be back at it at first light," he says. "Try to get some sleep tonight. You'll want to have your head in the morning."

I mumble something like *all right*.

"They do find people," he says, "even the second or third day they're missing. After that, well . . ." He glances at me in the rearview; he even has Dmitri's striking green eyes and neatly pressed shirt, the import of a tidy appearance drilled into the young Romanian while briefly serving in the French Foreign Legion. "Then again, a few years back, they found a lost hiker alive after seventeen days in the jungle. Aside from a broken leg, a few scrapes and bruises, and a third-degree sunburn, she was fine. Filthy and malnourished, of course. But thrilled to be alive."

"I heard about her," I say, hoping that will end the conversation.

It doesn't.

"That was up north," he says, "in the Makawao Forest Reserve. Ever hiked up there?" He doesn't wait for my answer. "A couple thousand acres of pure wilderness. Dense rainforest, steep ravines, falling lava rocks, and enough green that you can't see three feet ahead of you without a machete."

Mercifully, he pulls onto our road and rolls to a stop in front of our house.

"Off the grid?" he says.

I nod as I open the rear door and step out. He says something else, but I've already swung the door closed and started up the walk. The kitchen is lit, which means Zoe's home. I could not be more grateful. I don't want to be around more strangers today, least of all police, but I don't want to be alone either. I'm shaking; I need to be held, even if only for a moment.

"No luck?" Zoe says, crestfallen.

I shake my head and wrap my arms around her. Our hugs have become such a rarity that I allow myself to cherish this one despite the insufferable circumstances. As Zoe's warm tears blend with my sweat, I suddenly miss our home back east, an address we've both needed to forget entirely.

Despite our ongoing squabbles, Zoe is anxious to help. She's spread out a large map of Haleakala National Park on the kitchen table. Circled on the map is the Pipiwai Trail, where Eddie and I had started out early this morning. Only sixteen hours ago, yet a lifetime has passed since our sunrise hike for which we missed breakfast. It was the first night he'd ever stayed over; usually we sleep at his place, while Zoe slumbers soundly in Eddie's guest bedroom.

"I can't even look at this map right now," I say, surprising myself. "I feel like I'm going to be sick."

Zoe nods her understanding. "Go lie down," she tells me with a peck on the cheek. "I'll bring you whatever you need."

Oh, Eddie. If this is some wild stunt to mend the widening rift between me and Zoe, it's so far working like a charm.

If only.

"Thanks," I say, gently pulling away, "but first a quick shower before this reek on me becomes permanent."

When I finally fall asleep, after a handful of Advil and a token Ambien, I dream that Jeremy found us. In the dream, it proved inevitable. With Eddie (or his remains) unfound, the police started looking at me more closely. The media moved in. Pictures were taken, fingerprints surrendered. In dreamland, it couldn't be helped. I was at the mercy of the torturous circumstances of my own making.

My first desperate thought when I wake is that in the two years since we moved here, I've followed at least four cases of hikers who have gone missing in either Haleakala or on some forbidden trail off the world-famous Road to Hana. Two were discovered dead, one from California, another from New Mexico. Two others—one Maui resident and one Canadian tourist—were never found at all. That, to me, is the most terrifying outcome of any—never knowing what happened to Eddie after we separated near the spur trail leading to the top of the falls.

The idea sickens me. I nearly vomit when I glance at my phone and find it's just past midnight. I've dozed for two or three hours at most and feel too wired to make a second attempt at sleep. Though Ambien rarely fails me, tonight the pill hardly worked at all.

Too much adrenaline.

Now all I can do is sit and wait the agonizing six hours until sunup, when the search will resume regardless of how tired I am. I move to the living room couch, where images from the day blend into an abstract collage. I glimpse Eddie and myself starting up the trail with our light-weight packs and my trekking pole, see us crossing Oheo Bridge, watch myself gazing at the ancient-looking banyan tree a mile into the hike. But the fog of my memory is even thicker than the mist present this morning. Soon I've lost sight of Eddie, and I'm searching and searching, debating whether to call emergency services or continue looking on my own. Finally, I'm calling, listening to the soothing voice of a female operator who has me calmly describe my location and then remains on the phone until help arrives.

Dazed, I go to my bookshelf and scan the spines for an escape. Staring back at me, however, are dozens of murder mysteries, legal thrillers, and police procedurals. *Damn my reading tastes.* And damn Zoe for inheriting them.

Minutes later, I sink back into the sofa and reach for the remote control, which is mercifully button-side up—a powerfully reassuring reminder that it (and I) are presently out of Jeremy's reach. I punch the power button and immediately wish I hadn't. Because there on the screen on the local NBC affiliate is a photo of Eddie Akana—with his arm around a thirty-eight-year-old Hana woman, ostensibly named "Kati Dawes." The image is a candid shot from a recent barbecue we attended. Though my face is turned toward the photographer, I appear to be too intoxicated to even realize some random partygoer is capturing a Kodak moment.

2

Following breakfast, which for me consists of a tall glass of Lipton iced tea, Zoe and I depart for the park. At dawn we reach the trailhead, where we meet a gruff, balding man sporting a thin goatee and stubbled skull. Wearing an official-looking white polo and khakis, he's clearly from some state or county agency. He's tanned, muscled, and early middle-aged; ten to one he recently rose from a physical job to a desk position—and he's already wondering why the hell he ever coveted the promotion in the first place.

"Graham Gephardt," he says, "Maui County Ocean Safety."

In the post-COVID world, no one has yet returned to shaking hands, so I simply nod in acknowledgment. "Kati Dawes," I say, "and this is my daughter, Zoe. Yesterday I was told your agency would only be contributing a single Jet Ski operator."

"He'll be out there again today. I'm just here to coordinate information so that we can make the most efficient use of our resources as possible."

"Should we wait for the other agencies?"

"They'll catch up. Let's take advantage of the sunrise and silence."

I detect a slight southwestern twang; my best guess would be West Texas. But I've permanently barred myself from initiating the "Where you from?" game (*big* among mainlanders who move to the islands). If pressed into it, I occasionally allow the East Coast. If pressed further than that, I lie.

Minutes later, the three of us are winding our way uphill along the edge of the Pipiwai Stream. My heart sinks into my stomach as I imagine Eddie getting knocked off his feet, dragged under by the current, and painfully drowning in a flash flood.

"Any other people on the trail yesterday morning when you started out?" Graham asks.

"A few early risers. Not many."

"Anyone you recognized?"

"No."

"Anyone Eddie recognized?"

"Not that I know of."

The Pipiwai Trail is considered only moderately strenuous, rising to an elevation of less than eight hundred feet, making Eddie's disappearance all the more vexing. The trail is one of the most scenic the island has to offer. And consequently one of the most popular. On previous treks, Zoe and I have passed children and seniors, none of whom appeared to be winded or otherwise distressed.

Which isn't to say there aren't dangers—there most certainly are. But the vast majority of those hazards are highlighted by bright red signage. In spots where fatalities have occurred, the National Park Service spells it out: DEFYING SAFETY GUIDANCE MAY RESULT IN CATASTROPHIC INJURY OR DEATH. PROCEED AT YOUR OWN RISK.

Zoe suddenly slaps her arm, startling me. "I forgot bug spray," she says.

Graham slips his hand into a concealed fanny pack and retrieves a travel-size bottle of Off!. He tosses it to Zoe, who proceeds to spray her arms and legs before starting on mine as well. Though I'm grateful for the sweet gesture, the odor, even outdoors, is dizzying with my empty stomach.

Less than a mile into the trek, we come to the overlook that faces Makahiku Falls, a two-hundred-foot horsetail waterfall.

"This is where we were when Eddie received his call," I say.

"Any idea who called him?"

"Just that it was a client. He stopped walking, said he needed some privacy. He answered and motioned for me to keep moving. Mouthed something to the effect of 'I'll catch up.'"

"He was standing still when you left him?"

"He was pacing, as he always does on business calls."

Graham nods without looking at me. "Before we speculate on his movements, let's continue with yours."

"Why hers?" Zoe says a bit too defensively.

"Because Eddie was supposed to catch up with her. His movements should reflect hers, unless and until something distracted—or someone accosted—him on the way."

We continue along the trail, moving swiftly. We pass the hidden lava tube in which Eddie and I once stashed our packs to hike to a secret waterfall where we shed our clothes and skinny-dipped.

We pass through a gate and soon come upon the many-tentacled banyan tree that marks the entrance to yet another secret trail, currently closed by the National Park Service due to a fatal incident involving a ten-year-old girl. Something to do with a rockfall.

After crossing two bridges over the stream we've been hugging, we enter the lush bamboo forest. As we voyage in silence, the clack of the swaying thirty-foot bamboo canes sounds like soft music, wooden wind chimes caught on a light breeze.

"Bamboo is actually a type of grass," Eddie had said to me the first time we passed through here. "I know," I told him so that I didn't sound stupid (but the truth is, I had utterly no idea and was sure he suspected as much).

Zoe grabs a cane of bamboo to use as a walking stick and we continue upward, over a weathered boardwalk. On the way, we pass a small grove of guava and mango trees, and I feel a surge of hope that Eddie survived the night. That swell of optimism, however, is instantly overshadowed by a pang of dejection, because Eddie is nowhere near here. If he were, we'd have found him yesterday. Hell, he'd have found *us*.

A garbled transmission over Graham's walkie-talkie cuts off my thoughts. He holds the walkie to his ear, listens, then twists a knob, shutting it off. "Maui Fire just arrived at the park entrance."

"Should we go back there?" I say, hoping he'll respond in the affirmative. I've forgotten my Ativan and am on the verge of a panic attack. Despite Zoe's pacifying presence, I feel strangely alone and suddenly crave the circus atmosphere of yesterday. Especially the nearness of emergency medical personnel.

"Let's keep going," Graham says.

Near the end of the second mile, we hear the roar of Waimoku Falls, a stupendous four-hundred-foot giant that plunges down three sheer lava rock walls.

"Did anyone see you this far along the trail?"

"I passed two or three other hikers but wasn't really paying attention."

When the falls finally come into view, we stop and look up in awe, something that cannot be helped, apparently even under the most abhorrent conditions.

"How long did it take you to hike out here?"

"From the trailhead? Maybe an hour. A little over. I was moving at a quick pace."

"Any reason in particular?"

I shrug. "To work up a sweat? To make the trek feel more like exercise than a stroll."

"But Eddie was supposed to catch up with you, wasn't he?"

"I never left the trail. If he didn't catch me before the end, I should've met him on the way back."

"That was the plan?"

"There *was* no 'plan.'" I swallow hard, frustrated at betraying my irritation in front of this man, in front of any man, really. Weren't all those hellish years with Jeremy enough for one lifetime?

"All right," he says with the timbre of a despot, sweeping the area with a hawk's gaze. "Let's head back, then, shall we?"

Behind him Zoe makes an obscene gesture with her bamboo cane and, fleetingly, my eyes widen and the corners of my lips curl up in a smile.

When we reach Makahiku Falls on the return trip, we're no longer alone. Special Agents Lui and Harris huddle together, outfitted for a day of trekking. Oddly, Alana Lui appears just as intimidating in her pastel hiking getup as she did in her smart gray suit in the interrogation room. She also seems much taller. Worse, her hair looks as though she just stepped out of a salon.

"Good morning," Lui says with all the sincerity of a born politician.

I thank them for coming before introducing Zoe, who is her usual polite, charming self. A relief since I don't want it to seem as though Zoe's protecting me, despite my daughter's strong instinct to do just that.

Nothing better than a common enemy to bring together old foes.

The agents ignore Graham Gephardt, evidently not knowing or caring who he is.

"This morning," Lui says, "teams are conducting a grid search off trail. We're widening the radius since Mr. Akana could have traveled even farther last night if he's lost."

With his phone in hand, Harris looks around, nodding as if admiring his own freshly cut lawn. Suddenly, he turns to me. "*This* is where you parted ways?"

I like neither his tone nor his word choice. Nor his hiking outfit, which consists of simple earth-toned clothes with flashy and excessive branding. His metamorphosis into a hard-ass causes me to wonder whether they learned something overnight. Something about me, about *us*.

I show the agents the spot where Eddie received the call. I can pinpoint it—my memory of Eddie as he stepped away from me is as clear as the sky over the Pacific. Only, as hard as I try, I cannot *hear* him. *Because of the falls?* Who the hell called him yesterday morning? Why did he insist that I move on?

"Odd," Harris says without more.

Lui steps over to him. He shows her his phone. She removes hers from a pocket and holds it above her. "Seems there's no service up here," she announces to us all.

I retrieve my own phone. No bars whatsoever, and Eddie has the same phone, the same carrier, the same plan. This makes no sense, and I say so.

"Could he have had a second phone?" Graham chimes in. I'd all but forgotten he's here.

I shake my head, but suddenly I'm not so sure. Now I'm crushed beneath barrels of possibilities. Was he secretly seeing his ex-girlfriend from Tokyo? Or could it have been Noelle, his receptionist? Were her dirty looks (what Hawaiians call stink eye) and shade thrown in my direction more than just ordinary cattiness?

Lui holds her phone up. "Didn't you say you made your 9-1-1 call from here at the overlook?"

"I *did* make it from here." *Didn't I?* "Not sure why there's no signal now."

"Cell tower might have come down overnight," Graham suggests. "We've had high winds, high surf. Rained heavily here on the mountain."

Rained? I hadn't even considered a downpour. Would Eddie have been able to find shelter under an overhang or inside a lava tube? Only if he isn't hurt. Only if he can move.

Pursing her lips, Lui points off to the left. "Is it possible Mr. Akana hiked the spur trail to get a better look at the falls?"

"That trail's closed," I say without looking at it.

"Been closed for years," Harris cuts in. "Does that mean you never hiked it?"

I freeze, tingling with the remnant of childhood instinct to never admit you've done something wrong. "I have hiked it."

"With Mr. Akana?"

"With Eddie, yes, and once with Zoe."

Zoe lowers her eyes as if she's in the principal's office. Like mother, like daughter, I suppose.

"Let's hike up the spur trail, then," Lui says, "to make sure nothing was missed during yesterday's search."

We follow her lead.

"Did you look for him up here?" Graham asks on the way. "Before calling 9-1-1?"

"No," I blurt out. *Another damned lie—and why?* "It never crossed my mind he'd hike up here. That wasn't part of the plan." Although my memory's fuzzy, the spur trail was probably the first place I checked when I got back to the overlook and didn't find Eddie.

Graham stares at me. "Earlier you said there was no plan. You were rather emphatic."

"There wasn't really a *plan* plan," I say, frazzled again. "It's a figure of speech. I meant there was a presumed plan to hike to the end of the Pipiwai and return to the trailhead like we usually did."

Following a somewhat arduous hike (made all the more so by my mounting anxiety), we reach the end of the spur trail, which leaves us at the apex of Makahiku Falls, where a surrealness instantly overcomes me. My heart thuds, my flesh turns clammy. Dizziness and nausea hit like a tsunami.

The four others gaze longingly at the Infinity Pool. It's only 9:00 a.m., and everyone is already coated with sweat from exertion, despite the natural green canopy overhead. My sore left leg reminds me to recover my trekking pole. In the hopes that it wouldn't be stolen, I'd stashed it inside a lava tube near the overlook before searching for Eddie. *Why did I leave him in the first place? Why the hell didn't I wait?*

"Ever swim here?" Harris asks me, indicating the pool.

"A couple of times," I say.

"With Mr. Akana?"

"Once, yes."

His hands go to his hips, his brows climb up his forehead. "Pretty dangerous spot, no?"

The Infinity Pool is a superb spot for a swim when the waters are calm. But the pool does lie at the very top of Makahiku Falls, which means any flooding or strong current can wash swimmers two hundred feet down the face of the falls—and on a few occasions has done so.

"I always look toward the mountains," I tell him, half in the present, half in the memory of Eddie and myself swimming the Infinity Pool, bottomless. "If there's a single dark cloud, I don't risk it."

"Even still," he says. "During the rainy season, there are any number of flash floods." He points. "Just over that rise is a sharp bend. Most swimmers would never see it coming."

"I'm well aware of the danger," I say. "As was—" *Shit.* "As *is* Eddie."

Meanwhile, Alana Lui stands several yards away, getting friendly with Zoe. I want to break up their huddle, but Harris prattles on: "There was a heavy rainfall the night before last. There would have been flash floods yesterday morning."

"I don't doubt that," I say. "But Eddie didn't hike up here, and he certainly didn't go swimming. Can we get back to the overlook now?"

My tone causes Harris to eye me with fresh curiosity, which rapidly morphs into a look of raw suspicion. Why the hell did I say that? Why *is* this spot making me so incredibly fretful? Is there something I don't remember, something lost in the maelstrom that is my mind these days?

Harris glares again at his phone. "There *is* service up here, though, which means there's likely no cell tower down."

Could I have made the call from up here?

I stare down at the familiar sea of smooth gray stones edging the length of the Infinity Pool. Each is roughly the size of a softball but shaped more like a Frisbee.

If I called from up here, why did I tell the 9-1-1 dispatcher that I was standing at the overlook? Was I in shock, entirely unaware of my surroundings? Was I detached, outside my own body as I've felt so often in recent weeks?

Harris is about to say something more when Graham's walkie sounds off again. *Strike that.* It's Special Agent Lui's. Lui pivots away from the group to speak privately. I listen over the rush of the water spilling over the falls but hear little.

"You found what?" Lui says into the walkie.

". . . one slippah, yeah?"

"Size?"

I don't hear the response, but my heart is already lodged in my throat. Fear has settled in every millimeter of my body. I cross my arms over my chest, suddenly chilled to the bone.

Lui turns to me. "Remind me, Ms. Dawes, what was Mr. Akana wearing on his feet when you last saw him yesterday morning?"

3

Special Agent Lui fixes her gaze on my feet. "And you? You were wearing what you're wearing now? Timberland hiking boots?"

I lift my right foot to show her, inadvertently kicking mud onto Lui's crisp, clean trekking outfit. *I've been so clumsy lately.* I'm about to apologize when a young uniformed park ranger (maybe even the one who drove me home last night, the one who reminds me so much of Dmitri) hands Lui a plastic evidence bag containing a size 11 left sandal, which a firefighter fished from the water beneath the two-hundred-foot falls only minutes ago.

Lui holds up the bag. "Look familiar?"

Speechless, I bow my head. It's one of the pair of OluKai leather sandals I had bought for Eddie for his birthday a few weeks ago. Suddenly, I'm short of breath. I instinctively pat myself down for the antianxiety pills I know are back home on my nightstand.

"What does this mean?" Zoe says, evoking awkward glances all around.

Surprisingly, it's Graham who steps forward. "It only means Eddie Akana lost his shoe. Nothing more." He pronounces *Ah-kah-nah* like banana. So much for cultural sensitivity training.

Yet his answer calms even me, if only for an irrational moment. Then my heart starts racing with the speed of my thoughts. How would he have lost a sandal? How would it have ended up under the falls?

"Curious," Lui says. "Did he always wear sandals on strenuous hiking trails?"

"Moderately strenuous," I say, instantly wishing I hadn't. "But no, no, he didn't. He usually wore his boots, ones very similar to mine. We bought them together." I suddenly feel as though I'm listening to someone else speaking, someone manipulating my lips, my jaw, my tongue, my larynx. It's as if I have no control over my own voice.

"Why wasn't he wearing them yesterday?"

"He stayed at my place the night before," I mutter.

"Is that unusual?"

"We usually stay at his."

"How did you get to the park yesterday?" Harris interjects.

My eyes remain fixed on the plastic bag in Lui's hand. Could the sandal belong to someone else? Could Eddie have lost it without having had anything horrendous happen to him? Could he be—

Hands on his hips, Harris repeats the question, startling me out of my own head, a place I am spending far too much time in anyhow. "We took Eddie's Range Rover," I finally say.

"Why didn't he stop home and switch?"

"I don't know, it never came up. I suppose we were in a rush to catch the sunrise."

Lui jumps back in, making me feel like a tennis ball in a US Open match. "And the decision to go hiking was yours?"

"As I told you last night, the *idea* was mine. The decision was *ours*."

In my periphery, Harris is jotting down every word. At least it looks like that's what he's doing.

"What happens now?" Zoe says, the pale-blue pools of her eyes beginning to well.

I hate subjecting her to this after everything that happened on the mainland but remind myself that Zoe's nineteen, technically an adult. A fact she's thrown in my face during every argument since her eighteenth birthday.

"We continue looking," Graham says. "The sandal alone tells us nothing."

The doubt in Zoe's eyes mirrors my own. I briefly wonder if any of her doubt pertains to whether I had something to do with Eddie's disappearance.

Shit, shit. Double shit. Strutting toward us now is Eddie's law partner, Noah Walker. I never got the impression he likes me, but that could be because I had spent the past two decades surrounded by Jeremy's caustic friends who had already consumed generous amounts of poison about me courtesy of my loving husband and his mother.

"Hola," he says. A strange greeting given the situation. But then, Eddie would be the first to admit his partner is random (or "rando," as Zoe says). He described Noah as having the spirit of a sixties rebel who came of age in the nihilist nineties.

"Too much *pakalolo,*" Eddie once told me of his partner. *Pakalolo* being the Hawaiian word for marijuana. "Then or now?" I asked him. Eddie smiled, that big, beautiful smile that lit up the dimples on his bronzed chin and cheeks. "Both."

"Mr. Walker," Lui says with a bow of the head. Harris appears even more deferential to the attorney in the open aloha shirt.

"Agents," Noah greets them, running a reckless hand through his shaggy blond hair. If there was a book on how to look like a gnarly California surfer dude, he'd make a run for the cover.

Noah raises his brows in Graham's direction. Graham introduces himself and reaches out to shake Noah's hand. Noah grudgingly complies before reaching into his pocket and retrieving a travel-size bottle of Purell.

"It's getting a bit crowded up here," Graham says, catching the vibe. "I'm gonna get out of your hair. I've got enough info to help the county coordinate." Once I thank him, he stalks off in the direction of the trailhead, following the young ranger who delivered the sandal.

Meanwhile, I don't know whether to feel relieved or even more despondent that Noah and the detectives seem to share a rapport.

Although Walker & Akana is a general-practice law firm, Eddie primarily handles civil litigation and Noah mostly criminal cases. Has Noah dealt with the park service before? At this point, wouldn't he make a better friend than a foe?

When Noah finally acknowledges me, I jump at the opportunity. "May I speak with you in private?" I ask him.

"Sure," he says with so little enthusiasm I nearly tell him to forget it. Noah just made what I anticipate will be an uncomfortable conversation downright brutal.

Once we're alone with only the thunder of the falls to contend with, I say, "Obviously, my only concern at this point is finding Eddie. But Lui and Harris seem like they suspect me of something."

"They're just doing their job," Noah says in his usual relaxed manner. "Whether it's a missing hiker, an accident, a suicide, or something else, they'll have to write up a report and make a recommendation to the US Attorney."

Now, how to ask without asking?

"Maybe I've watched too many cop shows," I say tentatively, "but I fear innocent people sometimes get convicted of gruesome crimes they didn't commit."

"No, you're right," Noah concedes. "Mistakes are made. By cops, by lawyers, by judges, and certainly by juries." His tone suddenly shifts. "But listen, before you even ask, I should tell you that, under the circumstances, I would *not* feel comfortable stepping in as your attorney."

"I understand," I say, the heat in my cheeks betraying the lie. "But I *want* to answer their questions as openly and honestly as possible." I pause, trying to find the words; words are coming so much harder for me lately. "*Without* sacrificing my rights. If there's been some awful accident . . ."

Noah dips his head in understanding. "You're worried that while you're being helpful, the investigators will be building a case."

"Isn't that what they do?"

Noah turns his gaze away as if reading cue cards held aloft by the trees. He scrunches his features, agonizing over this monumental dilemma. "I suppose I can advise you in a limited capacity, just to keep the park service honest."

My stomach floods with relief; just now I *need* someone on my side.

"Do I hand you a dollar bill or something?"

"I'm afraid you are *vastly* miscalculating my hourly rate," he deadpans.

"I mean as a . . ." I again fumble for the words. "As a placeholder, an 'official' retainer to satisfy some legal technicality."

"Only if this gets made into a movie. Listen, I'm happy to represent you pro bono during the search. Just be aware that if evidence comes to light that conflicts me out, you'll need to retain new counsel."

He means if evidence leads him to believe I caused Eddie's disappearance.

"Mahalo," I say.

"You're welcome." He scratches the back of his head and sighs deeply. "Now that I'm your attorney, Ms. Dawes, I actually have one or three questions for you myself."

Sitting silently with Zoe, waiting for Noah in a sunlit conference room at Walker & Akana, I blush at the memory of Eddie taking me on this long mahogany tabletop just weeks ago. At the moment, losing him is too appalling an idea to even contemplate. There is simply no way to brace myself for it. Somehow I, an avowed pessimist, must remain optimistic for the duration of the search. Otherwise, I'll soon be tearing my hair out.

"I spoke to Eddie's mom on Oahu," Noah says gently as he enters. "His cousins are hopping a flight to Kahului today."

Veiling my concern that they'll only contribute to my problems, I thank him for reaching out to them. Trouble is, I've never met any of

Eddie's family members. Eddie's mother, Nani, doesn't travel off-island due to health reasons, and what little time his cousins Elta and Kanoa spend outside their busy boat-repair shop in Waianae, they spend on the sparkling waters off Makaha fishing, drinking, entertaining female tourists.

"There will be plenty of time for me to meet them," I told Eddie in a constant effort to put it off. "For the holidays, then," he said recently. "My cousins are giving me one last chance to prove I'm not being catfished by some old man in a fishing shack in Saigon."

Little does Eddie know, I have at least another year's worth of excuses for being unable to leave Maui, from lost wallets to a myriad of contagious (and rather loathsome) medical conditions, beginning with pink eye and rolling neatly into monkeypox.

Noah opens a yellow legal pad. "Personally, I have no problem with Zoe being present for this meeting, but as an attorney I need to strongly recommend against it. The prosecution—assuming there ever is one—can compel her to testify."

Zoe looks as though Noah just gut-punched her. "I'd never say *anything* that would hurt my mother."

Given the circumstances (few of which Noah knows), I understand my daughter's indignation. Yet our own experience with the justice system proves that you can hurt a loved one without aiming to. How to do this delicately, though? "School needs to be your first priority, Zoe. This is your senior year."

I want to rescind the words the moment I say them. Days ago when I'd mentioned senior year, Zoe had a meltdown. *"Senior year,"* she scoffed. "Senior year is meaningless! I already have enough credits to graduate, my SAT scores are through the *roof*, and I've applied for early admission to the only schools I'm interested in. *Senior year* isn't about academics, Mom! Senior year is about friends and football games, it's about boyfriends and *proms*. None of which I'll experience now."

What she left out was *thanks to you*. But it stung just the same.

"*Hire* me, then," Zoe says to Noah as if a light bulb just appeared over her head. "That way the attorney-client privilege will extend to me, right?" When Noah says nothing, Zoe steps back into the silence. "I'm already on the books, remember? From when I worked here a few weeks while Eddie tried that case in Honolulu."

"That was several months ago," Noah says. "A federal judge would never buy it. The Court would force you to testify, and if you refuse, you'll be held in contempt. If you take the stand and lie, you'll be indicted for perjury and obstruction of justice."

Zoe nearly knocks her chair over as she stands. "Whatever," she huffs. "You're both making a big fucking mistake." She hastily makes for the door. "But remember, Mom, it's your ass on the line, not mine."

I jump up and try to reason with her as she storms out. A moment of panic strikes as I pat down my pockets, searching for the keys to the Jeep. I sigh with relief when I find them.

"Do you need some time with her?" Noah asks, depositing a stick of Juicy Fruit into his mouth. When he catches me staring, he holds out the pack and asks, "Want one?"

As I retake my seat, I don't know whether to throw something at him or accept a piece of gum and chew away the day. He appears so *zen*, so in control. I'm envious. Maybe I could learn a thing or two from him. But not now, not while Eddie's still out there. Alone. Scared. Possibly injured, exhausted, dehydrated. Starving.

I decline the stick of Juicy Fruit.

"Listen," Noah says, "the expectation right now is that Eddie will be found alive and well—perhaps a little battered from the elements—and that charges will, therefore, never even be considered, let alone filed."

"I'm not worried about charges," I say, "I'm worried about Eddie." At least that last bit is true. "I can't help but think the state's search-and-rescue response is underwhelming."

"You're not wrong. Two unpassed bills are still floating around the state legislature in Honolulu concerning search-and-rescue operations."

I had pivoted to Eddie hoping Noah would regain focus following Zoe's tantrum, not launch into a lesson on public policy. Noah, however, is one of those few mainland transplants who truly comprehend "island time," an alternate reality in which nothing happens fast.

"The first bill," he says, "makes sense. Few years ago, after that missing hiker was found half-dead, she lobbied for the state to improve search-and-rescue operations by investing in technology: installing cameras, expanding the use of GPS, enhancing communications."

"Would've been extremely helpful now. What happened?"

"Hiker's family happened to be in the tech industry. After she generously offered the seed money collected by her new foundation, the loons came out of the woodwork with their conspiracy theories."

"About what?"

"Suddenly, folks were *sure* that the hiker set out to get lost on purpose—maybe even intentionally broke her own leg in three places—so that her family could make a little dough on state contracts."

"What possible evidence did they have?"

"That's the thing about conspiracy theories. You don't need evidence. Just the worm of an idea to slip into the ears of your fellow wackadoos. Some questioned her level of electrolytes after surviving two weeks on stream water. Others wanted more detailed accounts of how she bedded down most nights in a boar's den. Evidently, the wild boars *they* know are dead set against houseguests."

"Didn't the police conduct an investigation?"

"A *thorough* investigation, sure. Complete with polygraph tests. But these people live in a parallel universe. To them the world operates the way it does on television, where every word, every action, every little piece of evidence *means* something and is crucial to solving some puzzle."

Even where no puzzle exists.

"Get this," he adds. "The other bill would require missing hikers— or presumably their grieving families—to reimburse the state the tens of thousands of dollars spent during any rescue efforts."

"No one would ever call for help again."

Noah shrugs. "Call me cynical, but I strongly suspect that's the point."

After I take Noah through every detail of that morning for the umpteenth time, he pauses, his blue ballpoint hovering over a clean yellow page on his pad.

"Eddie talks about you all the time," he starts with the slightest hesitation. "But not a word about your life before arriving in Hana."

"Doesn't everyone move to a remote town like Hana looking for a fresh start?"

He thinks about this. "Sure. But some things follow you no matter how far you run or where you hide."

My spine chills. "Is my background really germane at this stage?"

"No, but if things go sideways, those subjects you absolutely *cannot* talk about to anyone? *Those* are things *any* lawyer is gonna need to know to properly represent you. Otherwise, you risk being ambushed on the eve of trial."

Before I can reply, Noah's cell goes off. He excuses himself and breezes out of the room, leaving me to sit alone in silence gazing at the walls, which sport a framed cover of a recent issue of *Honolulu* magazine featuring Noah and Eddie and a large-font caption reading TOP ATTORNEYS IN HAWAII. Next to it is a framed copy of *Pacific Business Week* with an article about Eddie's verdict against the Lanyon shipping company. A little farther to the right is a photo of a midsize boat called the *Reasonable Doubt*.

After a few minutes I stand and drift over to the window, relieved to see Zoe sitting under a shade tree, flipping through a magazine pilfered from the firm's waiting room. I look closer. Make that a *pile* of magazines pilfered from the firm's waiting room.

When he finally returns, Noah's expression is somber. "We need to head back over to the park. They won't disclose much over the phone, but apparently they discovered something salient to the search."

4

When we arrive at the park entrance at dusk, a number of reporters and photojournalists swarm Noah's white Ford Explorer. I instinctively lower my head and cover my face with the top of my shirt, exposing my midriff, one of the few body parts I doubt Jeremy and his family would recognize online.

Noah has promised to handle the media, but I cannot press upon him the gravity of my face being flashed on the evening news without telling him everything—from our vanishing act on the mainland to why we're living off-grid with new names and an anonymous online presence.

As we slowly pull around the visitor center to an area cordoned off by rangers, I'm relieved Noah had suggested we drop Zoe at home before coming. Pissed that I've barred her from taking selfies for Instagram for the past two years, I question whether my daughter could resist posing for the cameras.

Zoe understands the dangers, but the longer we stay hidden, the more complacent she's become—the more complacent *we've* become—and it could well get us killed. We cannot put anything past Jeremy's vengeful family and their motley army of well-compensated minions.

After being whisked inside the parks service building, Noah and I enter a private office presently occupied by Assistant US Attorney Charley Kay, a tall, broad-shouldered woman with short auburn hair and the sharp features to pull it off. As we sit, I can't help but compare the prosecutor's neat taupe suit, perfectly tailored, with Noah's pineapple-themed aloha shirt, with its three opened buttons at the top. *Strike that.* Now that I get a better look, those buttons aren't open, they're missing.

Books and covers, I remind myself.

Special Agent Harris arrives moments later and seats himself on a small sofa facing our backs, leaving space for Special Agent Lui, who I assume is moments behind him. His positioning makes me feel boxed in, vulnerable to verbal cross fire. This edginess is exacerbated by the fact that I'm still clueless as to what they found—a fact that doubtlessly serves their purpose.

Following a needlessly lengthy preamble, Charley Kay leans forward on her elbows and says, "An hour ago, a team of national park rangers, using a block search pattern of the area at the top of the spur trail, discovered a StartTrek trekking pole in the woods roughly fifty yards back from the Infinity Pool over Makahiku Falls."

I immediately try but fail to grasp the significance.

"That's it?" Noah says in a tone clearly reserved for adversaries. "*A walking stick?* You couldn't have relayed this information *over the phone?*"

The reason the prosecutor wanted us here is obvious: to gauge my reaction to the news. But why? I'm baffled about what this has to do with Eddie. He wasn't using trekking poles, only I was (and only one), and I dropped it off at the overlook before beginning my search for Eddie. I definitely did *not* have it with me when I hiked up the spur trail. It would've made it impossible to navigate over all those rocks.

Wait. Did I try? In my head, the clouds gather again. Suddenly, I'm less certain of my movements that morning, a pestering doubt that's as frightening as it is frustrating. Was I in shock? Or is my uncertainty something more, something serious, maybe even something permanent? Something progressive.

Charley reads the fear and confusion on my face. "Do you have a question for me, Ms. Dawes?"

I glance at Noah, who vehemently shakes his head and says, "What exactly does this walking stick have to do with Eddie's whereabouts?"

Charley's eyes remain on me. "Were you carrying trekking poles with you yesterday morning, Ms. Dawes?"

Noah holds up a stop sign. "Counselor, did someone *see* her with trekking poles? Is that why you're asking?"

I can't imagine why it matters. Beating back the prosecutor's questions will only cost them more time. Time Eddie cannot afford. "I *was* using a trekking pole yesterday morning," I say. "Only one, though. I dislocated my left kneecap in a skiing accident nine or ten years ago." My left hand instinctively cups my knee, which particularly hates the rain. "I've used one when hiking ever since."

"This pole," Charley says. "Was it manufactured by StartTrek?"

"That name sounds familiar; I'd have to check. But Eddie wasn't using poles, and I dropped mine off at the overlook before looking for him. So any pole you found must belong to some other hiker. Who knows how long it's been up there?"

"Where are your poles now?"

Over Noah's protests, I tell her I never went back for my pole. "It's still there, I guess. Just off the trail. The other must still be at home."

Charley bows her head, but her gaze stays locked on me. "According to Agent Harris, you never mentioned a trekking pole. You only said you and Mr. Akana were each carrying a light pack."

Affronted, words fly from my mouth like a gag reflex. "It must have slipped my mind, I guess."

"The fact that you were carrying a potential weapon?"

"Potential *weapon?*" Noah cries. "*Wait.* Is this an update on the search for Eddie or a criminal investigation into a missing person presumed dead?"

"Obviously, Mr. Walker, it's both."

Noah stands. "Then you might have troubled yourself to Mirandize your suspect." He holds his hand out to me as if I'm drowning. Maybe

I am and just don't know it. "Unless you intend to arrest my client, she has nothing further to say."

"She's not a suspect," Charley says with a calmness that irks me.

"Since when does law enforcement ever call a suspect a *suspect*?" Noah scoffs, still waiting for me to take his hand. "If you did, you might actually feel compelled to read someone their rights." He motions to me. "Let's go."

"She's a material witness," Charley says, "who came in voluntarily, *presumably* because she wants to aid in the search."

"I *do*," I say, rooted firmly in the chair. "I want to find Eddie more than anyone."

Noah turns around to face the park service investigator. When he speaks, I hear a fresh urgency in his voice. "Tell me something, Special Agent Harris. Where is Agent Lui right now?"

Divide and conquer. That's what Mac told me back on the mainland following the death of Jeremy's mother, Teresa Perotta. *It's a tactic used by all cops—and it works. Rest assured, if you don't talk, someone else will. Sometimes knowingly, sometimes not.*

Zoe, I think as I spring from the chair.

Rising behind her desk, Charley seems to tower over me. I, meanwhile, rose too fast. I haven't eaten. And I hardly slept at all last night. Like the thirty-foot bamboo canes, I sway in the gentle wind blowing in from the window. I'm about to collapse to the floor when Noah grabs hold of me.

He turns to Charley. "You have paramedics on-site?"

"Not far," Charley replies without affect. "Shall I call them?"

No matter what they say, I remember Mac telling me in his gravelly, old ex-cop, ex-con voice. *No matter what they do. No matter what kindness they show you, no matter what empathy you feel radiating from them. Police and prosecutors are not on your side. Not when your rights and freedom are at stake.*

"No, no paramedics," I say. "I'm fine, just a little lightheaded."

"Something from the vending machines?" Harris asks.

As a matter of fact, I *could* use that Kit Kat right about now (not to mention the Diet Coke). But no, no more distractions, nothing more to delay me. Because as Noah just intimated, I need to get home to Zoe now—*now*, before the rest of our little universe comes crashing down around us.

Hurrying outside, I forget the journalists as well. The moment the mob sees me and Noah exit the station, they charge at us like ants at a sugar cube, the earlier cordon nowhere in sight.

"Ms. Dawes, tell us . . ."

I shield my face, but a few flashes have already gone off. Spots dance before my eyes like dueling balloons as I try to blink them away to check my phone. *Damn it, no missed calls.* Noah's hand clutches my arm, and I allow him to guide me toward his Explorer.

"Kati, just a few questions . . ."

A persistent bunch, journalists, Mac said when the investigation into Teresa's death started garnering statewide attention. *But they're only doing their job. Which is to make everyone who passes in front of their cameras look "guilty AF," as my grandkid puts it. Only times the media use flattering photos in the crime section are when the suspect is a red carpet celeb or professional athlete, or when a young blond-haired, blue-eyed, upper-middle-class white woman's gone missing.*

The tap of Noah's key fob is followed by the chirp of his alarm and the click of the locks. I hear the car door open, and Noah helps me climb inside, where I immediately bury my head between my knees, a position that serves the dual purpose of concealing my face and preventing me from hyperventilating.

Through the glass I hear Noah briefly address the reporters before hopping behind the wheel. He punches the button that starts the ignition.

The SUV peels around, kicking up gravel, fending off our pursuers, some of whose tenacity nearly blinds them. As I gaze into the side-view mirror, Noah places a call and then speaks into a Bluetooth device.

"Kilo, I need a favor," he says. "Drive right over to Eddie's girl-friend's house. Her daughter Zoe is home alone, and we don't want her singing to the po-po. Got it?"

I can't hear the other end of the conversation.

"I'm gonna call her now," Noah says into the earpiece, "but a special agent with the park service may already be at the house. So be discreet."

At nearly four hundred pounds, with the oversize personality to match, Kilo is anything but discreet. But as Eddie's oldest and closest friend, I trust him completely to do his best to bail Zoe out of this jam.

"Just tell Zoe you need to speak to her alone for a moment," Noah says, "and get her *and* Hawaii Five-O *out* of the house toot sweet. We'll be there in twenty."

"Thank you," I say once he clicks off the call.

"About that. I'm gonna need you to remind me why I'm doing all this. I wasn't expecting to get bushwhacked by a federal prosecutor back there. Believe me, Charley Kay didn't fly over from Honolulu to help you work through your feelings. Her presence means they've found something that suggests foul play."

A niggling (and haunting) thought finally comes to the fore.

What if Jeremy is responsible for Eddie's disappearance?

But why? Jealousy after all this time? It's possible. Hell, he had a conniption years ago when one of *his* old high school chums hearted one of my more risqué photos on Instagram. But would he *kill* out of jealousy? Or would Jeremy only kill Eddie to get to me? To get to Zoe. To ultimately choke the life out of us both.

I need to get home to my daughter.

The twisting road up Haleakala Crater is no easier on the stomach on the way down, especially in the dark. About to paint Noah's beige interior neon yellow, I remember a simple meditation technique I picked up online. I close my eyes, breathe in through the nose, out through the mouth, while silently reciting some meaningless mantra, and the nausea gradually dissipates. But a problem arises when I try to envision my "happy place."

My *happy place* is with Eddie under the forbidden falls. Except Eddie is still missing. Maybe dead. As harrowing as it is, as callous as it sounds, there's little I can do about that now. But I *can* continue to protect myself and my little girl. After two days of incessant upheaval, all my focus must immediately shift back to my highest priority—keeping Zoe and myself hidden, keeping us safe.

"Can Lui question Zoe without me or a lawyer present?" I ask.

"She's interviewing a witness, not a suspect. Your daughter can refuse to talk, but the choice is hers."

And Special Agent Alana Lui won't couch it in terms of a choice.

As she did back east, Zoe might do me harm by trying to help. If Lui asks her about our past, Zoe knows what to say and how to say it. But how will she hold up under questioning? An interrogation by Special Agent Lui is an entirely different animal than a pop quiz from me on the backyard deck.

Noah drags me away from my thoughts. "Kati, I'm gonna need some honesty from you now. Any idea who'd want to harm Eddie?"

I can't think of a way to provide a truthful answer without revealing too much about Zoe and me. So again I lie, solidifying the denial. I briefly wonder if two years of around-the-clock lying has turned me pathological. *I can stop anytime I want, right?*

As we near my home, my stomach groans with hunger, a brief but misleading respite from the violent nausea that's plagued me since yesterday morning.

"Zoe's not answering the number you gave me," Noah says. "I'll keep trying."

"Thank you, Noah."

"Yeah, you keep saying that."

"And I mean every word of it."

"Then you're gonna have to be a little more forthcoming with me."

I heave an irritated sigh. "Can't we continue this conversation *after* we dig Lui's claws out of Zoe?"

I catch Noah stealing a sideways glance and instantly feel guilty for the outburst.

"I'm . . . I'm sorry," I say. "I know you care about him too."

Something in Noah's sad smile makes my chest ache. "Like a brother," he says, his eyes misting in the bright blue glow of his dashboard. "I've known Eddie Akana since our first year of law school. Without him, I'd never have stayed at UH, never have graduated. I just had no interest at the time." He nods, though not unkindly. "So, yeah, Kati, I care about him. He's not just my business partner, he's my best friend."

The Explorer's interior falls silent.

Finally, as we turn onto my road, I say aloud the only thought presently rattling around in my head. "He's my best friend, too, Noah."

That Eddie's also my *only* friend is probably best left unsaid.

5

Day Three

At sunrise Zoe and I sit on the rear deck drinking Kona coffee, as we did those first many mornings after arriving in Hawaii. Back then, there was so much to talk about, so much to do, even so much to look forward to. Our conversation had a perceptible electricity, a buzzing of excitement, an exhilaration only possible by moving somewhere new, I think. Somewhere exotic.

Today we sit in silence, listening to the distant mooing of cows, the chirping of birds, the occasional crowing of the rooster that resides in our yard. I'm not sure whether Zoe isn't speaking to me or I'm not speaking to her. Not that it matters. The way I flew off the handle last night, Zoe wants nothing to do with me this morning. Frankly, I've yet to decide how much I want to do with her.

Last night Noah and I arrived at the house just after dark to find Zoe and Kilo outside "talking story" (as we say in the islands) while Special Agent Lui stood off to the side, scowling, thwarted in her attempt to make my daughter her ally. Noah immediately sent Lui packing. After inhaling a loaf of taro, Kilo left too. Noah seemed ready to excuse himself from the kitchen table when instead he turned to Zoe and said softly, "How long was she in the house before Kilo arrived?"

"Not long," Zoe said, her cheeks suddenly crimson.

"What did she ask you?"

Noah's words rang like an accusation, even to me. Zoe swallowed hard, avoiding eye contact with either of us. Seated at the table with her back to the wall, she no doubt felt as trapped as I felt in the interrogation room at the ranger station. "She asked if Mom and Eddie ever argued."

"What did you tell her?"

"Who *doesn't* argue?" Zoe cried.

Noah frowned but maintained his cool; my blood pressure shot through the roof. "What else did she ask?" he said.

"What kinds of things Mom and Eddie argue about."

In my head, an irrefutable fury wrestled with raw agony at seeing my little girl again so distressed. When I finally found my voice, it was little more than a strained whisper. "And you said?"

Zoe eluded my gaze and shrugged. "The usual couples stuff, I guess. Money, politics, religion." When she continued, her voice faltered and nearly broke off. "Mom's drinking."

I gasped. Noah swiftly placed a hand on my forearm to keep me from jumping down Zoe's throat. "What else did she ask?" he said.

"She asked me when I last heard them argue."

An uneasy silence hung in the air as Noah waited for Zoe to elaborate. When she didn't, he prodded. "What did you tell her, Zoe?"

This time my daughter didn't hesitate. "The night before last."

My jaw fell open. "Eddie and I didn't argue *the other night*," I charged, tempering my voice only when Zoe flinched. My eyes narrowed to slits through which I could barely see. "We didn't fight the night before *he went missing*."

"You *did*, Mom. You had a few drinks, smoked a joint on the deck, and became super paranoid, remember?"

Noah clutched my shoulder to stifle my protests. "Did she ask you what the argument was about?" he said.

"She started to. That's when Kilo pounded on the door."

I finally wrenched away from Noah and stood. "I'd like to talk to my daughter alone for a few minutes."

Noah slowly rose from his chair. "Talk all night. I've gotta get home and catch up on my z's. I'm wiped."

Still steaming, I escorted Noah to the door. When he paused to say good night to Zoe, she folded her arms and turned her back to him. I could tell she *hated* him at that moment. Hated both of us. Maybe enough to turn on me as she turned on Jeremy back east.

With Noah gone, Zoe appeared almost . . . what? *Frightened* of me? This was no time to lose my shit. But then, how could I help it? As soon as I stepped back into the room, I started in on her. "How could you *say* those things?"

Zoe shrugged. She knew how much I hated that gesture, her primary response to me over the past few months. "Once I admitted you argued, I felt like I *needed* to answer Lui's follow-up questions or else she'd be suspicious." Genuine tears spilled down her cheeks like an overpour of pinot. "Mom," she sobbed, "I was so worried about saying anything about our past that I totally blanked on the present. The truth just spewed from my mouth like word vomit."

Even as my heart cracked like a delicate wineglass, I yelled, "Only it *wasn't* the truth."

"It *was*," Zoe shot back. "You argued that night."

"Over *what*, exactly?"

"Over *me*. Over where *you* think I should go to college. Over the length of my leash."

"Your *leash*? I treat you like a dog now?"

"Eddie's word," Zoe snapped. "Not mine."

"He said no such thing."

"You were drinking, Mom."

"A few glasses of wine with dinner."

"You downed two bottles of pinot, maybe three. *On top* of the Ativan. *On top* of all the antidepressants. And God knows what else." Zoe wiped away her tears and shook her head in disgust. "Then you wonder why you space the fuck out all the time?"

"*Language,*" I barked on autopilot.

A cruel heat crawled up my neck. Sweat beaded on my forehead. Ironically, I *hated* the tropics. I chose the islands as the last place on earth where Jeremy would expect us to flee. He'd look for us in Antarctica first, and just now, the shrinking ice continent sounded like a fine idea compared to Hawaii.

"Zoe, what were you *thinking*?"

"I *wasn't* thinking, Mom." Her eyes filled again. "I feel like I'm caught in a whirlwind." She paused, planted her face in her palms to hide the ugliness of her anger, something she's done since middle school. "I've felt like this ever since Grandma died."

Admittedly, I was on the verge of verbally slapping her down when I somehow managed to bite my lip and step back. Zoe's relationship with her grandmother Teresa had been a source of contention since it started. I concede that, to me, their closeness felt like disloyalty, like a spiteful betrayal. Together Zoe and Teresa played cards, laughed, watched daytime soaps, even took daily afternoon tea. Almost as if her grandmother was a real human being. Only, human beings *feel* things for others; Teresa felt nothing for anyone but herself.

"She died more than *two years ago*," I said with immediate regret. Last time I wielded that sword, Zoe asked just how long she was permitted to grieve her dead Grams.

This time Zoe leaped from her seat so fast it fell backward, clattering against the linoleum. "And two years ago," she cried, "I was a *normal* teenager in a *normal* house, enrolled in a *normal* school. I had a *normal* boyfriend, normal friends, a normal family." She sucked in her breath and added, "At least I thought I did."

When I said nothing—*What could I say?*—Zoe gained steam and advanced. "*Nothing* in my life is normal anymore, Mom. I have a different *name*, I go to school on a *computer*, I live 'off the grid,' which is way more complicated and nowhere *near* as cool as it sounds!"

"All for our protection."

"Is it, though? Is it all really *necessary*? Or is the whole thing just to feed more of your baseless paranoia? Everyone's after you, right, Mom?

After us. Dad, Grandma, Uncle Gunther. The past twenty years have just been one big conspiracy to make you think you're crazy!"

The shock from two years earlier returned. Only this time I didn't fall into a petrified stupor. "How can you *say* that? You were there."

"My experience back home was very different from yours, Mom."

Regrettably, I instantly returned to my old fallback. Perhaps every single mother's fallback. "Would you prefer to go live with your father, then?"

"*No.* It's just that . . ." Zoe finally drew some air and lowered her tone. "Now I have no boyfriend, no real friends, no family left but you. I have no email, no social media, no real identity; in other words, I have no *life*."

"That's exactly what you have, Zoe. You *have* your life."

"What good is it if I can't *do* anything with it? I feel like I'm no one, like I'm nothing, like I'm *air*. I'm not allowed online except for 'express purposes,' none of which are fun. I can't communicate with anyone back home. And my virtual senior class is the size of our *car pool* back east."

"So you *sabotage* us?"

"How is it sabotage? Is Eddie *dead*? Are you *really* a suspect? From everything you said earlier, it makes no sense. Why, Mom? *Why* is this happening again?"

Now, as I sip my iced tea, the rooster we christened Billy Fires for his magnificent colors crows. With a lump in my throat, I wait for Zoe to speak, to apologize or at least say something conciliatory. But that's not on the menu this morning.

"I'm sorry we argued," I say. It's the only kind of apology that Jeremy ever permitted himself, an apology that's not really an apology at all.

But Zoe's no dummy either. "Me too."

I immediately return to a defensive position. "Sweetheart, I *didn't* hurt Eddie. I *love* him."

"I know." She says it with all the conviction of a lapsed priest.

"I *am* worried there's been an accident," I tell her. "He could have stepped off the rocks in the fog." How to phrase this next part? "But, Zoe, we also *cannot* rule out the possibility that we've been found."

With enough cabbage, Mac told me, *anyone can find a person, period. The best we can do is make it so expensive and so convoluted that whoever's looking for you will ultimately give up and go home.*

What if he never gives up? I asked him.

Then you'll need to keep running.

Forever?

Or until he's dead.

There are times when your failures as a parent weigh most heavily on you, good intentions be damned. You dismiss all the positive you've done (or thought you've done), because none of it matters once you've so royally fucked up.

For Zoe's sake, I did everything possible to live with an impossible person for almost two decades. After all, he never directed his rage at Zoe. His lies, his false promises, his infidelities, his beatings—he reserved those for his bride.

So I stayed. I "sacrificed." Sacrificed by living in a mansion, by driving a Benz, by summering on Martha's Vineyard. I repeatedly tell myself that I didn't stay for any of our material possessions, but only sometimes do I believe it. Yet having grown up without a father myself, it's true; I didn't want to deprive my daughter of a dad, no matter the cost to me. And, yes, I was scared. Scared of being a single mom with no job, no experience or skills, no support system, and only a high school education and single semester of college.

Jeremy's father died when he was young, leaving Jeremy and his sister alone with a single tyrannical influence—Teresa. But then, *young* Jeremy was always the golden child in his mother's eyes. The boy who could do no wrong. When he was disciplined at school, Teresa dashed to the principal's office and immediately threatened to go over his head to the superintendent. The facts didn't matter, only Jeremy's word.

When he was benched in Little League, Teresa took to the field and confronted the coach. When he was arrested for public drunkenness, for assault and battery, for driving under the influence, Teresa hired the best lawyers in the state to defend him against the injustice. In the single case where the attorney failed to win him an acquittal, she turned to her state senator, who, through a series of bribes and threats in the judiciary, got the jury's verdict overturned, leaving thrice-arrested Jeremy with a spotless record.

At night I stay awake asking myself why I waited until I had to run, why I didn't leave him sooner. Sounds so simple now. Move north to Rhode Island or Maine, apply for a restraining order. But then, what good would a restraining order have done? *It's futile,* his sister Shannon once told me. *Even if you left the child . . .*

Which was something I could never have done. But Shannon understood the situation I was in. She was Teresa's permanent scapegoat, after all. The black sheep of the family, distinguished by her goodness, her empathy, her generosity. When, at age thirty, Shannon opened her wrists, no one was surprised. When she survived, her family made jokes around the dinner table in front of my daughter. *Can't even get that right, can she,* Jeremy said, to Teresa's delight.

At age thirty-four, Shannon got it right. Using the sharpest of her mother's $3,000 set of Miyabi Birchwood kitchen knives. (The knife, following a cursory investigation by police, was returned to Teresa, who had it cleaned and returned to the block within weeks.)

She didn't know how to live were the kindest words Teresa ever said of her dead daughter. *There's no one to blame for her death but Shannon herself.*

Breaking the painful silence, I say, "If Eddie hasn't been found, there'll be a vigil at Koki Beach this evening."

"Are you going?"

"How can you even ask me that?"

"Eddie's cousins are organizing it, aren't they? Have you even spoken to anyone in his family since he went missing?"

"What are you saying? That they won't want me there?"

"Mom, even if they send you an Evite, Eddie's a former state rep. There'll be tons of people there. Which means the media will be there too."

I fall silent. Zoe is right. Attending Eddie's vigil would likely be suicide. The last thing I need is my face plastered in the *Star-Advertiser*.

"What will people think if I *don't* attend?"

Zoe hesitates, then admits, "It'll inflame their suspicions."

Of course, she's right. "How would I explain it to Lui and Harris?"

"You don't *need* to explain anything. You don't need to speak with them."

Closing my eyes, I count silently to five. "I don't want to start another fight," I say calmly, despite the heat rising in my cheeks, "but why weren't you thinking that last night when Special Agent Lui came to our door?"

"I was caught *totally* off guard," she says. "I had no idea she was there to get dirt on you."

"But you met her yesterday morning. You knew she was federal law enforcement."

"I thought I was helping to find Eddie. She made her visit seem like nothing more than a formality. That she was just confirming information for her report."

"Did she show you her badge?"

"Sure. It says 'National Park Service,' remember? If she was FBI, DEA, ATF—part of the Justice Department's alphabet soup—I would've refused to speak to her. But who the hell fears the National Park Service? Aren't they with the *Department of the Interior?*"

A solid point. The fact that Zoe even knows all these acronyms is a testament to how I allowed her to grow up too fast. From a young age, I exposed her to all the ugliness in the world through books, movies, and television. Not just fictional stories that could later be dismissed as make-believe, but true crime—brothers killing brothers, husbands killing wives, mothers and fathers slaughtering their own daughters and sons.

It's all my fault. And though it doesn't aid me one iota in the investigation, I at least realize I have nothing to be angry at her for. When the Department of Justice or Homeland Security crop up at your door, it's one thing. When the National Park Service comes a-knocking, no one cowers. In a significant way, I'm to blame since I didn't apprise Zoe of Lui and Harris's interrogation the previous night. And our meeting at Noah's office was abruptly cut short by Zoe's tirade, then by Charley Kay's call summoning us to the ranger station.

"Let's put this past us, all right, Zoe?"

She says nothing.

I stare hard at my daughter, willing her to agree to a truce, to a temporary ceasefire. Because with Eddie missing, with Jeremy possibly on-island, with Lui and Harris and Charley Kay sniffing around our lives, this perpetual battle with Zoe is all too much.

"Why not?" Zoe says, rising from her chair. "That's what we always do anyway, isn't it? Leave things and people and places in the past and run away?"

Zoe

She wants me to lie for her again. She wants me to keep her secrets, our secrets, the secrets she forced on me.

But how can I say the right things when I don't know the whole story, when I don't know what's important and what's not?

All I know is that she's been behaving super strangely these past few months. She's spacey and flaky and tries to cover it up by pretending and agreeing with whatever the hell is said to her. Someone's bound to take advantage of that sooner or later.

Which brings me to the lawyer. What's his game? Why shut me out of her defense unless he and I have vastly different objectives? That's all it can be—one of us clearly wants her in prison, while one of us would risk anything to see her stay free regardless of what she's done. If that's the case, Noah has no idea who he's up against.

I need to get out of this suffocating house before the walls close in any more. Which means you, my friend, need to return to hiding. If she found you, she'd take you from me—and that, I couldn't handle. I've already lost the only person I thought I could turn to, and if I can't talk to you, I'll go insane in the membrane.

Given my family history, it wouldn't take much to trigger whatever gene I inherited from my parents and grandparents. Before long I'd be fucking cray-cray. Just like Mom.

6

Over her strenuous objections, I refuse to allow Zoe to leave the house. When she screeches, *"Why not?"* like a banshee, I remind her that Eddie is missing, maybe dead, that her grandmother's killer may be on Maui, may be in *Hana*, and that *we*—either or *both* of us—might be his next target.

Tramping upstairs to her room, she hurls one last nasty, *excruciating* jab at me before slamming her door. "Maybe *you're* not safe," she shrieks. "People keep dying around *you*, Mom, *not* me."

I give chase, but she instantly dead-bolts the door, locking me out. A series of six beeps emanates from her keypad as she arms her room's individual alarm. Not the first time she's used our intricate security system against me. I'm about to plead through the door when a loud knock comes from the front of the house. I instinctively pluck my phone from my pocket and open the Fish Eye peephole app.

On the screen is Koa Pualani of the *Honolulu Star-Advertiser*, whom I recognize straight off from the thumbnail photo next to his byline in the paper.

How did he find me? Unless . . .

Unless there's a leak at the park service.

I tap a button. "Please *leave*. I've nothing to say to the press."

"Just give me five minutes," he begs.

A local quasi-celebrity, Koa writes articles that often dominate the top half of the front page. Given his good looks and fluency in Native

Hawaiian, he also spends a fair amount of time as a guest on the morning shows of the local television stations.

"Direct your questions to my attorney," I say, descending the stairs. "Noah Walker of Walker & Akana."

My fingers flutter to the pang in my chest from the mere mention of Eddie's last name. Which, if he's still alive, in a few short months will be *my* last name. Which will be *Zoe's* last name. A name with a connection to someone meaningful in our lives. Briefly, my calves turn to rubber, and I nearly collapse in the kitchen before grasping the counter and regaining my balance.

"Come on, Kati," Koa says as if we've been besties since preschool. "'Talk to my lawyer' isn't the quote you want in the *Star-Ad*. That's the quote of someone with something to hide."

"I've *nothing* to hide," I say, holding the phone up to my mouth. "Prove it."

"I've nothing to *prove* either."

"*Two* minutes," he says, staring into the camera with the same hangdog expression he's used to flirt with every attractive anchor in the islands. "Just talk about your relationship with Eddie. What kind of man is he? What do you love about him? Make people *care*."

You'll be tempted to talk to the press to refute the worst of the bullshit you're going to read online, Mac said early in the investigation into Teresa's death. *Don't do it. Nothing anyone writes or says about you will have as crushing an impact as the slightest mistake that spills from your own kisser.*

But then, *here* isn't there. Hawaii is a different world from Connecticut. People view life through a different lens. Eddie taught me that. As a litigator, he never passed on an opportunity to speak to the press. *If I can connect with readers and viewers,* he'd say, *I can connect with people in the courtroom.*

On my phone's screen, Koa continues his spiel. "The more I know, the more I write, and the more I write, the more attention—and *resources*—my words will bring to Eddie's search." He pauses, then:

"It's worked in the past. That hiker found alive after two weeks in the wilderness? She was only rescued because her family never gave up, never relented. Her family wouldn't *stop* talking until they got her back."

I see the logic, know he's right, yet . . . my first priority is to protect Zoe. But then, what if I could get Eddie publicity *without* putting Zoe in danger? Better yet, what if I could protect Zoe *while* bringing more awareness to Eddie's cause?

"I'll need a promise from you first," I say into the mouthpiece. "No photos of me or my daughter will ever grace the pages of your paper."

"I'm a writer, Kati, not the editor. That's outside my domain, above my pay grade. Choose your cliché."

"Then you're as useful to me as tits on a wild boar." I immediately shut the app and step toward the window. Carefully, I part the blinds to find the reporter making like a statue on my doorstep instead of retreating to his rental car.

Seconds pass before his knuckles finally rap my door again. *Hard.* Hard enough to make me jump.

When he steps back, I jab the "Listen" button on the Fish Eye app, half expecting him to curse me out. "I *promise*," he cries.

I tap the "Talk" button. "And you have the clout to make the paper honor that promise?"

"It'll cost me, but yeah." Then, more definitively: "Yeah, I do."

"When I say *leave*, you leave."

Koa throws up his hands. "I'd be breaking the law otherwise."

"Good," I say, "because it's been a while since *True Blood*. I can't recall the rules once you've invited a vampire inside your house."

As I open the door, a vehicle peels away, its tires screaming against the blacktop. I try to catch sight of it, but it's already been consumed by the surrounding jungle.

"Your ride?" I say.

He glances over his shoulder. "Just another lost tourist making a K-turn, I think."

Somehow I doubt that. But Koa's rented Mustang convertible (90 percent of all rentals on Maui are Mustang convertibles) sits silently in the dirt driveway leading up to our not-so-supersecret house. I step aside to allow him in.

"We need to make this quick," I tell him. "In twenty minutes, I'm meeting with someone from Maui Search and Rescue." Coincidentally, to discuss our dwindling resources, how best to use them, and how to obtain more. Somehow I don't expect good news.

As Koa settles at the kitchen table, he takes in the room around us. Good, let him describe our kitchen for his readers; let him tell them about my perfectly benign obsession with sea turtles, which adorn our fridge, hang from our walls, are woven into our dish towels. *Sea Turtle City,* Zoe mockingly calls our place. *Honu House,* Eddie always corrects her, using the Hawaiian word for *sea turtle. Sea Turtle City sounds . . . cheap and cheesy.* Zoe rolls her eyes. *Hell-o!* she tells him. *At least you don't have to* live *there!*

"No doorbell?" Koa says instead of commenting on the decor.

"We don't want visitors."

"Lots of cameras, though."

"We don't want intruders either," I add a tad too defensively. "Our closest neighbors are miles away." I open the fridge and gesture to its slim selection of offerings like the poor man's Vanna White. "Something to drink?"

"Just water, t'ank you." Only rarely does Koa slip into Pidgin, which is spoken by roughly half the islands' population, including Eddie and Kilo at times.

"It's like space," Koa says as I hand him one of Zoe's plastic Island Pure water bottles. Ordinarily, Zoe is as green as green can be, but having witnessed the construction of our water catchment system, she's decided she'd rather kill the planet than drink the runoff from our storm gutters, filters notwithstanding. But then, it's always something. Back east, she refused to drink from the tap because municipally treated water contains too many added chemicals, one of which is the fluoride that afforded her a pristine set of teeth. She *hated* brushing as a child, and it took me and a nanny to hold her down to get a dab of toothpaste into her mouth.

"'Like space'?" I say as I pour myself a tall glass of iced tea from the frosty pitcher.

"Your neighbors are miles away, you said. So it's like space." He grins as he unscrews the cap on his Island Pure. "No one can hear you scream."

I take a step back from him, my stomach suddenly doing somersaults.

As he gulps some water, he reads my expression. "My bad," he says, holding up his free hand as if to show me he's not carrying a weapon. "That was a stupid thing for me to say."

I replace the pitcher in the fridge without turning my back to him, and although he appears sincere, I make sure there's a chair between us when I select my seat. He clears his throat and slowly produces a micro voice recorder similar to the one Zoe used as an audio diary back home. I absently nod my consent, simply relieved that it's not a .22 or a switchblade. I'm afraid of *everyone* these days.

Clearing his throat, he starts with, "You and Eddie Akana were engaged to be wed, yeah? For how long?"

"Months?"

He makes a show of inspecting my unadorned ring finger.

"He was saving up for the right one," I tell him.

Generally, injury lawyers in the islands don't starve. Eddie would have no trouble affording an engagement ring. But they don't necessarily feast like litigators back east either. Unlike the mainland, people here pride themselves on being nonlitigious. Most slip and falls are resolved with a handshake (or its post-COVID equivalent) and an apology rather than tens of thousands of dollars and years of senseless litigation.

Truth is, I want no ring. Although Eddie isn't aware, I've done that dance before. The magnificent three-carat diamond Jeremy placed on my finger twenty years ago ushered in not a moment of happiness and now rests five thousand miles away at the bottom of Candlewood Lake.

"I don't know if you saw the footage last night," Koa says, glancing at the small white television on my kitchen counter, "but in an interview with KITV, Eddie Akana's mother, Nani Akana, says she doesn't want you attending her son's vigil at Koki Beach tonight."

"I hadn't heard." Something catches in my throat as my eyes fall on the small TV remote, grateful as always to see it button-side up. "But I'll respect his mother's wishes. Even if I don't understand her reasons."

Koa comes right out with it. "She implied that she believes you're responsible for his going missing."

I desperately cling to one word. *"Implied?"*

"She says her son has been around waterfalls and other hiking hazards his entire life. Presumably, he was experienced and sure footed, yeah?"

He was. He *is*. Eddie is strong, athletic, even graceful. Nani's right—he's as familiar with the Pipiwai Trail as he is with all the other trails we hiked. Which is why I'm still holding out hope. If anyone can survive days lost in the wilderness, it's Eddie, dropped sandal or not.

"There was a dense fog that morning," I say more to myself than to him. "Maybe even flash floods. And Eddie wasn't wearing the proper—"

Out of nowhere, he says, "Do you believe it's possible he jumped?"

With a flash of anger, I surface from my thoughts. "Absolutely *not*. Eddie and I are happy and have everything in the world to look forward to."

Koa sips from his bottle, then sets it aside. "Federal prosecutor Charley Kay said this morning that even if Eddie is never found, criminal charges will remain on the table. Do you believe the federal authorities view you as a suspect?"

"Of course not," I lie.

"But you *were* questioned more than once. You're at least considered a 'person of interest.'"

What have I done? I've invited the enemy into my bed. Started something not so easily stopped. *Stupid, stupid.* My vision blurs; my heart thumps. Between slurps of sweetened iced tea, I shake my head in a fruitless effort to clear it. Now that we've come this far, I can't back out. I can't risk forfeiting Koa's promise not to publish our photos.

"I returned to the ranger station *voluntarily.* Of course they want to speak with me. I was the only person with Eddie when he went missing."

Following Teresa's death, the media did the prosecutors' work for them. For months, they parroted our names and made sure their readers and viewers had our faces seared into their retinas. They predicted (more like *fantasized about*) indictments, interviewed and reinterviewed irrelevant witnesses, and marshaled the evidence in a way that persuaded their audience that both Jeremy *and* I were guilty of cold-blooded murder. Worse, *blue*-blooded murder. They practically convicted us on tristate television every night at ten and spent countless hours on social media reminding followers to tune in. MATRICIDE AT MEGA-MANSION, their banners screamed in a conspicuous effort to turn their fantasies into reality. One station even gave the case its own ominous theme music.

"Do you believe it's possible someone harmed him?"

"I don't—" I shake the cobwebs loose again, my eyes returning to the remote control on the table. It's impossible not to think of Jeremy at this moment. His jealousy, his temper. The way he shouted at me whenever I left dirty dishes in the sink or placed the remote control button-side up on the coffee table. The way he threw things, the way he *hit* me. "I can't answer that. I don't know."

"Yet you just noted you were the only person with him at the time."

"*On the hike.* You're putting words in my mouth."

He raises the recorder. "Shall I rewind?"

Suddenly, there's another string of reverberating thwacks against my front door. I don't bother excusing myself, just leap from the chair and rush to the front of the house, phone in hand, my fingers already opening the Fish Eye app. It's Noah.

When I open the door, Noah looks as angry as I've ever seen him. Inside I'm filled with equal parts terror and relief. He shoots past me and heads straight for the kitchen, where he finds Koa with his micro recorder sitting at the table.

Noah points a finger at the startled reporter. "You, get the hell out of here before I call my buddy Chief Stetler at Maui PD and have you hauled in for trespassing."

"She invited me in," Koa says, rising to his feet.

"Maybe you haven't noticed, but there are two truths to everything these days. And each has just as much of a shot of winning the day."

"I have it all *right* here," Koa says with an arrogance he's never exhibited on television.

In one fluid movement, Noah snatches the recorder from Koa's hand and plunks it into my tall glass of iced tea. "And now you don't," he says. "Now *get out!*"

7

Noah waits until Koa's rented Mustang vanishes behind the dirt it kicked up in our driveway, then turns to me. "What the hell were you *thinking?*"

My memory's a little fuzzy now, but I think I'd put the same question to Zoe last night. I'm embarrassed, though I shouldn't be. "It's *my* life," I toss at him.

"Yeah, well, it's my case. The public *knows* I represent you. Which means anytime you do something monumentally stupid like talk to a reporter, *I* look like a legal neophyte."

The words *I'm sorry* just aren't there for me at the moment. "You smell like the inside of a rum bottle," I observe. I glance at my phone as if to check the time, but who needs to? It's too early for *anyone's* attorney to be drinking, and his bloodshot eyes scream he's had more than a few. I didn't even know he was a drinker, let alone a day drinker.

"Yeah, well." He runs a hand through his product-free hair. "I'm having one hell of a time dealing with all this myself, Kati. You're not the only victim here."

"I never said I was a *victim!*" My shout silences him. But the silence is short lived because I'm not finished. "What are you doing here anyway? Shouldn't you be home on your lanai smoking a doobie with Captain Morgan?"

"Listen," he deadpans with a finger leveled at me, "there's no need to disrespect the Captain."

I try on my best scowl. Moments pass while I glare into his hazel eyes, my mind floating back to his office, back to the stick of Juicy Fruit and, that easily, the tension parts like the Red Sea despite my fierce will to keep it whole and between us.

Before shifting my gaze, I let fly one final sardonic scoff to make it absolutely crystal clear to him that the word *victim* is not allowed in this house.

"What's going on down here?" Zoe's on the landing between floors, peering down at us. There's no telling how long she's been standing there. Until age fifteen, she couldn't enter a room without fireworks and fanfare; now she skulks around the house like a frigging ninja. I swear I'd tie a bell to her if she'd let me.

"I'm taking your mother back to the trail to find her trekking pole," Noah says without inflection.

"I'll come with," she says, starting down the steps.

"Actually, I need to use the time to speak to your mom alone."

Zoe freezes midstep. "I'll wear headphones and blast ZZ Top."

ZZ Top? I didn't think she even knew who they were. But then, of course I didn't. I've no idea what Zoe listens to these days. Since moving to the islands, her music no longer blares through the house but through headphones. Her TV watching, too, has become a wholly inward experience. No longer do we sit on the couch, scarfing gummy bears, laughing our asses off at *Curb Your Enthusiasm*. Now she hides in her room, watching whatever she's watching on a screen the size of a postage stamp, giggling only to herself. At times I stand by her door, my knuckles ready to rap on it, and I suddenly feel like I'd be intruding on one of the "cool kids" back in high school, where I was, needless to say, a monster geek. Maybe I need to knock on that door more often rather than run away. Maybe I need to make more of an effort, to spend less time protecting her and more time just loving her, more time getting to know her, the *real* her, not a mother's perfect illusion. We're around each other *constantly* yet we've somehow drifted miles apart.

"I'm afraid ole Billy, Dusty, and Frank Beard won't suffice," Noah says.

Frank Beard? One of the band members was named *Beard?* How did I not know that? Or did I once? It's not like ZZ Top ever made it onto my playlists. Or my mixtapes. But still . . . This is what's scaring me the most. Forgetting what I know is one thing; more and more I've been questioning whether I've always been ignorant of the things I don't know—how to tie a man's tie or braid Zoe's hair (Zoe swears I used to do it all the time)—or if these things, once there, are now lost to middle age or something even more insidious.

Under her breath, Zoe mutters, "Go to hell," before turning on her heel and retreating up the stairs. A few moments later, the door slams. This time Noah's presence prevents me from chasing after her. All the better since all I can think of is to promise her a trip to her favorite Japanese restaurant, Nama, an extremely out-of-the-way eatery in Haiku on Maui's North Shore. Come to think of it, I'm not even sure Nama survived the pandemic. So many restaurants didn't.

"Do me a favor," Noah says. "I'd like to inspect the second trekking pole. Can I see it?" He reaches into his pocket and pulls out a pair of nitrile gloves. "Wear these while you handle it." He retrieves another pair for himself but holds off slipping them on.

The other pole.

Did I forget to look for it last night?

How could I have forgotten *that?*

"All right," I tell him, slowly leading him up the stairs, "but fair warning: Zoe has dubbed my wardrobe the 'closetocalypse.'"

An hour later, after grudgingly canceling my meeting with Maui Search and Rescue, Noah and I are hiking the Pipiwai Trail, heading toward the falls. Most of the search-and-rescue activity has moved deeper into the wilds, but a few searchers—mostly senior volunteers who can't handle anything more strenuous than the Pipiwai—still lurk along the edge of the trail. Every moment I'm in public I feel thousands of eyes on me, and they itch like my legs, which are now covered ankle to ass in mosquito bites.

The pole wasn't in my closet. When I realized it was missing, Noah's face fell a yard. The news just sucked the life out of him. Does he think I'm lying? Are its whereabouts more important than I realize?

"Could you have left it somewhere else?" he said, standing before my closet.

"I don't think so. Maybe at Eddie's?"

He shook his head. "I've already received an inventory of the contents of Eddie's house. There was only one old set of hiking sticks, and they were his." Biting his lower lip, he says, "Who, besides you and Zoe, have been in this house?"

I think about it. Over the past two years we permitted more people inside our home than I would have liked. The off-grid community in Hana is close. It has to be. People who don't rely on traditional technology often need to depend on one another. Swapping spare solar parts, borrowing specialized tools or gas for a generator, it seems there's always something that needs fixing or building or maintaining. And Zoe and I aren't particularly good at any of it. Our worn copy of *Off-Grid Living for City Slickers* and single toolbox would get us only so far. Anyway, to shun these folks would have invited suspicion; it's not as if they don't have connections with the on-grid world. There are organized monthly supply runs into town, ham radio stations, even satellite phones. People talk. If word got around Maui that a woman and her daughter were living off-grid, evading their neighbors, it would eventually make it to the tourists, and if it made it to the tourists, it would make it to the mainland, and if it made it to the mainland, it could make it to the East Coast, to Connecticut, to Bridgeport, to Jeremy.

A few of the neighbors have teen daughters, and I brought them over hoping they'd make a connection with Zoe. The first friendship lasted four days, the second almost a week. The third lasted thirty minutes, and I decided to stop trying. Zoe had nothing in common with any of them. She'd never taken an interest in fishing or hunting or surfing—all things these kids took for granted. A couple of them didn't even know what Instagram was, never mind using it. A few months later, I befriended a few off-grid neighbors with teenage sons. Zoe was fonder of them, and those relationships lasted anywhere from a weekend to several weeks. All made visits to our house. Although Zoe never truly bonded with any of the kids, we showed the community we were "normal." We showed them we had nothing to hide.

After that, however, Zoe completely shut me out. It would be easy to blame it on Eddie, but it started before I met him. Anyway, Zoe got along well with Eddie. She liked having a real father figure, and Eddie always took her side during our arguments, making Mom out to be the bad guy. If Zoe's account is accurate, it happened most recently the night before Eddie went missing.

Noah's voice pulls me back to the present. ". . . nearing the overlook," he says. "Hey, you seem a little out of it. Are you all right? We haven't passed the spot yet, have we?"

"Of course not," I say. We *totally* almost passed it. "It's right up here on the left, past the first copse of trees."

"I'm still not getting how all those rangers, rescue personnel, and volunteers could have missed finding your pole two days straight."

We step off the trail, duck under low branches, and I point toward the lava tube where I had stashed it. "They searched the cave," I say, "but . . . Well, you'll see."

The tube is just large enough for me to navigate without ducking my head, but Noah learns the hard way that he's several inches taller than me. "It gets larger a bit farther in," I tell him.

"Something to look forward to," he sneers with his palm pressed against his forehead.

"I told you I'd get the pole and come out." My voice makes a pleasant, slightly trippy echo. "You didn't need to join me."

"It may become evidence, Kati. Besides, Lui and Harris are gonna want to know how first responders missed it. Best if I see it with my own eyes. And get pictures."

I stop suddenly, just as Noah stumbles into another lavacicle, or what you'd call in every other cave a stalactite. "If you become a witness, you'll be barred from being my attorney, won't you?"

"Only if I'm lucky," he says with a pained groan. "Anyway, I'm all we've got. I'm currently on the outs with my usual investigator."

I inadvertently shine the flashlight directly into his eyes, causing him to throw up a hand and smack the back of his head on the wall again. If he was smiling a moment ago, he isn't anymore.

"It's right up here," I say.

Here the tube stretches higher, permitting Noah to tread upright, but he has to dodge the lavacicles overhead. "Do these ever fall?"

Ignoring him, I turn toward the wall and put on the nitrile gloves. On my tippy-toes I reach up. "See, it's right here in one of these nifty grooves." These nifty grooves, or striations, Eddie explained, actually mark the levels of former lava flows.

Feeling along the shelf for the pole, my stomach tightens. In the glow of the flashlight, Noah reads the rising panic on my face. "It's not here," I say, my voice pitching high. "It's not where I left it."

"Are you sure we're in the right spot?"

"Positive. This is one of the caves Eddie and I stashed our—" I pause and reconsider telling him *our clothes*. Noah doesn't need to know about our skinny-dipping. "We stashed our . . . stuff in here a few times before so that it wouldn't get stolen."

He looks back toward the entrance, then again at me. A thin trail of blood runs from his hairline to just below his left ear. "Could someone have found it the first day of the search and moved it, left it to be found again up near the Infinity Pool on day two of the search?"

"I'm still not understanding why this is so important."

Noah sighs, clearly about to share something he doesn't yet want to share. I'm not so sure I want to hear it. "Look," he says, "Charley

Kay calling this pole a weapon didn't sit right with me, so I did a little research . . ." He trails off, staring up at the stalactites overhead.

"And?"

"StartTrek doesn't make your average hiking stick. They make poles that double as survival tools and weapons of self-defense."

Zoe

Mom still treats me like a child, as if some arbitrary birthday will somehow bestow on me all the wisdom of adulthood. Age is so fucking important to people. Until you're twenty-one, you're too young for just about anything fun. Then eight years later you're shitting your pants because you're about to turn thirty and your biological clock is ticking and you still have time but, hey, what if the next ten years produce similar results to the last ten and you've gotten nowhere?

On your fortieth birthday—Mom's just two years away—you're deemed unfuckable in certain circles, and that's the end of your usefulness as a human being. At least that was Mom's greatest fear before we fled to Hawaii. Dad would eventually inherit Grandma's money, and he'd have given Mom just enough so that she wouldn't have to work, i.e., complain too much. She could have gone on to stardom in The Real Housewives of Bridgeport. *She's always been terrified of such a transparently useless existence.*

Funny how she's been talking about going back to school for as long as I can remember yet she's never even perused a course catalog at the local community college. Why say something you know you're never going to follow through with? It makes no sense. Who was she trying to impress? Who was she trying to fool? When she talks about "missing college," she's always referring to the debauchery, not the education. By being conceived I ripped all the fun right out of her life.

And that's why she puts herself in a pinot-Ambien coma every night. Because why deal with serious issues when you can avoid them? Why exist in a rotten, unfair reality when a fantasy world is attainable by prescription or over the dark web?

She talks of how intense her feelings were at my age yet ignores that I have feelings at all. She's certainly not concerned with my happiness. She chose to seclude us in a remote jungle rather than lose ourselves in a big city overseas like I wanted. "Your father knows you love Europe," she said. "It's the first place he'll look." I didn't bother telling her he also knows how fucking selfish she is and that she wouldn't choose a refuge based on my preferences.

The worst of it is how she complains about the tropics. As if Hawaii wasn't perfect for her. She could get me away from everyone and everything and control me the way Grandma controlled my dad. It's amazeballs how much my mom hated Grandma given how much they had in common.

Now she's still playing dumb about the trekking poles. As if she doesn't know they're really weapons. She and Noah just looked for one of them in her closet which, as always, looks like a fucking sharknado hit it.

I'm not surprised they couldn't find it. I wouldn't be surprised if they never find it.

There's no other way to put it—everything she's doing points to her guilt. Why else wouldn't she admit that she carries the pole for self-defense? And why deny that she and Eddie argue constantly?

Above all, why is she so worried about what I say to the park service when this morning she talked to the fucking press!

Noah, her newest knight in shining armor, came and put a stop to the interview. He was beyond flustered when he left. He knows how things look. He may have handled high-profile island murder trials before, but this time he's in over his head.

Yet no one wants my help. No one is interested in my opinions.

Well, Mom, I finally feel entirely invisible.

Invisible, ugh. When we ran, Mom was obsessed about being "invisible." She stacked her supersecret Kindle with titles like How to Disappear *and* The Art of Invisibility, *books on how to erase your digital footprint, how to leave false trails, how to quote-unquote vanish without a trace.*

Of course, she demanded I destroy every electronic device I owned. Only some last-minute cleverness allowed me to keep you. Regardless of what she thinks, we can't completely erase the past. We need to confront what we've done and didn't do and redeem ourselves or pay for our mistakes.

Which leads me to wonder who Mom was really running from—my father or the justice system. Our running became more urgent with every police interview, with every tidbit of information released about the investigation. With the police watching their every move, Mom saying she was frightened of what Dad would do was so disingenuous. Unless she meant she was afraid of what he'd say.

Mom's hatred of Grandma was common knowledge. From Great-Uncle Gun to her hairstylist, she never shut up about her. About how she supposedly lied and threatened and manipulated, how she had my father wrapped around her little finger, how Grandma was quote-unquote trying to poison me against her. Gee, Mom, projecting much?

The past matters. It's how we learn, how we grow, and it affects every damn decision we make moving forward. How can she of all people not see that?

So what do I do now? That's the question.

I can't just sit here and think. I'm so damned tired of sitting and thinking.

I just want to get away from all this—

Shit, there's someone at the door again. Sorry, but for the moment, you're going to need to hide where the sun doesn't shine.

8

After departing Haleakala, Noah drives us back to his office, where he shows me the inch-thick binder of research he's printed out about StartTrek's newest model, the Trek-n-Deck, little brother of the Hike-n-Strike, first cousin of the Slog-n-Slug and Stump-n-Thump, and a not-so-distant relation of the Plod-n-Prod, which is a fully functional trekking pole that also provides 950,000 volts to anyone or anything stupid enough to come within a few feet of you.

"You recognize yours from any of these?"

I sure do. I point at the sleek new Trek-n-Deck.

"You never noticed the heavy brass bottom?" he says, making it clear he's—*How would Zoe put it?*—a little sus. Or maybe *I'd* be the one who's sus, I don't know, and who cares? I've got bigger fish to fry, taller mountains to climb. Choose your frigging cliché, as Koa Pualani would say. *Or are those idioms?* I should know this. I write articles for Scary Mommy and HuffPo for chrissakes.

"How long have you had these poles?"

"I had an old set when I met Eddie. He replaced them, gave me these as a present five or six months ago."

"What kind was your old set?"

Hike-n-Strike, Slog-n-Slug, Stump-n-Thump? Who the hell knows? But I wasn't strolling through the jungle with Zoe completely defenseless. A mother needs to protect her child. What if we encountered a pack of wild boars? What if we encountered Jeremy? What if we encountered *both*?

This time the idea of *not* lying never even occurs to me. "I don't know, Safe Stroll? Something for old bags with osteoarthritis."

A chirping sound emanates from Noah's briefcase, which rests at the far end of the conference room table. He ambles over to it, reaches inside, and retrieves a watch.

"Is that a *Casio*?" I (perhaps) overreact.

"You betcha. See, this bad boy not only tells me the time. It tells me the date and . . ." He stares at it. "Well, that's pretty much it. But that's enough, right? It's shock resistant, water resistant, solar powered. It backlights so that I can read it in the dark, *and* it's great for extreme sports."

"You play extreme sports?"

"I watch them on ESPN plus-plus when there's nothing else on."

"In the streaming era, there's never nothing else on."

He sighs. "I'm still with Oceanic Cable. Who needs more than seventy-two channels?"

Me. Me, me, me. Because streaming became mainstream just in time, not only for the pandemic but for the escape from the East Coast when what I needed most was, well, an escape. I'm not ashamed to say I *needed* twenty-two seasons of *Law & Order* and all seven of its spinoffs. I needed *Bosch* and *The Lincoln Lawyer*, *Reacher* and *The Chestnut Man*. I needed an endless supply of true crime documentaries, even though half are about husbands killing their wives. It didn't matter; I used other people's lives as an escape from mine, and I needed an escape. Especially once Zoe started pulling away.

Noah holds up his Casio. "I'm sorry, but I need to motor."

"Oh, right. The vigil."

"Wanna join me?"

"I'm not sure I'd be welcome. What would you advise?"

"As your attorney?" His lower jaw shifts to the left as he thinks it over. "I'd say maybe it's best if you don't make an appearance this evening."

When Noah drops me outside the house at dusk, the first thing I notice is that all the windows are dark. They are *never* all dark. A light always burns in the Dawes residence. It's another rule, one even Zoe has happily followed the past two years. Is she that angry with me? Is this her way of lashing out? To make us less safe? To make us vulnerable?

But no, Zoe has nightmares too. In the small black hours I hear her cry out in her sleep. Not just any old sound but a holler for help. The many times I've attempted to intercede, though, have consistently turned into shouting matches. *I don't need you* now, she'd say. *I don't need to be saved. Just go back to your own fucking room and your own fucking dreams.*

My own fucking night terrors, she means.

Our Jeep remains parked in the driveway, which means Zoe's home. Maybe we can finally sit down and have a long talk that doesn't devolve into a murderball match. That's not too much to ask, is it?

I reach the stoop only to find the door ajar. The words cross my vision like a movie title. *An Open Door.* Coming soon to scare the living shit out of you. My stomach takes an unexpected ride on the Tilt-A-Whirl, and I almost lose my balance at the top of the cement steps before clutching the iron rail and steadying myself. Could I have left the door open? *Impossible, right?* I gently push the door wider, the dark mouth of the foyer yawning open like a monstrous maw.

"Zoe?" I call out.

Could Noah have been the last out of the house when we'd left earlier? Could he have left it open by mistake? But no, I'm almost sure I was last out of the house. Locking the door is as automatic to me as breathing. Could I have been so thrown by the missing trekking pole that I left the house not only unlocked but wide open to intruders? Could this be another of those clouded moments, time lost to some dangerous disorder now making itself more and more apparent?

Did something happen while I was gone? I look back. The dark has already pushed dusk aside. No stunning Maui sunset tonight. I cross the threshold.

Faint music emanates from upstairs. It has to be Zoe's stereo. Only she never plays it out loud, not even while I'm out. One of her two speakers is busted; the sound is a thousand times crisper through her wireless headphones.

In the foyer I freeze in place. The tune is familiar, *too* familiar. It's the Stones, Jeremy's favorite band. Mick Jagger belts out the chorus, and dread washes over me like a rogue wave. Goose bumps spring up along my arms. It's Jeremy's favorite song. What he called his anthem. Back when I was *under his thumb*.

After Zoe was born, he crooned along with Mick every morning to make certain I knew that the balance of power in our relationship had dramatically shifted his way. The subtext was simple, blunt; subtlety was never his forte. *The bitch* (his mother's adorable pet name for me) would *pay*. I would *pay* for once being unsure I wanted to be with him. I would *pay* for weighing abortion against having his child as a teenager. I would *pay* for any sleepless nights he'd spent pining for me or fretting over his zygote.

I would pay for the rest of my life.

I've no doubt it's a promise he still intends to make good on.

Especially now that I'm no longer *under his thumb*.

Feeling around for the light switch, I knock over a ceramic vase on the counter. Before I can reach it, it rolls off the granite and smashes to pieces on the kitchen tiles. I cringe at the racket, bend to pick up one of the larger, sharper shards, then wait to see if the noise prompts anyone upstairs to come down.

"Zoe?" I call out again.

As I pull out my cell phone, the Stones song ends, only to begin all over again. *It's on a loop.* With a couple of practiced swipes, I turn on the flashlight app, which is brighter than I anticipated. Almost too bright. I feel like a target. I'm about to turn back toward the wall to locate the light switch when I notice the moonlight illuminating the kitchen table and, more vitally, what sits on it. *The remote control.*

Backside up, button-side down. *Definitely* not how I left it. I finally turn toward the wall and hit the light switch. *Nothing.* My dread morphs into paralysis until I realize my fingers are already crawling across my cell phone. After tapping in 9-1-1, I tap on the speakerphone so that I can continue to use the flashlight to search the house.

I pump up the volume. Let the bastard know the cops are coming. If he's here, let him run like he made me run. Like he made his daughter run. I set down the shard, and from the wooden block on the counter I pull out the eight-inch chef's knife.

Let him run for his life.

Forever?

Or until he's dead.

I'm about to send the call when the conversation I'll likely have with the dispatcher runs through my head like a court transcript.

"Nine-one-one, what's your emergency?"

"I think someone's inside the house."

"Where are you right at this moment?"

"Heading upstairs to find out."

"Ma'am, that's not a good id—"

I thumb the red button to cancel the call and continue up the stairs, suddenly too afraid to call out Zoe's name. Something's wrong. I can *feel* it. But calling the police right now would only add to our troubles, would only draw more attention to me, more attention to *us*. It could lead Jeremy straight here—that is, if he hasn't found us already.

Upstairs I shine the light on Zoe's door, which is closed. *Please be home, please be safe. Please just be in bed sulking and hating me like a normal teenager.* Cautiously, as if it were a thousand degrees, I reach for the knob, clasp it, and turn. The door opens. I peer inside.

"Zoe!" I scream.

9

Keys in hand, I dart outside and jump into the Jeep, twist the ignition, hit the lights, and back out of the drive like a shot before realizing I'm not wearing my seat belt. Between the twisty, turny Hana Highway and the way I've been driving recently, even a brief ride to Koki Beach could turn into another *Poseidon Adventure*.

Minutes later, my head is every bit as hazy as the road stretched before me, but I'm nearly there. I lower my window and savor the fresh ocean air. A few hundred yards away, heat-resistant white cars ironically blanket the lot nearest the beach like Hawaiian snow. People are everywhere. A hundred of them or more. All with burning candles, all chanting something in Hawaiian with near-perfect harmony. It's an ancient chant, somehow both melodic and ominous. The closer I get the more it looks like some in attendance are carrying wooden torches and pitchforks. But no, just bamboo tiki torches and surfboards. Though I never met any of them, Eddie had—*has*—many close friends in the surfing community, most of whom live on Oahu's North Shore.

I pull up onto the grass across the street and park. Leap out of the Jeep and scramble across the highway toward the beach. Once I hit sand, I'm instantly swallowed up by a sea of strangers. Luckily, after a couple of minutes of frantic searching, Noah notices *me*. "Over here," he calls out, beckoning me. I veer toward him, nearly tipping over from the slight shift in direction. He catches me, though I don't know whether I needed catching. My money says I could have recovered without his help.

But maybe that's because I'm mad at him at the moment. Livid, really. I tried calling on the way over and he didn't answer. He could have saved me a whole lot of stress by picking up and, hopefully, telling me my baby was there on the beach with him, having a lovely conversation with Eddie's cousins. Or maybe that *is* asking too much.

". . . she here, Noah? Tell me she's here, tell me she's all right, that she just—"

"Whoa, slow down, Millie Bobby Brown. What's going on?"

"Zoe, *is she here?*"

"I haven't seen her, but there's a lot of . . ."

I'm already free of his arms, navigating the human tide, sneaking looks around shoulders, above heads, in the crooks of people's necks.

"Zoe!" I call out involuntarily. I know I shouldn't attract any more attention to myself than absolutely necessary, but my head and my heart are grappling and my head's losing right now.

I glance over my shoulder to find Noah following me, but he's having much more trouble struggling against the human current than I am.

Finally, I see the back of Zoe's head.

"Zoe!"

She turns around.

Not Zoe.

I stop, suddenly all discombobulated, my high hopes fallen to new lows. I spin, spraying sand up between my toes. In which direction was I heading? I turn again, first one way, then the other. Where was I coming from? Suddenly, hands clamp on the back of my shoulders, large hands, strong hands, man hands. Noah's.

"Catch me up, Kati. What happened to Zoe?"

"I don't *know*! She's not at home, the door was open, the house was completely dark. *Pitch. Black.* Like I've never seen it before. Even though we're off-grid, we always keep some lights on—and I went upstairs to her room, and . . . and . . ."

I'm out of breath, but not only out of breath, I've lost track of what I was telling Noah. Staring at me from only a few yards away are two large men I recognize from Eddie's photos as his cousins Elta and Kanoa. They don't look happy to see me. *No one* looks happy to see me.

"Her room?" Noah says, prodding me from my stupor. "Zoe's room, what happened?"

Signs of a struggle. Only that's not what I want to say, is it? Isn't that a term used by police detectives and the actors who portray them on television?

"Her computer was *gone*," I cry out, "her desk chair *knocked over.* Things she cherished are broken and strewn all over the room. It looks like . . ."

"Signs of a struggle," he says.

I was going to say *like a tornado hit it*, but I just dumbly nod, my body numbing, mouth dry, eyes watery.

Noah, meanwhile, takes it all in.

"Eddie's cousins," I murmur as they approach us.

"I'll talk to them," he says, stepping between me and them.

I stand stock-still, waiting, taking in the smell of shampoo and perfume, of body odor and ocean and sand and burning wood. In the mist of my mind, I see Zoe's room as clearly as if I'm still in it, rifling through her drawers (*Her passport is missing!*), sifting through her handbag (*Her wallet and credit cards, even her emergency cash is still here!*), and finally rummaging through her closet, where all her luggage and clothes remained undisturbed.

Next to me, a woman's cell phone goes off. Then someone else's. Another. Then another. And another, and another. I spin, watching one by one as each person pulls their phone from their handbag or pocket, checks the screen, swipes, then holds it up to their ear. Mouths move, but it's one great jambalaya of sound. Nothing makes sense. I can't understand a word being said, even as the chanting quiets, then fades altogether, even as individuals turn to face me, first an outer circle of them, then a middle, then an inner, until everyone's gaze converges on me at once.

This isn't my imagination.

Finally, Noah's phone rings. He plucks it from his pocket, swipes, and holds it to his ear. A moment later he stares at me. "It's Maui Fire. They've just found a body."

My lips part.

"I'm sorry, Kati," he says. "I really am."

PART II

THE SLAYER RULE

10

Zoe is missing.

In the full dark Noah and I travel along Hana Highway toward Kahului Airport. Minutes ago I was on the verge of coming clean, of telling the police everything, even if it meant facing the music back home. Then Noah received a phone call from one of his old buddies from the FBI forensics lab in Honolulu. Instead of sending it to his Bluetooth, he tapped on the speaker. Suddenly, a young female voice emanated straight from the dashboard like *Knight Rider*'s KITT, with what sounds like a slight Ukrainian accent.

"Anca, what have you got for me?"

Okay. So it's that kind of buddy.

"Just a heads-up," she said. "We found something on the pole."

"Prints?"

"All right, *two* somethings."

Blood. The other was blood. *Is* blood, at least I think. According to Anca, the findings are preliminary and they're still running tests. Not that any of us are deluding ourselves after hearing the news on the beach. There's no doubt in my mind that it's blood. And there's no doubt about who it belongs to.

Eddie is dead.

There on Koki Beach, just like that, the world as I knew it ended and a new one, a *darker* one, emerged like a ghost ship from the mist. No more weekend-long Netflix marathons cuddling next to Eddie on the sofa. No more hikes or bike rides or Sunday drives along the Road to Hana. No more Native Hawaiian folktales by a romantic campfire for two. No more skinny-dipping at the bottom of hidden waterfalls, no more making love on our black-sand beach under the stars. It's official. Any hopes for a future I still desperately clung to are gone.

And so is Zoe.

Immediately following the call from Anca, I ran through the potential consequences of coming clean to Noah in my head. If I told him, told him everything, Noah would doubtless abandon me. Would even turn me in to the police. To hell with the attorney-client privilege; he's old chums with half the force, and he'd have no choice but to believe that this woman wanted for questioning in Connecticut in connection with her loathsome mother-in-law's murder *killed* his best friend. He'd make a single "anonymous" call and I'd be behind bars, detained while Maui PD connects with the Fairfield County district attorney's office back in Bridgeport.

I can't do anything for Zoe from a holding cell. As for Maui PD, there's only a few hundred officers spread across the entire island. If all their attention turned to me, they'd dismiss my worries about Zoe. They'd consider her a runaway, a disgruntled teen who, after two years living anonymously off-grid, finally fled from her fugitive mother. As for Zoe herself, once she hears I've been arrested, she'll vanish like a puff of smoke. She's smart, she's resourceful, and as she always says, *Mom, I'm independent AF.*

And disappearing is precisely what I taught her to do if I was ever detained by the police.

Of course I'd never considered that Zoe could go missing. That if she vanished, I might never know whether she'd run or been taken.

As we approach the central part of the island, I run through the possibilities in my head again. Zoe *could* have run away, but the state of her room makes that unlikely. Unless . . .

Unless that's what she wants me to think.

Zoe is clever enough—and savvy enough thanks to our shared taste in movies and books—to stage a crime scene that would stand up to my scrutiny. But, no, no. No, I can't think like that or I'll twist myself in knots. No, I need to assume the scene is genuine and that someone, maybe Jeremy, maybe one of his minions like Dmitri, has her. But where would they take her? All I see in my head is Kahului Airport. But Jeremy's smarter than that.

And shit, shit, shit, his best friend Ozzie Bent owns a private jet. And a damn yacht.

"We need to turn around," I say.

Noah looks at me like I'm wearing a tinfoil hat. His confusion is understandable. The plan was to scour the airport for my missing daughter and inquire of security and the clerks on the ticket lines if they'd seen her. I've already selected the photo on my phone: a candid headshot of Zoe turning toward the camera, laughing like the old days. I snapped it the night Eddie proposed.

"Turn around?" Noah snaps. "Where to? What for?"

After the airport, we planned to head over to the Maui County coroner's office in Makawao. As Eddie's fiancée, I have no right to see the body, but evidently another of Noah's "buddies" works as an assistant to the chief Maui County medical examiner.

"Hana Airport," I say, instantly realizing I can't say more. Can't tell him that if Zoe was abducted, it's most likely by her father, the quasi-infamous venture capitalist Jeremy Perotta, whose friend Oz owns—and flies—his own private plane (and has a penchant for young girls and a reputation for roofies and date rape).

"Just one airline uses that airport," Noah says. "Mokulele. There's practically no traffic at night. I'll just call over and ask if anyone's seen a teenage Caucasian girl."

"Let me guess," I mutter, not quite knowing why. "You have a fuck-buddy who's an air traffic controller."

"She happens to be an airfield operations specialist. And my local connections—male *and* female—might just help us find your daughter."

I'm living my worst nightmare.

Like a horror movie playing out in real time. That's what crime *is* to the victims of violence. All this time I've been watching mysteries and thrillers and procedurals, but they're all the same; they all stir the same emotion. *Fear* with a capital *F.*

I so dreaded this happening that I never thought through what to do if it did. For two years, I obsessed about hiding out and locking in while I should have been preparing for this very night. There was never a way to completely protect her, never a way to keep my eyes on her 24/7, 365. Not a willful teenage girl. Not Zoe.

How did I not see that?

Worse, how did I not foresee that Jeremy would do just this? Of course he'd come after her. He *knows* what would most hurt me, and it isn't a knife in the chest, at least not a literal one. I bet this was his plan all along. Kill Eddie, take Zoe. That's how he thinks. But what *then?* Would he harm his own little girl to finally slice my heart in half? Is he truly the malignant narcissist, the unabashed sociopath, that I long suspected him to be?

If he took her by force, then yes, I need to assume he'd kill her. She was already dead to him anyway; he'd said so a number of times. Zoe told the Bridgeport police things Jeremy would never forgive her for, daughter or not.

Even if he could forgive her treachery, he could never forgive her for fleeing with me. In his mind, abandonment is the ultimate sin, an action for which there *is* no forgiveness. Early in our relationship, I suggested we see other people. The change in him was instant, like Jekyll and Hyde. He screamed at me. Blocked the door of his dorm so I couldn't leave. Took out a bottle of his roommate's pills and threatened to commit suicide right before my eyes.

Later he convinced me that this behavior was atypical for him. That his passion for me drove him to it. In no time, he made me fall in love with him all over again, actually made me question how this smart, attractive young man from a wealthy East Coast family could even be interested in an average-looking girl from a broken home in the middle of nowhere.

"We're still headed in the wrong direction," I say.

Noah needn't remind me that this is Hana Highway. There are precious few places to turn a car around without getting killed.

"There's a scenic lookout just past this curve," Noah says. "I'll turn there. But are you sure you want to go to Hana Airport rather than Kahului?"

"I'm *sure*," I say with much more confidence than I feel. I'm not sure of anything. Right now I can hardly think straight. *No, I'm thinking like a storyteller when I should be thinking like a true detective.* "Wait," I tell him. "Pull over at the lookout. I need to thin—"

I never get the word out. Because as we round that final curve an oncoming pair of high beams blinds us, throwing Noah's Explorer into a spin.

But this is Hana Highway. There's nowhere to spin but into the mountain or the ocean.

Zoe

So dark in here, and cold. I haven't been this cold in two years.

I think my nose has already adapted to the rotting smell, but the memory of the stench alone is enough to make me want to vomit.

But she'll come for me. I know she will.

I know deep down she loves me and wants to protect me. I know she does what she thinks is best for me—even when it isn't. Hell, if she only made good decisions, I wouldn't exist. She's said so herself in not so many words.

I know, too, that we can't always protect what's precious to us, no matter what that is. Sometimes it's obliterated, sometimes it's taken away.

Sometimes it's both.

I just want this to be over. I'm so fucking scared. I can't possibly predict the outcome of all this, and the possibilities are infinite, most of them terrifying. But unless I think of something, this is now out of my hands and in hers.

Who am I kidding? It's always been in hers.

But she's smart. God knows she's consumed enough crime stories. Wine and illicit substances aside, books and TV and movies have been her escape for the past two decades. They're the islands she hid in before we fled to Hawaii. I've read the books and watched the shows, too, so I know how she thinks.

She'll find me. The question is when. And what state I'll be in when she does.

11

When I come to, Noah's Explorer is spun backward just a few yards into the lookout. I'm lying on the ground farther in and Noah's hovering over me, cell phone in hand. *Shit, he called the police.* Strangely, my vision is crisp, my head clear, but there's blood on Noah's hands, and he's pressing a University of Hawaii T-shirt against my scalp. And *ouch.* There it is, the pain surfacing like a shark fin, cutting through my head like a chain saw. And, *Ew, oh my God,* there's blood in my mouth.

"Don't move," Noah says when I try. "You can't help Zoe if you're in a coma."

Coma? "Is it *that* bad?"

"I'm not a doctor, Kati, but there's a lot of blood, and you lost consciousness for a few moments."

The scalp bleeds profusely, I tell myself. Lots of blood vessels near the surface, I'd read somewhere. *BFD,* as Zoe would say. On the other hand, even seemingly minor head injuries can be fatal. You can be fine one minute and gone the next.

Talk and die, they call it, Mac said the day he came clean to me about his criminal history. *One punch, not even a good one. Just hard and in the wrong place. When the guy I hit left the pub he seemed jim-dandy. Not so much as a stumble. Next day I'm arrested for first-degree manslaughter.*

OMF'ingG. Am I going to die? How long will it take for an ambulance to get this deep on the Road to Hana? What if there's traffic? What if a single spiteful tourist in a rented Mustang holds up the single-file line? What if a breakdown blocks both lanes?

No, I can't think like this.

"Noah," I say, my eyes reflexively making like the falls. "I *need* to find her."

"We *will*."

His conviction is so genuine that a warm feeling passes through me as he says it. *Hopefully that's not internal bleeding.* Somehow I believe, as if by magic, Noah can make it happen. We *will* find her. It's more than just words, more than an optimistic assessment. It's a vow, it's a pledge, it's a promise . . .

That's when my vision clouds and everything around me rapidly fades to white.

When I regained consciousness seconds later, I was back in Noah's Explorer, headed to Maui Memorial Medical Center in Wailuku.

Here, in the examination room, Kilo sits beside me. He's just ended a call with Noah.

"Has he found her?" I say, though I hardly recognize my own voice.

"Not yet," Kilo says, hurriedly looking over his shoulder for a nurse. "But no worries. He'll find her." He finally lifts himself out of his seat and labors toward the door. "Hey, we need one doctor here, yeah?" When he turns back to me, he speaks in his usual soft, gentle tone. "He went to Hana Airport like you told him."

Did I place Noah on the right path? Would Jeremy and Oz have taken Zoe straight to the airport, or would that have looked too suspicious? Maybe the plane is still there. If it is, we still have a chance to recover Zoe. Borrowing Kilo's phone, I text Noah, instructing him to check for a Gulfstream G350. That's as much as I can tell him right now. But unless Oprah's giving away Gulfstream G350s these days, it should be enough.

I glance toward the room's lone window. Still dark outside. How much time has passed since the accident? *How much time did we spend in the waiting room?* There's an analog clock on the wall, but it's one big blur. I can't even see any hands, let alone what numbers they're pointing at.

My phone. Maybe Zoe called in the past few minutes.

"Easy, easy," Kilo says as I twist my body to search for my things. He reaches out and hands me my phone.

No texts.

No missed calls.

No notifications whatsoever.

And the phone is fucked. Even worse than I originally thought. Simply seeing its condition drains me of all remaining energy. It's almost as if the phone is my battery, the only hope I have of hearing from Zoe. I swipe left and right, up and down, to make sure the touch screen still functions. I slump back down on the ER bed and stare into its shattered face again.

Ten p.m. Do you know where your children are?

It's a public service announcement I remember from childhood. Ten p.m. every night after back-to-back reruns of *Cheers. Do you know where your children are?*

Only for me it was, *It's ten p.m. Do you know where your frigging mother is?*

I squeeze my eyes shut tight. I'm lost in my head. I need to come out of it, need to think of Zoe, need to figure out a way to tell someone that Jeremy—*maybe Dmitri? Or Oz?*—is responsible for our crash. Back at the scene, it didn't seem plausible. Now I realize it's not only plausible, it would have been easy. If they have Zoe, they have Zoe's phone, which they could have used to pinpoint my location on Hana Highway, right? Or someone could have been tailing us, calling ahead, telling Jeremy or Dmitri or Oz, *"They're twenty seconds from the curve."* They could have timed it perfectly.

". . . somet'ing to drink?" Kilo says.

I point to the pitcher in the corner of the room and think of Koa's recorder submerged in my glass of iced tea. *Like space,* he'd said. *No one can hear you scream.* Suddenly, as if a trapdoor opens beneath me and swallows me whole, I'm racked with powerful *doubt* about whether Jeremy was involved in the accident, in Eddie's death, in Zoe's disappearance. Is my hatred for Jeremy so great that I've developed tunnel vision?

"Kilo," I say gently, "did Eddie know Koa Pualani well?"

Handing me a Styrofoam cup of ice water, he says, "During the big Lanyon case, yeah, they were boys. Eddie got publicity, Koa got the story. After that, though, I dunno. Eddie never told me what happened. A falling-out over somet'ing, eh?"

Could Eddie have promised Koa a payoff upon the verdict and reneged when the shipping company appealed? Was dirty money past due? Eddie had boasted about the impact that Koa Pualani's articles had on the case nearly every time he mentioned it.

"Kilo," I say, "who would want to hurt Eddie?"

Kilo looks at me like I just asked him to assist me in taking my own life. His silence is like a siren call.

"Eddie would want you to answer my question," I say.

To break his silence, I ask him whether Eddie was having an affair, whether he was afraid of any disgruntled clients, whether he was in serious debt. At debt, *that's* when Kilo turns his head away.

"He *was* in debt, wasn't he."

A nurse finally enters the room, a real-world Ratched if ever there was one. Stiffly, she checks my vitals, reviews my chart, asks me routine questions I don't really know how to answer. This is the first time I've received medical treatment in Hawaii. It's a wonder how healthy you can stay when your husband's not tuning you like a piano every other night.

With Kilo on the cusp of spilling his guts, I want Ratched out of the room. "Can you *excuse* us?" I say with more annoyance than I intended. She gives me one last Ratched glare, and for a moment I think she's about to pull up a seat next to Kilo and join the conversation. Instead, she huffs and puffs and blows out the door. *Did I read her name tag right? Midge?*

When she finally leaves, I shoot Kilo a look like the one that chased Ratched away.

"I realize there's a bro code that maybe extends beyond death. But my freedom and, more crucially, my daughter's *life* are at stake. I need you to be straight with me."

For a moment it seems as though it was all for nothing. Kilo's face is a stone slate.

Finally, though, he draws a deep breath and closes the door for privacy. As he exhales, he emits a slight wheeze, then knocks his fist against his chest and clears his throat. "Awright," he says. "This whole t'ing started . . ."

According to Kilo, Eddie's love affair with gambling began during their first semester of college at UH. Like most addictions, it started off innocently enough with a few bets on professional football games between friends. Since Hawaii doesn't have its own professional sports teams, bets lent some mild excitement to *Monday Night Football* and the game of the week.

Early on, Eddie proved a competent gambler. Each Sunday he won money, and each Monday he won (or nearly won) the weekly football pool. Although Kilo was less interested in gambling at the time, he was grateful to see his best friend partake in spectator sports. Eddie had always been an athlete. Prior to gambling, Kilo spent most weekends alone in their dorm's common area watching television while Eddie played soccer, basketball, or beach volleyball with their friends.

When they graduated, Eddie proposed their first trip to Vegas. Until then, they'd spent most summer and winter breaks on "staycations." Why leave paradise for a lesser destination? But Eddie was itching to get into a casino. Elta and Kanoa were too busy with their shop, but Kilo worked on his own schedule and could perform his job from just about anywhere. Lacking a good excuse, Kilo agreed to eight days, seven nights at the Bellagio on the Las Vegas Strip.

For two young guys who'd never left the islands, the lights and sounds of Vegas offered a new kind of paradise. While the pair took advantage of the town's many offerings, they spent the lion's share of their time in the casinos. Roulette, craps, poker, blackjack—they loved it all. Even the slot machines.

As in most things, Kilo came out a loser and Eddie a winner. But Eddie shared his winnings, and they splurged on all-you-can-eat prime rib buffets, alcohol, shows (and doubtless other forms of Vegas entertainment Kilo is too shy to share with me). Soon Eddie and Kilo started racking up the frequent-flier miles, heading to Vegas at least once per season. For Kilo, four weeks a year were plenty. For Eddie, it simply wasn't enough. A fire had been lit. He wanted to bet big money every week of the year. So his cousins introduced him to a young man named Makoa Urima, a small-time Honolulu bookie with aspirations of expanding his business across the islands.

Like most addicts, Eddie denied having a problem yet became super secretive about his betting habits. Kilo first realized that his friend's sportsbook gambling was no longer restricted to football season when Eddie suddenly renewed his childhood interest in pro baseball, basketball, hockey, even college athletics. Kilo never learned how much Eddie was betting, but his daily mood swings suggested gambling had become more than a hobby—and that the stakes were steadily increasing. He was like a baseball team down six runs, trying to get it all back in one swing.

This went on to some degree for two straight decades. Meanwhile, Eddie's trips to Vegas became more frequent and bore a new kind of urgency that for Kilo soured the entire experience. Hawaii's "ninth island," as the locals call it, eventually became Eddie's home away from home.

Listening from the hospital bed, I close my eyes and a single tear slides down my cheek. Only now do I realize I never truly knew my husband-to-be. Not the whole Eddie, not the real deal. I saw what he wanted me to see, heard what he wanted me to hear. His secrets were his secrets, and he never had any intention of sharing them with me, even if we shared our lives.

But then, who am I to get angry about secrets? Eddie never knew where I actually grew up, never knew I was married, *am* married, never even knew my real name.

By the time Kilo completes his story I'm even more convinced that Jeremy *could* well be innocent. Eddie was a compulsive gambler. Maybe he was in debt to the wrong people. Maybe they threatened him, maybe they tried and failed to collect, maybe they killed him. What if Eddie's luck simply ran out?

My eyelids fall, stretch wide, and fall again. So sleepy, so hungry, so thirsty. But the antiseptic smell of the hospital is also making my stomach sick, while a mix of emotions rumbles through my head like an L train. Images of Zoe's birth, memories of cradling her in my arms for the first time, feeding her, burping her, breathing in her aromatic newborn scent.

Along with those images come images of the emergency room visits for stitches to my lips, cheeks, and hairline—all trips made with creative and well-rehearsed lies on my tongue. And I remember Mac's heart attack. Though he survived, he wasn't the same man he'd been. For a while, it almost felt as though I actually lost him after all.

12

Unable to keep my eyes open, my chin finally drops to my chest. I nod off in the ER with Mac on my mind and snap to with him again at the forefront.

No contact, he said. *None whatsoever, I'm sorry. This entire plan is modeled after WitSec, the federal witness protection program. No contact with anyone from your life in Connecticut, not even anonymously. You are now Kati Dawes and your daughter is Zoe Dawes—and I get to bask in the knowledge that I named you both.*

Why those names? I asked.

Katharine and Zoe were the names I picked out for my own daughter, but her damn loon of a mother won the argument.

"Kilo," I say, thankful to find him still sitting beside the emergency room bed. "The other car . . ."

"They *awright,*" he says quickly.

"They?"

"Coupla newlyweds in a white Mustang convertible, Noah told me."

I let fly a deep sigh of relief. *Newlyweds, honeymooners—shocker— tourists.* Not Jeremy, not Dmitri. But that leaves me back at square one: *Who has Zoe?* Not knowing your child's whereabouts is a terror that ages you months for every minute they're missing. Every bone, every muscle, every organ cries out for her. My brain feels like it's caught fire, my heart as if it's exploding in my chest. How I *wish* I could contact Mac. But he was clear: if I tried to contact him, I'd soon find that *he* disappeared.

For your own protection, he said. *And for Zoe's.*

Only Zoe *needs* him right now. And so does her mother.

I was roughly the same age Zoe is now when I met Mac. I started college younger than Zoe will—my mother so wanted to be rid of me when I was three that she paid to enroll me in pre-K at a Catholic school rather than wait another year for me to go to public school. So I was seventeen when I started college at a small liberal-arts school tucked away in a rolling green valley in Bumblefuck, Pennsylvania.

College. A fresh start with a full ride. Only a few miles away from my mother Joanne, away from seventeen years of pain, but far enough. No more of her yelling and screaming, no more of her slapping and smacking, no more of her wishing me dead. At least not to my face. No more worrying about someone from school seeing us together at the mall during one of her conniptions (or *shit fits*, as I called them). No more of *her*, period.

And no more *me* either. In high school, I hadn't made connections yet never understood why. I was super shy, sure, but other shy kids had friends. What was it that made me so *different*? I was pretty, sort of; I saw that despite my mother's hateful criticisms about how I wore my hair, the clothes I favored, my taste in shoes. In any case, I'd made a conscious decision to entirely reinvent myself for college.

With few social interactions over the previous few years, I worried about being an outcast from the start of freshman year. The great thing, though, about not having friends is that it gives one time to read voraciously—and that's how I read. Not the crap my high school English teachers pushed on me but genre novels and crime stories. I was in love with the Los Angeles painted by Raymond Chandler. I was addicted to Mickey Spillane's intensity and Dashiell Hammett's elegance. So I fabricated an entirely new character. A *hard-boiled* bitch who was *cool* in high school, too, and who, oh, so, so, *so* missed her besties back home!

For me, college was akin to Rumspringa, the Amish rite of passage during adolescence when the repressive restrictions on clothing, driving, prayers, and alcohol are mercifully relaxed until the individual chooses baptism or banishment. Nine out of ten Amish return home. But I knew my decision the moment I stepped on campus. I had no intention of returning.

College opened my eyes in so many ways. The first few weeks were by far the greatest of my life, and I somehow shed my shyness and inhibitions like a snake's skin. Alcohol helped. But I became a different person when sober as well. I made friends, I went to parties, I hooked up. And, finally, I fell in love.

Only not with one guy but two. One a fellow college student, the other a townie. Jeremy and Glenn. Jeremy was the sort of man I dreamed of being with before I even met him. The one who could instantly give me a large family, with a sister-in-law, mother-in-law, and plenty of aunts and uncles and cousins. On the underside of my roommate's top bunk, I scrawled *Mrs. Jeremy Perotta*. It just sounded so right at the time.

Then there was Glenn, in so many ways the opposite of Jeremy. Jeremy was flashy, Glenn was grunge. Jeremy was popular, Glenn was anything but. Our school, Center Valley College, was too small to have its own football team, but if it did, Jeremy would have been the starting quarterback by default. Glenn's only friend, as far as I could tell, was Georgie Porgie, his Portuguese water dog. Meanwhile, Glenn had a "family" like the one I'd just run from. Only instead of an overbearing mother, he had an authoritarian father. A blue-collar worker at a steel mill who broke his ass and wanted Glenn to break his as well and start "earnin' his keep." Glenn had started a few courses at the local community college (he wanted to be a small-town veterinarian), but his father made it impossible to continue. Glenn dropped out after showing up for final exams his first semester.

Small college towns like Bumblefuck often have only one hangout, and ours was the Black Pepper Pub. Almost within walking distance of campus, you either got *in* the Black Pepper Pub or you were *out*. Without admission, it was virtually impossible to have a social life. So the first weekend after arriving on campus, my suitemates and I drove down to Philadelphia and bought ourselves some expensive fake IDs.

Mac was an older guy even then, *much* older. Late middle age, grizzled, scarred, bald or near bald with white peach fuzz wrapped around his head like Caesar's laurel crown. As the bouncer and doorman at the Black Pepper Pub, he wielded more power than Dean Kenderman back at school. The first time I approached him with my fake ID, I was utterly terrified. But others had gotten in with similar fake IDs, so why shouldn't I?

Of all the frigging luck, after one glance at mine, he pulled me aside. When he did I almost pissed myself. Was I going to jail? Would it affect my scholarship? Could I be expelled and forced to move back in with my mother?

Mac's voice was gruff yet gentle, even soothing. "How old are you really, young lady?" I swallowed hard, looked toward the line at the door, but my suitemates had fled. I so wanted to do the same. "If you answer truthfully," he told me, "you'll have a much better shot at making it inside."

"Eighteen," I sneered, still peering sideways for someone I knew. I needed a lifeline. *Help me! SOS.*

"Close enough, I'm sure." His hands went to his hips. "Are you responsible?"

"Responsible for what?" A reflex from Catholic school.

"Do you *drink* responsibly? Or do you get shitfaced like most of the young ladies who come in here?" The *shitfaced* kind of shocked me. But then, he looked like a retired boxer or wiseguy or both. "Do you drink and *drive*?"

"No," I said, "but it doesn't matter anymore. My friends left." I was too traumatized to go inside.

"Then go in and make new friends," he said. "Or better yet, here." He dug into his back pocket and handed me an old BlackBerry. "Go inside. Wait five minutes for your friends to get back to campus, then call them from this. Tell them the old guy's all right. They can come in too."

At that moment, a thousand questions ran through my mind. Can't he get in trouble for this? Like serious trouble? Law-type trouble? Why's he even doing this? Is there some ulterior motive? Is he hoping I'll get "shitfaced" enough to go home with him? No, he couldn't possibly believe I'd go home with him willingly.

What if my willingness is the last thing on his mind?

Before I'd made a conscious decision, he shuffled me inside.

In a quiet corner of the bar, I ordered a light beer and stared at his BlackBerry, waiting to call my suitemates. The place was *packed*. Bored, I scrolled through his contacts. There were only a few numbers in his phone. A few women with age-appropriate names like Agnes and Elanor, Iris and Ruth. I scrolled farther down to a contact labeled "CVC—Ives." CVC was the acronym for our school, Center Valley College.

Who was he in touch with there?

Whether it was someone on the faculty or administration, or even a student—especially a student—I found it curious. All right, suspicious. I glanced over my shoulder to make sure he hadn't stepped inside. I opened the contact but found only a phone number with the local 215 area code. Surreptitiously, I jotted the number on a cardboard coaster and stuffed it into my pocket.

With the coaster safely socked away, I checked my watch and dialed the dorm phone number and my suitemates' extension.

"Guess where I'm calling you from, *bitch-es*?" I said.

Their first guess was jail. I thought, *How cool is that?*

Kilo's admission about Eddie's gambling addiction leaves me to wonder what else I don't know about Eddie Akana, the man Kati Dawes was about to marry. "Kilo," I say from my hospital bed, "tell me about Eddie's love life."

"I'm lookin' at it," he says.

Heat rises to my cheeks. "That's sweet, but you know what I mean. *Before* me."

"Before you, he loved only the *'aina* and the law."

The land and the law, that much I knew. Eddie had loved the law since high school on Oahu. He also loved Kilo and his cousins, Elta and Kanoa. The four were like brothers ever since they started kindergarten together at Kamehameha Schools, a pre-K through twelve educational system dedicated exclusively to children of Native Hawaiian ancestry.

Following high school, all four friends were admitted to the University of Hawaii and were scheduled to begin classes in the fall. But that summer, Eddie's cousins spotted an opportunity too good to pass up. The owner of the boat-repair shop, where they both worked for years, was selling and moving to the mainland. When Elta and Kanoa sniffed around for an asking price, he offered them a superb deal, which they immediately took to their aunt Nani, who controls the purse strings of the extended Akana family. It took some persuasion—Nani wanted Elta and Kanoa to go to college—but after she spoke with the owner and inspected the books, she decided the shop was a solid investment and that it would be detrimental to the family to not allow the boys to go their own way. As long as Elta and Kanoa would commit themselves to the shop for five years, she agreed to provide the down payment. The owner accepted a promissory note for the remainder.

Kilo, meanwhile, started at UH as Eddie's roommate. While Eddie felt right at home on campus, Kilo—though only thirty miles away by car—quickly became homesick. He didn't thrive in class, lectures put him to sleep, and reading just made him hungry. He missed his mother's home cooking and didn't like getting up early in the morning (a must for freshmen). And then he, too, was given a unique opportunity.

Because of his prodigious computer skills, he was offered freelance work from several large companies based on the mainland. These businesses constantly needed to update their cybersecurity measures to stay one step ahead of criminals, so he became what they call in the industry a white hat hacker. Working remotely from home, he tested the businesses' latest security systems, updates, and fixes by finding new ways to work around them, thereby exposing his client's cyber vulnerabilities. Ever since Eddie was sworn in as an attorney, Kilo's work has focused on large white-shoe law firms, and he's done quite well for himself.

As for Eddie, when he graduated from law school at UH, he went to work for the trust established by the Bernice Pauahi Bishop estate, which endowed Kamehameha Schools with fifteen *billion* dollars (greater than the combined endowments of Harvard and Yale Universities), making it the wealthiest charitable organization in the United States.

Early in his legal career, Eddie defended a case against Kam Schools, in which an unidentified student charged that the preference of Hawaiian applicants over non-Hawaiians violated provisions of the Civil Rights Act. The Ninth Circuit Court of Appeals shockingly agreed. Ultimately, Kam settled the matter (over Eddie's fierce objections) for high seven figures, creating one hell of a windfall for one "luckless" unidentified white boy from the wealthiest neighborhood in Honolulu, who (the *poor* thing) had been excluded from a school whose chief mission is the advancement of Native Hawaiians in the face of a century of discrimination, following the unlawful overthrow of their monarchy in a bloodless yet indefensible coup. It was *this* case that convinced Eddie to run for US Congress.

After losing the primary to a former lieutenant governor, Eddie set his sights slightly lower and ran for the state legislature, where he'd spend the length of his political career. During that time, he championed bills to keep the North Shore of Oahu rural, to curb commercial land development on Maui and Kauai, and to provide everyday Native Hawaiians from Hilo to Kilauea with more autonomy and economic opportunities. The centerpiece of his work was a proposal for the development of a Polynesian-themed casino that would provide similar revenue to Native Hawaiians as those enjoyed by certain Native American tribes.

Despite high approval ratings and unquestionable charisma, Eddie refused to become a career politician. After two successful terms he decided against running for reelection, yearning to test his talents in a different arena. He wanted to be a litigator.

For one year he worked as an associate at a busy personal injury firm in Honolulu. Many of his cases took him to neighboring islands, and while on Maui for a series of depositions, he visited his old friend Noah Walker from law school. Following graduation, Noah started a criminal practice by hustling clients at various courthouses on Oahu. In criminal defense, a good lawyer can eke out a living. A *great* lawyer can make a killing. Which Noah did. After only a few years, he had built such a reputation that he could practice anywhere in the islands. Noah chose to hang his shingle in the sleepy town of Hana.

Eddie admired Noah's fearlessness and attitude toward the law, as well as his lifestyle. After sitting in on a three-day jury trial in which Noah won an acquittal for a young woman charged with attempted murder, Eddie decided to open his own law practice. Noah offered Eddie the use of his office until he got things off the ground, a task that didn't take long given his statewide name recognition and endless political contacts. Once Noah recognized Eddie's natural ease with clients, he offered to bring him aboard as a full partner. Over a single morning, they hammered out and executed an agreement, and the law firm of Walker & Akana was born.

Eddie found his calling.

When I look up, Noah enters the examination room. My eyes ask the question, his own provide the reply. Hana Airport was a bust. Zoe remains missing.

"I need to get out of here," I say.

"Doc tells me another hour before they can do a CT—"

"Not then. *Now.*"

He shakes his head in feigned bewilderment. "Why?"

Because the police will be here any minute to take my statement. And I need to find my daughter.

"I'll tell you when you drive me away from this place."

"That's gonna be a little difficult considering the Explorer was towed to Manny's Auto twenty minutes after we got here."

"How did you get to Hana Airport?"

"Taxi." His Adam's apple bobs in his throat. "Kilo offered his car, but I'm not getting behind the wheel again anytime soon. I'm still pretty shaken up."

I immediately want to smack myself in the head. I'd completely forgotten about his post-traumatic stress disorder. About Tammy and their prom night twenty-plus years ago.

"Anyway," he says, "Kilo left to grab some grub at Zippy's and is gonna be gone for at least an hour."

"Get us a Lyft, then," I tell him as I gradually, painfully, sit up. "We need to get to your office, fast."

13

I spend the long ride back along the scenic road to Hana with my eyes closed. Sneaking out of the ER without my discharge papers was simpler than I anticipated. I just put on a Rainbow Warriors T-shirt Noah picked up from the gift shop and sauntered out the door when no one was looking. The hospital was so busy I'm not sure I even needed to take those precautions.

"Now," Noah says, "tell me what's going on."

I owe the truth to him; he's trying so hard and I'm giving him so little. But the situation hasn't changed and neither have my calculations. If anything, what little Kilo told me about Noah over the long hours at the hospital reinforced my decision to keep Noah in the dark, despite my sympathies. Commendably, the lawyer has a rigid code, which means he'll throw me to the wolves if he believes me guilty of killing his partner.

"I need to see Eddie's files," I say, wondering for the first time whether his love of the law—not gambling (and not *me*)—actually *could* have gotten him killed.

"Eddie's files are confidential," Noah says. "His clients are now my responsibility, and I'm still bound by privilege. Tell me what you're looking for."

I nearly go off, forgetting again that Noah is no stranger to loss.

Eddie had told Zoe and me the story of Noah's tragic past. The night of his senior high school prom, Noah and his girlfriend Tammy planned to spend the whole night together for the first time. For them it was a big effing deal, less about the sex and more about waking up next to one another for the first time.

Listening in, Zoe thought it was romantic, how as teenagers, Noah and Tammy loved each other "so fucking much" they were committed to spending their lives together. When I called bullshit and said they were just stupid teenagers who still believed life was a fairy tale, she promptly reminded me that, by that time in my life, I'd gotten knocked up and married a man I would later despise. Yet twenty years later, by all accounts Noah still loves Tammy, still grieves her.

Noah told Eddie he still sees Tammy every day, sees her in her red prom dress and oversize corsage, sees the flashes from her parents snapping pictures, sees her in their limo with her hand in his lap.

"It's so fucking romantic," Zoe said. "Like he had Insta before Insta."

Eddie didn't necessarily disagree. "Noah isn't haunted by her," he said, "just constantly reminded of her like there's a string fixed permanently around his finger or an eternal rubber band wrapped tightly around his wrist."

On that fateful prom night, Tammy had made Noah promise: no drinking until after they reached the motel. At the time he said it, he meant it. Which is probably true of most promises people make. It's the follow-through that's the problem.

Once they arrived at the dance, Noah's friend Quigg snuck in a sixer and a couple of forties. Noah shotgunned a can of Coors, then gobbled a few Altoids and joined Tammy on the dance floor. After a few too many bathroom breaks—shocker—Tammy got suspicious. When Noah finally admitted to drinking, she stormed off.

After that, things get foggy, but he remembers searching for her, questioning her friends, and finally heading back outside and finding her waiting for him in their limo. She demanded to go home; he begged her to stay. Said stuff like, "This only comes around once in our lives, Tam." She told him, "You should've thought of that earlier. I want to go home."

Noah finally relented. Told the driver to drop them both at her house, where Noah had left his old pickup.

Next thing he remembers is wearing her down at the park up the street from her house. "The room is paid for. There's a chilled bottle of champagne waiting. There's a king-size bed. A complimentary breakfast tomorrow morning! How can you pass on all that?"

"You were drinking," she said.

"Two hours ago! I'm perfectly fine to drive."

At the time, he believed it. And technically, legally at least, he was fine to drive. Immediately following the wreck, Noah blew a .09, just under the state's legal limit back then. But that changes nothing in his mind. He says, for all the good he did, he might as well have held a gun to her head and squeezed the trigger.

I pull myself out of Noah's past and ask him, "What do you know about Eddie's finances?"

"We never talked about money unless it was the firm's."

It's what Kilo said too. As close as Noah thinks he was to Eddie, Eddie kept a lot from him too. Eddie's real friends, his *close* friends, his brothers, were Kilo and his cousins Elta and Kanoa. He had nothing against Noah—at least nothing Kilo knows of—but the simple fact is Noah is a *haole, haole* being the Native Hawaiians' term for Caucasians. When spoken by locals, it's often meant to be derogatory. Yet most mainlanders, even longtime white residents, wear it like a badge of honor, prompting Eddie to once tell me, *Dumb haoles, yeah? They even t'ink their slurs are superior.*

Thing is, I'm a *haole* too. Why, then, should I be so surprised that Eddie hid stuff from me as he did from Noah?

"I'm convinced Zoe didn't run away," I say. "I think she was kidnapped."

"Why's that?"

I decide to be completely straight with him for once, since I now know he's far more likely to let me root around Eddie's office for gambling slips than he is to let me trawl through their client files fishing for a killer.

"Did you know Eddie was a heavy gambler?" I ask him.

Noah releases a mournful chuckle. "Of course I did. He was a personal injury lawyer, for chrissakes. His entire career was one giant roll of the dice."

"Did you know he was deeply in debt?"

Noah's silence and thousand-yard stare hint that there's something he's not telling me. Finally, he shakes his head, says, "It wasn't necessarily Eddie's debt that worried me. It was who he owed that was most troubling."

"What do you mean?" But I know what he means, if not who.

He turns to me. "Ever hear the name Tim Jedrick?"

Jedrick. The name sounds familiar, but with all this stress, I could search my brain for months and still not recover any memory of him. *But wait there it is. How could I miss it?* Zoe herself mentioned Tim Jedrick—and not in a good way. Jedrick is the head of the Hawaii Hotel Coalition, one of the many private and powerful hotel advocacy organizations in the islands.

Plastic water bottles aside, Zoe is a zealous proponent of the environment, never more so than since we arrived in Hawaii. Working remotely, she eagerly volunteered for an organization dedicated to pushing forward a bill to cut funding for the Hawaii Tourism Authority. Jedrick and his Hawaii Hotel Coalition, of course, lobbied against the legislation—and won.

But Zoe wasn't yet finished. She and Eddie put their heads together and envisioned an evolved path forward. A way to protect Hawaii's delicate ecosystem while still sharing the islands with the world. A way to preserve the economy *and* the environment while primarily benefiting Native Hawaiians, who have taken it on the chin for the past century.

"During the pandemic," she said one night at Eddie's dining room table, "when tourism dropped, when a quarter of a million tourists a day weren't pecking away at the islands' natural beauty, the land, the 'aina, healed far more than expected. Wildlife returned to their habitats. The air quality improved dramatically. The highway leading into Honolulu was no longer a parking lot. And the locals, the Native Hawaiian businesses, finally got a chance to thrive among the mainland giants."

"Sure," I said, a true dunce about just how passionate my daughter was at the time, "but people also lost their jobs. The overall economy took a huge hit. Tourism is Hawaii's largest industry. It makes up, what, at least twenty percent of the state's GDP?"

"The point is," Zoe said as if she were speaking to a five-year-old, "it *doesn't have to be*. We need to create a more sustainable approach to tourism. If the state won't defund the Hawaii Tourism Authority, we need to force the Tourism Authority to make a dramatic shift in policy by *exclusively* promoting ecotourism."

Days later, with Eddie's help, Zoe crafted a petition and had in place a solid plan to collect thousands of signatures within the first sixty days, without ever leaving the house.

"Rainforests cover only seven percent of the earth," she said over the phone to anyone who would listen, "and those left in South America are being wiped out by corrupt politicians and land developers, not to mention the millions of acres burning to the ground due to climate change."

"You're fully behind this?" I asked Eddie while we watched my daughter work.

"Traditional tourism's greatest impact is on Native Hawaiians," he said. "We endure the desecration of our sacred places, the forced reburials, the needless pollution of our reefs and rivers, all while being priced out of our homes by foreign investors. This economy doesn't benefit us." It was true: Natives were the poorest of all the people in the islands. They had the highest unemployment, the highest number of welfare recipients, the lowest life expectancy, and they dominated the state's growing prison population.

After a particularly heated call, Zoe hung up the phone and cursed Tim Jedrick and at least a half dozen other hotel lobbyists she knew by name. "Almost every major resort in Hawaii is owned by transnational corporations. *They* are the ones exploiting Native Hawaiian culture, values, and traditions, all while crowded beaches and commercial tour boating destroy the shorelines and coastal fishing. It's horrific."

Suddenly fully alert in the Lyft, I ask Noah, "What *about* Tim Jedrick? He's a lobbyist."

"He's a little more than that." In the moonlight coming in from the back window, Noah appears to weigh how much to tell me. "Do you know anything about his past?"

Suddenly, it comes to me. "He's originally from *Vegas*, isn't he?"

"He's *originally* from here, Honolulu to be exact. He moved to Vegas with his family when he was still a kid and grew up to become one of the Strip's wealthiest hoteliers." He paused, wet his lips. "But my point is, in Vegas he had a reputation. One for eliminating those who oppose his objectives."

"Eliminating?"

"Through intimidation, blackmail, and extortion." Noah swallows hard and draws a deep breath. "And failing that, violence."

Zoe

As hard as it is to get things done, I enjoyed working with Eddie on the environment. Baby steps aren't going to save the planet, but no one wants to sacrifice now for a generation they haven't yet met. It's my children and grandchildren who will inherit a boiling planet constantly overflowing with seawater.

The pandemic changed our world more than any event since September 11, 2001. Although I wasn't around then, I know plenty of people who were. Many of Dad's closest friends and colleagues lived and worked near the World Trade Center in New York. I know plenty of people who lost people and still have a tough time talking about it two decades later.

In some ways, man-made climate change is 9/11 in slow motion. We can stop this. We can stop the terrorists from ever boarding our planes. So why the hell aren't we?

All I ever wanted was a normal life. But when there's a new normal nearly every day, it's impossible to keep up. Who the hell has the time and energy? Not all that long ago, only introverts worked from home. Now nearly everyone who can do their job from home at least has the option. Is that great for individual employees who hate to commute? Sure. Is that good for society as a whole? Doubtful. But then, who cares, right? Individuality seems to be all that matters to many, and they're usually the ones with the same cars, the same clothes, the same toys as everyone else.

I miss Bridgeport. I miss our house. I miss our neighborhood. I miss our plumbing. How differently I pictured my senior year of high school. I would have been editor of the yearbook. I would have been snapping thousands of pictures: selfies, friends, landscapes, buildings, all while growing my Insta-brand.

Mom fucked everything up by running. She should have faced Bridgeport PD—and Dad—when she had the chance. Our lives would be very different right now. She makes me so damn angry sometimes that I could scream. But I've screamed before. At her, at others, at the world. It's never done me any good. It'll certainly do me no good to scream now. Not here, where no one can hear me.

I feel sick. I'm beginning to doubt Mom will find me. What clues does she really have? If she notices my passport is missing, she'll start at the airports. When the airports prove to be a bust, she'll try to determine how else someone could have gotten me off the island.

If she can expand her tunnel vision, to see past my father, she'll begin asking questions about Eddie and eventually come to realize how little she knew him, how little she wanted to know him.

She erased her past and mine and insisted on remaining clueless about the one man she wanted so badly to love—even if she had to play dumb to do it.

Because playing dumb, pretending that things happening right under her nose aren't happening, is how she got through all those years back home in Connecticut.

When she finally sees Eddie for who he is, she'll spot his lies. See his weaknesses and vulnerabilities. She'll find out about his gambling, his trips to Vegas. Then she'll search for some link between me and Eddie. She'll look for a name.

If she can't figure it out on her own, she'll turn to Eddie's case files.

That's where she'll find it. The name Tim Jedrick. Then she'll fit the pieces together and know where to go.

That's how she'll ultimately find me.

Hopefully, in time.

14

Once we reach the firm, I rush straight to Eddie's office and rifle through his desk drawers, then his filing cabinets, and finally the loose files scattered all over the floor.

I'm no longer sure just what I'm looking for. Gambling slips, sure. But also anything that might possibly indicate that it was Eddie's love of the *land* that got him killed. As hard as I try, I can't evade the logic that if that's what got him killed, it probably also got Zoe kidnapped. But I flatly refuse to follow that train any further.

"Find anything?" Noah says from the doorway. I've no idea how long he's been standing there. Bent over, I'm suddenly sure my thong is showing like a plumber's ass crack.

"Not yet."

Jedrick, Jedrick, Jedrick. Now I can't pry his name from my skull.

"Why are you staring at me like that?" I snap.

"I'm not. It's just that . . ." Searching for the words, he steps into Eddie's office. "After Hana Airport I went and saw the body."

When he doesn't elaborate, I'm not sure what to do. I'm not sure how much I want to know. Maybe nothing. Maybe something, if it'll give me a clue as to Zoe's whereabouts.

"He was definitely struck in the back of the head," Noah says. "This was no accident; that's been all but ruled out." Quietly, he adds, "Someone murdered him."

Does he think it's me? Is he about to turn on me? Turn me in?

Unable to look at him, I return my attention to the large file sitting on Eddie's desk in front of me. I need to think not like Bosch right now but a real cop, a homicide detective like the ones in true crime documentaries. Only problem is, who is the most obvious suspect in any murder? The spouse or soon-to-be spouse. *Me.* Moving on.

"Who did Eddie date before me?" I say.

Distracted by what must be the horrifying image of Eddie on that cold metal slab, Noah has me repeat the question, then says, "This girl Jun."

Jun Sato. Eddie mentioned her, showed me a photo even. After meeting Eddie while on a two-week vacation a few years ago, she relocated here from Tokyo just to be near him. They dated for roughly a year before Eddie decided she was too clingy, too cloying, what he called "a bottomless pit of need."

"Who else?" I ask. Maybe there were others; maybe it was Eddie's love of *love* that got him killed.

Noah's eyes flick toward the door to the firm's storage room containing clients' closed case files, which lawyers are required to retain for seven years. I've neither entered the room nor desired to since Eddie and the receptionist Noelle both gave me fair warning: the dust inside is several inches thick and could make a rhinoceros sneeze.

Could the answer be in one of his old files?

I'm casting too wide a net. If the answer *is* in those old files, we'll never find Zoe in time. Now that there's no question that Eddie was murdered, there's no question in my mind that Zoe is in danger. She may be running out of time regardless of whether she was kidnapped *or* ran away from home. If we can deduce who killed Eddie—who was there at the falls that morning—we'll be one step closer to finding her and keeping her safe.

But how do I even begin to figure that out?

I need to think like a cop—or a criminal. I need to think more practically. I need to think more like Mac.

Mac didn't bother me that first night at the Black Pepper, or the next. Or the next after that. Or ever. Quite the opposite, in fact. He always made sure that my friends and I had a ride home and that none of us did anything too stupid while on Black Pepper property.

When I finally asked him why he let us inside, he said, "What would you girls be doing tonight if you weren't here?"

"Studying?" I told him.

"Oh, really?"

"Drinking," I admitted.

"Where? In the dorms?"

"No, the dorms are dry. We'd probably go off campus, maybe to a frat party over at Lehigh."

"Yeah, that's what I thought. You're safer here, kid. So as far as my conscience goes, it's clean. At least about allowing you young ladies inside."

Other students joined me and my friends from time to time, and no one questioned why Mac permitted them inside. No one, that is, until Jeremy questioned me about the coaster he discovered while digging through my coat pockets one morning.

I'd met Jeremy at an off-campus party near school, one held every Thirsty Thursday and every other Sloppy Saturday.

Jeremy wanted to know why Mac allowed me and my friends into the Black Pepper when he turned other students away, especially guys. "Maybe he's a rapist," he said. "Or worse. We don't know. Have you ever gotten into a car with him?"

"Of course not," I told him.

"But you've left the bar late at night? *Drunk*, I presume? I need to know who this fucking guy is. What else do you know about him?"

"Nothing, except that he hangs with chicks named Esther and Gertrude, so . . . yeah."

"Well, whose number is on this coaster?"

I considered the coaster. "CVC Ives," I said.

"CVC as in *our school, right?*"

"I assume so."

"And that doesn't concern you?"

I shrugged my bony shoulders; sometimes I felt so stupid around him.

"Ives, huh?" he said, pocketing the coaster. "We'll find out who it is and what this old bastard's hiding between his ass cheeks."

Jeremy did nothing. Except, that is, to phone his uncle Gunther, an attorney back in Bridgeport. He told his uncle about the old man at the Black Pepper Pub and how he had the handle CVC Ives in his BlackBerry. Gunther had his investigator look into it. Two days later, I was in Jeremy's dorm room when he got the call from Connecticut.

"Parole? I *knew* it. What was he in for?" His eyes flew open as wide as they'd go. "No shit? *Christ.*" He shook his head at my idiocy and grinned. "Yeah, I will. Thanks, Uncle Gun." He hung up. "Your good buddy Mac? He did time. A ten-year stretch at SCI Somerset and not all that long ago. CVC is Center Valley Corrections. Ives is his parole officer."

An intense apprehension crept up my spine, though I tried not to show it. "What was he in for?" I asked as casually as I could to maintain my reputation as a big-city badass instead of a Bethlehem, PA, bore.

"Oh, just . . . *attempted fucking murder,*" he said. "And guess where he committed his crime? At a bar. Talk about your fox shitting the henhouse."

"Who did he attempt to kill?"

"Some lady named Francis Summers. Probably because she wouldn't put out."

I didn't go back to the Black Pepper Pub that semester. When I returned from winter break, I heard Mac was gone. Fired, someone said. "For letting in minors?" No, he'd lied about something on his application. Like he was a child molester or something and didn't report it to his employer.

I didn't need to ask anyone to know what really happened. Jeremy's uncle Gun had called the Black Pepper Pub and given them an ultimatum: fire the ex-con or get shut down by the liquor authority for serving at least a half dozen underage college kids.

I felt so damn guilty about the part I played in getting Mac fired, but soon enough, I had my own troubles to deal with. Things had taken a turn. Choices needed to be made. About Jeremy. About Glenn. About an unplanned, unexpected, and (frankly) unwanted teenage pregnancy.

In Eddie's office, as I flip through the pages of each folder, suffering papercut after papercut, I try to marshal my thoughts. Eddie is dead; Zoe is missing. The only links between them are Tim Jedrick and myself.

I spot a large file labeled PANDEMIC.

Inside the file are reams of correspondence between Eddie and the lieutenant governor, all apparently relating to the governor's political decisions about whether to keep Hawaii "open for business" or shut it down to prevent the rapid transmission of COVID-19, which at the time virologists still knew very little about. Eddie and the lieutenant governor agreed that leaving it up to the state's individual counties made the governor appear feckless and weak.

The correspondence continues for months, then ceases abruptly in the middle of the summer of the first year of the pandemic. On the reverse side of the most recent letter are a series of Post-it notes with names and phone numbers: Artie D., Dale P., Charlie K. I slip the Post-it notes in my pocket, turn the most recent letter around, and lay it flat on the surface of Eddie's desk. It's from the lieutenant governor.

The governor has made his decision, Ed. Now it's up
to the mayors. As you well know, as goes Honolulu,
so go the neighbor islands.

I flip to Eddie's letter to the lieutenant governor dated just two
days prior.

You need to get the governor to reverse himself. If he
consigns these choices to the counties, he might as
well delegate them to TJ himself.

TJ? Tim Jedrick? As the head of the Hawaii Hotel Coalition? Makes
perfect sense. Of course the hotel and restaurant industries wanted
Hawaii to remain open for business. Waikiki was like a ghost town;
the hotels were desolate, and nearly half the nonchain restaurants went
under with no hope of coming back.

I call out to Noah, who had stepped into his own office. When he
returns, I hand him the letter. "Eddie didn't just oppose Jedrick on the
environment," I tell him. "They were on opposite sides of the pandemic
as well. I think maybe *that's* when this feud started."

Noah sets the letter down and shakes his head. "Kati, the feud
between Eddie Akana and Tim Jedrick started long before that."

15

According to the Book of Noah, the first clash between Eddie Akana and Tim Jedrick kicked off more than fifteen years ago and had nothing to do with the environment or any global pandemic. The warring began over Eddie's proposal for the Polynesian casino.

Prior to that, Jedrick worked behind the scenes for years to get a gambling license in Hawaii. "Look what we accomplished in the fucking desert," he's quoted as saying. "Imagine what we could achieve in a real-life paradise."

By all accounts Jedrick was on the cusp of obtaining that gambling license when then Hawaii state representative Eddie Akana took his proposal for the Polynesian casino to a rookie reporter named Koa Pualani of the *Honolulu Star-Advertiser* in an effort to gain advance support for the legislation.

It was Koa Pualani's first major story, and it changed the playing field in ways Eddie never anticipated. Not only was there little support for a casino that would exclusively benefit Native Hawaiians, but support for *any* casino in the islands dropped precipitously from 48 percent the previous year to 32 percent. The only explanation for the public's change of heart, Koa concluded in a subsequent article, was that the great majority of Hawaii residents only desired gaming in the islands if it would directly benefit *them*, but certainly not to empower the struggling Native population.

Not everyone agreed that was the reason, and, of course, some readers took offense at the suggestion that racism played into their reasons for voting against the Polynesian casino. What *was* clear to everyone, however, including Eddie Akana and Tim Jedrick, was that there would be no casino whatsoever in the islands' near future. Jedrick's shot at obtaining a gaming license was gone, baby, gone, including the tens of millions of dollars he allegedly spent bribing local politicians and other state officials, who now could not possibly sanction the construction of a casino for the benefit of a quasi-gangster from Vegas. There would be a revolution, an uprising, and rightly so.

"So Eddie *literally* cost this guy tens of millions of dollars and potentially billions by tanking his casino," I say aloud to get it straight in my head. "Then during the pandemic, Eddie tries to persuade the governor to shut down the state which, right or wrong, would have cost the tourism industry billions of dollars. *Then*, Eddie backs a proposal that will *upend* Hawaii's multibillion-dollar tourism industry in favor of its silly little ecosystem."

"That about sums it up," Noah says.

"But there has to be countless ways for a man with that much money to take revenge. And this *isn't* the Nevada desert. A single high-profile murder here could chill tourism for another year, maybe more. Has Jedrick killed politicians and lawyers in the past or just gangsters?"

"Only fellow gangsters as far as I know. But here's the rub. You initially asked if Eddie was in debt to anyone dangerous. Well, that's how Jedrick retaliated. He went around Vegas *and* Hawaii and bought up Eddie's massive gambling debts. Including those of a former client of mine, some ruffian named Makoa Urima."

"But *why*? It's not as if that makes killing Eddie legally justifiable."

"Kati," Noah says patiently, "Jedrick was making a statement. He was telling Eddie, *'Your debt to me doesn't die with you.'* And by making good on that threat, he'll be sending an incredibly powerful message to anyone considering crossing him in the future, especially in the islands, where he still wants to build a gaming empire."

If that is indeed the message he intends to send, Zoe is definitely in danger, whether she simply ran away or was taken. I need to know more about this guy. Now.

"Where would they take her?" I hear myself saying. "If Jedrick does have Zoe, where would they be?"

Noah chews on his lower lip. "I suppose he'd take her on his private jet, but we already have eyes on Hana Airport."

For a moment I don't know what the hell he's talking about. Then I remember. *Jeremy.* As focused as I've been on him for the past two years, the last few hours have seen my attention turn to Jedrick with equal intensity. I picture Ozzie and his plane, then recall he also owns a yacht. "Jedrick," I say, "*he* would have a yacht. Where would we find it?"

Noah nods as he absorbs the question. "There's currently only one place on Maui where large noncommercial vessels can dock—Lahaina Marina all the way across the island on the southwest shore."

"We need a car," I say.

This time he doesn't question me, doesn't stall. "I'll call the big guy, pronto. But you're driving. My hands are still shaking from our earlier mishap in the Explorer."

Steeped in history, Lahaina, land of the "cruel sun," stretches along scenic Route 30 and remains the most popular spot in West Maui. Its main drag, Front Street, runs parallel to the water and boasts dozens of boutiques and eateries that would have made the old me, the material me, *Jeremy's* me, salivate. As packed as Waikiki, Lahaina is a shore town that doubles as a downtown, while Front Street consistently ranks among the top ten greatest streets in the country. Zoe *loves* it here. The place has its own personality.

As we fight through the crowd, we keep our heads low, trying not to draw too much attention to ourselves. Despite a double dose of Ativan, my anxiety continues to skyrocket. The isolation of our off-grid home has altered me, permanently, I think. Maybe it's partly my age, partly the pandemic, but I want to be around fewer and fewer people these days. Right now, I just want to be home alone with Zoe.

But then, Zoe and I may never be able to return to our home again.

I drove Kilo's pickup the seventy-five miles from Hana to Lahaina as cautiously as an expectant mother, transforming the two-and-a-half-hour drive into a roughly four-hour nightmare. I had no choice; every time I put my foot on the accelerator Noah started having a panic attack of his own.

The morning was bright, and we were both fighting Kilo's visors to shield our eyes from the oncoming sun, when Noah's cell phone went off. He sent the call to Bluetooth, so I caught only his end of the conversation, which consisted of a few *when*s, a couple of *how*s, a *why*, and finally a *thanks for the heads-up*.

"Who was that?" I asked when he ended the call.

"The *who* doesn't matter, it's the *what*. And it's bad—a federal magistrate is about to sign a warrant to search your premises."

Our prints are all over that place. If the feds don't already have them, they will after the search. My eventual arrest and extradition to Connecticut are now a given. Unless, that is, the feds want to prosecute me here in Hawaii for Eddie's murder first.

What else will the feds find in their search? The über-elaborate security system, our computers, our burner phones, not only our cache but the ones we recently used. In all likelihood they'll discover the panic room and the dozens of secret compartments and hiding places Mac's contractor built into the structure.

Probably a good thing now that we couldn't afford the underground tunnel.

What matters most, though, as far as Eddie's murder is concerned, is what they *won't* find: the second trekking pole I told investigators was there in the house.

What all this means is the clock is ticking faster than ever. I need to find Zoe before the feds and Maui PD find me. Once they do—Zoe or no Zoe—it's game over.

As we near the marina on foot, the throng thickens along Front Street and sidewalk vendors get a bit too friendly, a bit too personal, a bit too pushy.

When we finally get some breathing room, the olfactory part of my brain lights like the night sky on the Fourth of July, with smells of straight-from-the-water seafood, freshly baked cookies, cakes, pies, and pastries, and every kind of candy Willy Wonka could ever fathom, all permeating the salty sea air. Even in the middle of the day, the place buzzes with such energy I can almost imagine this bustling boulevard as it was a hundred years ago, when Lahaina was the capital of the Kingdom of Hawaii and, before that, a whaling town visited by Herman Melville himself.

"The marina's just up here," Noah says, pointing toward the water. "If Jedrick departed for the mainland, the coast guard will have a record of it. If he left for international waters, he'd have to inform Customs too."

At the coast guard station, another of Noah's friends informs us that yes, Jedrick has a yacht called the *Ramblin' Man*, but she hasn't seen it in weeks. As Noah thanks her, I turn and head toward the dry dock, while uttering some unintelligible reason as to why I still want to take a look around. Moments later Noah hustles behind me to catch up.

As we cross the dock we have a crystal clear view of Lanai, an apostrophe-shaped island that for nearly a hundred years served as one large pineapple plantation. Today, 98 percent of it is owned by the tech billionaire who founded Oracle. I know little else about the island. Zoe had been begging to go there.

We reach the marina, and it's significantly larger and far busier than I hoped. Dozens of boats, large and small, dot the harbor in the distance.

"Want to tell me what we're doing here?" Noah says.

"Not really." I shuffle a little faster.

Should I just give up? Give in? Tell Noah everything? Do I finally admit to myself that I'm in over my head and always have been? That I became an imposter my first year of college and never stopped? After becoming the badass, I became the devoted wife, the loving mother, the abused spouse, the doting daughter-in-law, and most recently, the large and in-charge mama bear who will protect her young cub by any means necessary. All I really am, though, all I ever was, all I ever will be, is a cowardly fugitive who endangered her teenage daughter by refusing to turn herself in.

We never crave isolation so much as when we need people most, Mac told me. *Look, I'm always on your side, no matter what. But I'm like the hammer that sees everything as a nail. I only know one way you and your daughter get out of this. And like everything else I do, deary, it's fairly extreme.*

With Mac 86'ed from the Black Pepper Pub, the harder I fell for Jeremy, the more he isolated me from my friends. I saw my world shrinking but thought, *Isn't this just part of falling in love? Especially for the first time?* While watching my world shrink to nothingness, the unthinkable happened. Despite the birth control pills and the spermicide and the condoms, I somehow became pregnant.

One morning I woke with what felt like a particularly vicious hangover that followed a rare night of sobriety. When the pink stuff didn't work, I thought maybe I had the flu. Only it wasn't flu season, and no one else in the dorms was sick. So I cut morning drama class, slipped away from school, and went to a pharmacy.

In a public restroom, as I waited the agonizing three minutes for the results, I couldn't help but think of life with Jeremy as the father of my child. Already when he went out with his friends, he expected me to stay back in my dorm room, studying. It's how my relationship with

Glenn flourished in the first place. I was sure Jeremy was cheating on me, and what was good for the goose was good for the . . .

Gosling.

That's the word that popped into my head, and it wasn't of the *Ryan* variety. Because while staring down at my home pregnancy test, a second line materialized like a new crewman just beaming onto the *Enterprise.* There was indeed a new passenger aboard, and once I left the toilet stall, no matter what happened, no matter what I decided to do, my life would never be the same again.

Forgetting the misery of my childhood, my first instinct was to run to my mother and that's just what I did. True to form, she shamed me, practically made me parade the streets naked like the queen from *Game of Thrones.* Still, still, *still,* I sought her advice. *Run back to whatever prick put this in you,* she shouted at the top of her lungs.

It wasn't what I wanted to hear, but it was the only guidance I was going to get.

So that's just what I did.

As far as Jeremy was concerned, what we would do about the pregnancy wasn't even up for debate. Marriage, he said, was a no-brainer, then I would carry our baby to term and give birth. He dismissed my concerns that we were too young (*How old were your grandparents?*). He undermined my academic achievements and goals (*What's really more important?*). He even told people around school as a way of forcing my hand. Roughly half of those students were happy for us, the other half thought me a slut.

When he introduced me to his family, they were all on their best behavior. Teresa was every bit as superficially charming as her son. She fawned over me, while Jeremy ushered me around their mansion, convincing me that, even if things didn't work out between us, our child would want for nothing. He even used what I'd told him about my own childhood, how my mother constantly reminded me that she'd wanted an abortion (*I should've killed you in the womb!*), that only her own Catholic parents "saved" my life. As if I'd begged to be born.

Jeremy wore me down, weakened my spirit, even tried to frighten me with images of hellfire despite my insistence that I didn't believe in God. Before long, he even developed sympathy symptoms (*We're going to get through this together, babe*). When that didn't seal my decision, he outright shamed me—in front of his mother, in front of his sister, in front of his friends. Although he was the one who constantly demanded sex (*Let's do it in every building on campus!*), he convinced me the pregnancy was entirely my fault.

At the time I didn't realize I was a live lobster in a pot about to boil. Jeremy continued turning up the heat—until I was showing, until the child was viable, until our daughter was born.

What little I know about boats I learned from Eddie, who once took Zoe and me whale watching on his catamaran, the *Pilialoha*, which is the Hawaiian term for friendship. While I half expected to see nothing more than a small school of dolphins, the humpbacks were particularly active that day, leaping high out of the water and showing off their sexy forty-ton figures. *Look da size of dat buggah?* Eddie shouted with the excitement of a small child. *I nevah see one dat big befo, eh?*

Here in the marina there are boats of every kind and every size, all with disparate names like *Black Bear, Hobson's Choice, Green Man, Ted & Jo's,* and *Here Today, Gone to Maui.* None appear large enough to be Jedrick's, and I can't remember what Oz's yacht looks like, even though I've been aboard it before. I only remember its name.

Noah comes up behind me, startling me for a moment. "I went and spoke to Customs," he says. "Jedrick's yacht hasn't entered the marina in at least two months. At least not from international waters, and he usually takes the yacht between here and Australia."

I'm about to suggest we return to the coast guard station to beg his friend to allow us to see who's been in and out of the marina the past couple of weeks when I suddenly see a boat I *do* recognize. Only it's not Ozzie's. It's a twenty-seven-foot Yamaha called the *Reasonable Doubt*.

"You have a photo of that boat," I say, pointing toward it. "On the wall in your conference room."

"Of course I do," he says. "It's *my* boat."

"Eddie never said you owned a boat."

"Eddie never saw it, except in photos," he says. "I only bought it a few months ago, and I don't get many chances to get out here."

I look up toward Lanai. In the distance, a much larger boat appears to be anchored in the calm sea. With the sun in my eyes I can barely see it until a cloud mercifully provides some cover. The name becomes visible for only an instant, but an instant is enough for me to read it. To read it and remember.

"We need a closer look at that boat," I tell Noah as I turn back toward the pier to get the binoculars Noah's coast guard friend wears around her neck.

"*Which* boat?" Noah says, following me. "There are six or seven of them out there."

But only one that I recognize.

Her name is *Dorothy*.

16

From our second-floor lanai at the Lahaina Waves motel, we have an unobstructed view of the yacht. Noah's coast guard friend says the *Dorothy* checked in upon arrival a week ago. She hasn't seen any of her passengers since.

"Could be they're out there diving," Noah says, gripping the rail. "Maybe fishing off the other side of the ship." He turns to me. "It's time you told me what the hell is going on here. I thought we were searching for Jedrick and the *Ramblin' Man*. Who's aboard the *Dorothy*?"

How much can I safely tell him?

I breathe in some of the chill ocean air, steel myself, and exhale. "When I moved to Hana, I *was* running from something, Noah. From *someone*. My ex."

And the police, I dare not add aloud. At least not yet.

Instead I convey what I need to and nothing more: that my ex is violent, that he's vengeful, that he will never forgive us—Zoe and me—for abandoning him.

"You think your ex killed Eddie?" Noah says with a healthy serving of doubt.

I concede the truth that I don't know, that I've more than entertained the notion he's behind this. That if he *is* responsible for Eddie's death, I'll never forgive myself, never even try to seek absolution. As self-serving as it sounds, even as I say it, I know it's true. I feel the loss of Eddie deep in my bones, and the hurt is worse with every passing hour, even as my gray matter focuses solely on Zoe.

"And now you think your ex has *Zoe?*" he says, his voice laced with genuine concern. "Do you think he kidnapped her? Or that she went willingly? You don't really think he'd harm her, his own flesh and blood, do you?"

The truth leaves my lips once more. "Noah, I don't know whether Jeremy has Zoe and, if he does, whether he took her by force or she went of her own volition. I don't know if he'd harm her." I bite my lip. "I don't even know if Zoe is his own flesh and blood."

I was seventeen and knocked up and didn't necessarily know whose child it was. In my heart, I held that the baby was Glenn's. But Glenn, though a good person, was penniless, with dirt-poor parents who might love the baby to death but could never give my child what Jeremy offered. I resolved to keep Glenn a secret from Jeremy and the baby a secret from Glenn. So one rainy morning I just showed up at his parents' crumbling concrete doorstep to tell him how unhappy I was, how I needed space, how I was so sorry, but . . . yeah.

Glenn sobbed. He tried *so hard* to calmly discuss the matter, but I couldn't afford to hear him, couldn't afford to give in. I needed to hate him but couldn't, so I did my damnedest to get him to hate me. I told him I'd cheated. More than once. With more than one guy. He wept harder, *begged* me to give it some time. In my head, I wept with him, hating myself for every word leaping off my tongue. But I needed to end it, to *end* it end it, so before leaving his house I warned him not to come to my school. "Campus police already have your photo," I said, knowing it was unnecessary. Glenn would have stayed away had I simply asked him to. That's just the kind of guy he was. An old soul, a gentleman from another era clothed in grunge. A genuine intellectual who'd never have the diploma, salary, career, and trophy wife to prove his true worth. And there I left him, teary eyed and brokenhearted. The first man I ever loved.

Noah lifts the receiver from the handset of the room's landline. "We need to call the police."

I snatch the receiver out of his hand and hang it up. "What if Zoe's not on the *Dorothy*? What if Maui PD shows up and makes a scene and my ex and his friends are watching the yacht just like we are? Once they see something's wrong, they'll go to ground. We'll *never* find them."

Pinching the base of his nose, Noah sighs deeply. "I can warn MPD to use stealth. I'll explain the situation. Let the professionals handle this tactically. I know these guys, and they *know* what they're doing."

Oh hell, I suppose there's no more dodging this.

"Noah," I say, hoping my soft tone will ease what he's about to hear. "There's more to it than that. Before we moved here, something happened back home."

When I first discovered Jeremy's mother in a pool of blood at the bottom of our staircase, my palms stifled a horrified scream. I spun around with my head pointed skyward like a child lost at a crowded open-air fair. I called out for Jeremy, but nothing. Could I possibly be alone in this mammoth house with Teresa's fucking *corpse*?

Was she even dead? Unsure, I stepped in the blood, kneeled in it actually, and checked for a pulse. She was already gone. A flood of mixed feelings washed through me, from horror to elation to confusion and apprehension about how this happened.

She must have fallen, right? But then, why so much blood? Why was there blood on the wall? We'd recently watched *The Staircase* documentary. I summoned the scenes in which the prosecutor successfully argued that this *bloodbath* couldn't possibly have resulted from an ordinary accident. That the victim must have been struck from behind.

Except Teresa appeared to have been coming down the stairs rather than going up. Didn't that make a fall more likely? She was old, she was frail, she was infirm. That was her excuse for moving in with us in the first place. Yet she refused to stay in the smaller guest room on the bottom floor. Looking up, the stairs suddenly seemed to go on forever, and I fleetingly wondered how it could have taken her this long to have such an accident.

You've no one to blame but yourself, I wanted so badly to say to Teresa's lifeless body. Yet I was ashamed of my thoughts, my indifference, my coldness, despite how cold and indifferent she was to her own daughter Shannon's suicide. Because, as mind boggling as it was, Zoe loved her grandmother. She would be heartbroken. I glanced at my watch. *Shit.* My daughter would be home from school any minute.

Just then came Zoe's terrible scream from behind me. "What *happened*?" she shouted at me. "What did you *do*?" Tears poured from her eyes like from the fountains at the Foxwoods Casino. "Mom, how *could* you?" Then the dam burst, and it was the most painful thing I've ever seen.

"I *found* her like this two minutes ago," I cried.

She stared at my jeans now soaked in Teresa's blood. She stared at my hands, still wet and bright red.

"I checked for a pulse," I added, sounding more defensive than credible by that point.

"Why haven't you called the *police* yet?" she yelled.

The moment I imagined the police at the door, I froze. "No one saw it happen," I told her. "What if the police get here and jump to conclusions like you did?"

"So *what*! It's not the *truth*, is it? They can't prove you did something *you didn't do*."

Then why were there so many overturned convictions? Why were there hundreds of stories of criminal lawyers defending the *innocent* against a big, bad, heartless, brainless criminal justice system?

"We need to call your father first," I told her.

"Dmitri and I just saw him peeling away a few minutes ago."

That was the moment I wondered: Was Jeremy capable of matricide?

He was certainly capable of violence. My own contusions and scar tissue and mended broken bones could attest to that. And as much as he kissed Teresa's wrinkled old ass and laughed at her odious jokes, he privately claimed to loathe her. He'd even once told me how she abused him as a child, withholding food and affection, handing down draconian punishments for minor infractions, and berating him for things no child should be berated for. Shaming him for being himself.

Could he have killed her?

He damn well could have, I thought. We'd joked about it several times over the four nights we consumed the eight-hour *Staircase* documentary.

At that moment I began to fear for our *own* lives, mine and Zoe's. Because if he could kill his own mother, what would keep him from killing us?

He'd never hurt his daughter, though, right?

Any relief I felt quickly withered and died on the vine. Jeremy's uncle Gunther was the shrewdest bastard I'd ever met. What if, after seeing no family resemblance, he already told Jeremy to snatch a lock of my daughter's hair to perform a paternity test?

What if Zoe is Glenn's?

What if Jeremy already knows it?

"I don't understand," Noah says, back on the balcony, gripping the rail. But I think he does. I think he wants to confirm it, to go over every detail so that he can later testify that I confessed to him, confessed to everything from killing my ex's mother to knocking my fiancé over the falls. "You're not just running from this ex, you mean? You're running from the *police*?"

I suddenly feel very exposed on the lanai and need to head inside. Noah follows me back into the motel room, shutting the sliding glass door behind him.

"Was there an autopsy?" he says.

"It revealed she'd been hit in the head." *Like Eddie.*

"So you *fled* an open homicide investigation?"

I move to the front window and peek out the curtains that smell like smoke despite this being a nonsmoking room. Outside I count at least a half dozen uniformed officers, two on each block I can see. Are they here to control the crowds? Or are they here for me?

When I turn, Noah is sitting on the bed, shaking his head, his mouth a squiggly Charlie Brown frown.

"I need to use the can," he says, rising to his feet again.

"Noah," I shout, though I don't know why. I don't have any means to stop him from calling the police. I stare hard at the cell phone now in his hand.

He looks down at it. Tosses it underarm in my direction. It bounces off my chest and falls onto the bed. "I'm not calling anyone," he says. "Not yet." Then he disappears behind the closed bathroom door.

I pick up his phone. It's locked, but there I can see a notification on the screen. A missed call from . . .

No, it can't be. The name instantly sucks the air from my lungs. If I don't pop an Ativan under my tongue within the next sixty seconds, I'll be in the grip of another harrowing panic attack.

I fumble with the pills but manage to dissolve one under my tongue before Noah's flush. Why would he have that name and number in his phone? Then again, he knows virtually *everyone* on this island, male and female, doesn't he?

I recall the two of them standing there on the trail, facing one another and making introductions. It makes no sense. They didn't even speak again after that, at least not that I know of. But there's no mistaking the name.

Graham.

"I need to get out of here," Noah says, stepping out of the bathroom. "I need to clear my head." He takes his phone out of my hand. "You're safe here, Kati. Or whatever the hell your real name is. I have no intention of turning you in. If and when that changes, I'll give you a running start."

With that, he's out the door and I'm more alone than I've ever been before.

Zoe

I'm so alone.

It's the middle of the night, I can't see my hands in front of my eyes, and everything is still.

By now the police are probably looking for her. She can't risk going to them. She won't risk it. Not even for me.

She'll find me herself or I won't be found at all.

I'm so tired.

I can't sleep. How can I sleep with him in the next room?

I'm hungry too.

I don't know how—if—I'm going to get through this.

I'm weak. Almost too weak to lift this micro recorder to my lips and whisper into it.

And if I'm to have any hope of this ending well, I'm going to need my strength.

One way or the other, this needs to end soon. I don't think I have another full day left in me.

I just want to lie on the beach.

Swim in the ocean.

Breathe fresh air and feel the sun on my flesh.

I just want her to find me.

I just want to go home, wherever that is.

17

Day Five

I haven't slept, not a wink, not a nod, not a single, solitary z. I fear surfacing from a night terror only to feel a few fleeting moments of relief before realizing that my reality is even worse than the nightmare I just woke from. It's how I felt in the days following my ugly breakup with Glenn. I felt a loss, a gaping hole in the pit of my stomach that I'd never experienced before. Shamelessly, I tried to fill it with Jeremy, my drug, my original addiction.

Once I forced Glenn out of my life, I went all in with Jeremy. I said yes to the baby, yes to the wedding, yes to moving to Connecticut. I even agreed to take a year (*ha!*) off from school to care for our child full-time. The wedding, which according to Teresa had to take place before I was showing (*We're Catholics, goddamn it!*), was like nothing I'd ever seen before. Somehow, even on super short notice, the Perottas were able to book the world-famous Saint Patrick's Cathedral in New York for the ceremony. The reception was held at the iconic Carlyle Hotel. Something like two hundred people showed up to wish us well and pay their respects to the matriarch of the family. It was any girl's *dream* wedding—except mine. Unready to move from a family of two to a family of hundreds, I'd begged Jeremy to elope. But he refused, and as a consolation he booked our honeymoon at the Ritz-Carlton in Grand Cayman, an exquisite destination he chose not for its cyan seas or Seven Mile Beach but so he could visit his money in offshore accounts, to actively conduct business amid our bliss. When I complained, he exploded in the crowded lobby, saying, *Christ, babe, how much cock do you need?*

During our honeymoon, I stepped away from my body for the first time and imagined myself with Glenn, not in the Caymans but the Poconos, with one of those cheesy heart-shaped Jacuzzis and a single double bed with a dubious bedspread. Instead of the five-star restaurants Jeremy and I dined at, we ate pizza and McDonald's and bad Chinese food, followed by putrid diner coffee and a shared slice of day-old key lime pie. It felt as if my life had branched off in two opposing directions and I'd never be whole again.

Yet in the months immediately following Grand Cayman I convinced myself I'd made the right decision. Jeremy acted like the perfect husband, showering me with love and attention, yet allowing me whatever space I needed. When I had a rough day, he seemed to genuinely want to hear about it as much as I wanted to hear about his day. I naively felt relieved, thinking that prospective fatherhood had matured Jeremy in a way college never could. I was so damn certain of it.

While I don't doubt he had always been a monster, he revealed his full self slowly in the world's most disillusioning striptease: an unnecessary jab at a waiter who took too long with his burger (*oh, he's just hangry*); a few harsh words when he was irritable and I didn't have his martini waiting as promised (*he just needs routine*); an occasional off-color comment or dig about my clothes, my makeup, or the aroma of whatever I was eating at the time like, say, brussels sprouts (*poor thing, he can't help but be a dick*).

When our arguments intensified, I blamed myself. After all, I didn't *really* have a good reason for turning him down for sex that morning. I probably *should* have told him earlier that I ran into a quasi-ex-boyfriend from high school in the frozen-food section at Wegmans. I certainly *could* have acted more enthused when he announced we were spending the weekend at Foxwoods Resort Casino, again.

Meanwhile, I convinced myself the little things shouldn't trouble me. So what if he didn't like my college friends? Maybe he was right, maybe I *had* outgrown them. So what if he found my volunteering at the soup kitchen too inconvenient now that I had such a large house to clean? So what if he was selfish in bed? I still had my vibrator. I still had memories of being with Glenn.

On days Jeremy imposed the silent treatment, I wondered what I'd done to upset him. At moments when he suddenly went from warm to cold, I begged him to tell me what I did wrong. And the moment he noticed I gained a couple of pounds, I vowed to lose them, even though he'd trashed my stationary bike because, like me, it was "stupid" and "a complete fucking waste of space."

When I first learned he was cheating I actually tried to make myself sexier for him. When he threatened to divorce me over something as trivial as burnt pancakes, I promised to do better. When I caught him in obvious lies, I kept silent. When he blew up each of his friendships one by one (except for Oz), I always sided with him, no matter how obviously wrong he was.

As for Jeremy's mother, it took her somewhat longer to reveal her true colors. But once she did, she never held back. She berated her own grown children over life choices having nothing to do with her. She reveled in seeing Jeremy and Shannon at each other's throats, competing for her affection. When she became bored with Shannon, she turned her full attention to me, blatantly attempting to drive a wedge between me and Jeremy. When that went well for her, she went right to work on me and Zoe.

But our bond was much stronger: the bond between mother and daughter. Yes, even as a teenager. Because despite what mothers like Teresa and my own believed, a child isn't something you love only until it turns six.

Hearing something land with a thud outside my motel room door, I steal a peek through the curtains. Resting on the weathered welcome mat is a complimentary *Honolulu Star-Advertiser*. I slowly twist the knob and push it open. In a flash I bend to pick up the paper, causing a fresh surge of pain to shoot up my back—no doubt from the car accident. When I finally straighten, I duck back inside and pull the paper out of its plastic. Glaring at the front page, I nearly fall into a dead faint right between the room's double beds.

On the front page are photos of me, three of them, and the headline screams: Woman Suspected in Death of Local Attorney Also Suspected in Death of Mother-in-Law and (surprise, surprise) it's authored by Koa Pualani.

Honolulu—Who is Kati Dawes, the woman suspected by the National Park Service of killing her reputed fiancé, Hana attorney Eddie Akana, at Haleakala National Park five days ago? While authorities have been looking for answers since the lawyer went missing, today we finally learn the truth.

Kati Dawes's true name is Sara Perotta of Bridgeport, Connecticut, wife (yes, *wife*) of wealthy venture capitalist Jeremy Perotta. If that name sounds familiar, it's likely because it's been in the news several times over the past two years.

The death of Jeremy's mother, Teresa Perotta, grabbed statewide headlines in Connecticut after an autopsy performed by the Fairfield County medical examiner revealed that the cause of death, specifically a cervical fracture, most likely resulted from a violent strike delivered at the top of a flight of stairs in her home.

Mere weeks into the investigation, Bridgeport police returned to question both Jeremy and Sara Perotta only to learn that Sara had disappeared with the couple's teenage daughter.

Following a two-year search, Sara Perotta's possible involvement in the death of Hana attorney Eddie Akana may prove to aid authorities in closing cases at both ends of the country.

The article goes on to say that federal prosecutor Charley Kay dubbed the development "disturbing, if not wholly surprising" and vowed her office will continue its investigation in earnest. The attorney for Sara Perotta (a.k.a. Kati Dawes), Noah Walker of Walker & Akana, could not be reached for comment.

Shit, shit, super shit. Kati Dawes is dead and gone. Now only Sara Perotta exists. Sara Perotta who is wanted for questioning in her mother-in-law's murder.

Thing is, this isn't only the death of *Kati* Dawes but of *Zoe* Dawes too. Next time I see her—*if* I ever see her again—she will be Sydney Perotta of Bridgeport, Connecticut, and daughter of a fugitive from justice.

And what if I don't see her at all?

The thought, though always there, chokes me as if I'd just swallowed a horsefly. A world without my daughter is an earth devoid of oxygen.

Suddenly, a rap and another horror movie title crawls across the screen. *A Knock on the Door.* Coming soon to frighten the fuck out of you.

I keep silent, listen for the word *housekeeping* but hear nothing.

Then *A Second Knock.* My pulse speeds up.

Noah has a key, he wouldn't need to knock.

Quietly, I backpedal toward the sliding glass door, the room's only other exit. Thing is, we're a couple of stories high, and on the other side of that balcony is nothing but open ocean.

18

Where the hell is Noah?

Where did he run off to last night?

When will he be back?

Another rap on the motel door, followed by another, then another. Heel after heel, I retreat to the rear of the room, never once taking my eyes off the front. The scraped brass knob turns, and stops. Turns, and stops. It's locked, dead-bolted. The chain is in place. But whoever it is, the son of a bitch is persistent. Whoever it is *knows* I'm inside.

It's Jeremy. I'm sure of it.

I need to open the door and confront him. I *need* to know where Zoe is, even if it gets me killed. Swallowing the bile rising in my throat, I slowly step forward, one foot in front of the other, practically on my toes to avoid making any noise. When I reach the door, I push myself up, lean against it, and stare out the peephole.

Blackness.

Another booming knock causes me to jump, to instantly become faint with fear. Who the hell else but Jeremy would block the fucking peephole?

The police?

Then a long, loud cough, a wet, unhealthy hacking, issues from the other side of the door. It's a sound I haven't heard in the past two years, yet I recognize it.

Mac?

I open the door, my eyes immediately locking on the strip of tape covering the peephole.

"Sorry," he says. "Force of habit."

After he was fired from the Black Pepper Pub, I didn't see Mac again for years. First there was the pregnancy, then the wedding, the dropping out of school, the move to Connecticut. Zoe was almost three years old when I next ran into him. I didn't see him in Pennsylvania (I never returned there, not to college and certainly not to my mother Joanne) but in Bridgeport at the local Wegmans supermarket, where he was bagging groceries at the end of register seven.

The first time I saw him I was so startled I pretended not to notice him. If he recognized me, he gave no indication. For the next several weeks, I let the nanny do the grocery shopping. Finally, on the day before Zoe's third birthday party, I found myself with no choice. I fucking *needed* cupcake frosting.

With no one around to babysit, I brought Zoe with me. At Wegmans I made a beeline for the baking aisle and spotted the Betty Crocker frosting I'd seen advertised on TV. I snatched it off the shelf and spun . . . right into the old man himself.

"I thought you looked familiar," he said. His voice was even gruffer than it had been a few years earlier.

I once again stood speechless, paralyzed with fear, as if I were once again standing outside the Black Pepper, cold, alone, abandoned by my friends, holding a fake ID that could get me expelled if not arrested.

"Is this your little girl?" he said, gently lowering himself to one knee. "She's beautiful."

"Wh-what are you doing here?" I asked.

"I work here." His eyes locked on Zoe as he spoke. "Bagging groceries, stocking shelves, cleaning messes left in the baby food aisle. It's minimum wage," he chuckled, "but at least the hours suck."

I smiled awkwardly as he studied my daughter. Could this be nothing but a big coincidence? A case of "small world" and all that?

Returning to his feet, Mac read the relief on my face. "Did I frighten you?"

"Do I look frightened?"

"Petrified."

"Good," I said. "Because I am." I tried to make light of it, but my shaky voice betrayed me. "What the hell are you doing in Bridgeport?"

He grinned. "I thought you knew. I got shitcanned from my gig at the Black Pepper a few years back."

My first thought was that it seemed extreme that this strange old man drove hundreds of miles and took a job bagging groceries just to exact revenge four years later. Unless . . .

Unless he wasn't only fired.

"You were inside again, weren't you."

The old man looked surprised, as if he hadn't counted on me being that clever.

"So he admitted to you what he did?"

"What *who* did?" I asked.

"Your old boyfriend Jerry."

"Jeremy."

"If you say so." He lifted a random box of cake mix and stared at its cover as he spoke. "He had an uncle call the pub to get me fired. No big deal. *Then* he called my parole officer. A real hard-ass by the name of Ives. Told him I had a stash of blow in my apartment above the Black Pepper. So my PO came by, conducted a search." He turned the box over to the recipes and ingredients, then raised his cold blue eyes to meet mine. "Guess what he found—almost an ounce of blow. Only I haven't put anything up my schnoz in forty years, and I sure as hell wasn't pushing it."

"Then why was it in your apartment?"

"You'd have to ask your old boyfriend that."

Freaked the fuck out, unsure what or even *whether* to tell Jeremy about meeting Mac, I avoided the supermarket for the next few weeks. But as time wore on, my curiosity won out. I girded myself and gradually returned to Wegmans. Mac said hello and goodbye and smiled at me and Zoe, exhibiting no signs of anger or aggressiveness, so after numerous times avoiding his checkout line, I finally returned to register seven.

Several more weeks passed before he offered to buy me coffee at the Starbucks wedged inside the supermarket. When I agreed, he immediately removed his apron, told the checkout attendant that he was going on break, and joined me for a small latte.

During our conversation, he admitted he'd done time before he worked at the Black Pepper and why. Though I remained on guard, I felt more sympathetic than threatened. He'd been a Philly cop when he got involved in an off-duty bar brawl. The victim—Francis (better known as Frank) Summers—had a long history of domestic violence against his wife. Meanwhile, Mac's explanation for being in Bridgeport was both credible and benign, even noble: he had an estranged daughter who lived on the outskirts of the city, and he wanted, if nothing else, to be near her and her rug rats.

Coffee soon became a regular thing. Each time he shared more about himself, and I eventually came around to sharing too. More than I ever expected. When I told him that I'd married that "old boyfriend," he seemed surprised, possibly even disappointed, but wanted to hear more. As time passed, my depiction of Jeremy devolved, just as he had in real life, from a hot-tempered control freak to a cruel and physically abusive savage. I told Mac how Jeremy collects ammunition on *everyone*, from his enemies to his best friends and family. How he *files* it, *stores* it, and uses it when the opportunity presents itself. How he starts rumors, harmful rumors, lies really, and retaliates for every little missile fired back in his direction. Sometimes outright, sometimes through others, like his mother, like his uncle Gun, like his friend Ozzie Bent. I told him about Jeremy's hypocrisy. How he believes in rules, only they don't apply to him. How respect, patience, politeness were everyone's duties but his.

I saw pain creasing the old man's face as I opened up to him, and before long, I cared about him more than I ever did any Perotta other than my daughter.

From there our friendship evolved quickly. Far from being a dangerous stalker, Mac was a gentle, caring soul, a profoundly wise (if not well-educated) man with the street smarts of both a big-city cop *and* an ex-con. Within months, Mac went from being a friend to a confidant, from a confidant to a mentor, and finally to the kind of surrogate I needed most in the world.

Now that I've opened the door and allowed Mac inside, my stomach strongly suggests it was a mistake. I feel more confined than ever. This seafoam-green motel room seems to be shrinking in on me. Instinctively, I step backward until my ass hits the desk. There's no way to get around him unless I strike him with something. Maybe the lamp, maybe the landline.

Damn it, what if I chased Noah away for good with all my lies?

If only he were here now.

If only he'd come back.

Truth is, as much as I trusted Mac before his heart attack is as little as I trusted him after. Following his recovery, I could see something in his eyes—there *is* something in his eyes even now—that portends violence.

"How did you find me?" I say, recalling his adamance that I not tell him where we were heading. *If I don't have the beans,* he said, *I can't spill 'em, even under torture.*

"I've always known where you were," he admits without hesitation. "How the hell else could I keep you and your daughter safe from that bastard?"

My panic rises. *Has he lost it completely?* "What are you doing here, Mac?"

"I kept even better tabs on *him*," he says with a boastful wink. "When he and Iggy—"

"Ozzie," I say.

"Ozzie, Iggy, what the hell difference does it make?"

I note the irritation in his tone when I correct him and take a careful step back, my eyes darting to the open bathroom door.

"Anyway," he says, "when he and Iggy set off in their boat from Mexico heading west, I hopped on a commercial flight. I've been here more than a week already."

"More than a week? Where are you staying?"

"I travel light, like your pal Jack Reacher." He holds up a travel-size toothbrush, the bottom melted and molded into a prison shank.

Can I make a run for it? Lock myself inside the bathroom? If I could, though, what happens next? If an ocean didn't stop him, how would a paper-thin door?

And what if I'm wrong in distrusting him? What if, like Noah, I need Mac in my life even more than I realize?

Following his heart attack, Mac morphed into a different person altogether. Where before he advised and guided and consoled, he now pushed and persuaded and cajoled. "You *need* to leave him," he'd tell me. *"It's time."*

But the timing made absolutely no sense. Not when I was so close to Zoe leaving for college. Throughout my marriage the specter of the prenuptial agreement I signed hung over my head. If I left Jeremy, I'd end up with nothing. *We* would end up with nothing. Worse, if I filed for divorce, Uncle Gun would surely insist on a paternity test. What if Zoe *was* Glenn's? What then? Would Jeremy disown my daughter? Would he throw both of us out on the streets? Where would we go? Not back to Pennsylvania. My own mother was less than useless, and I had vowed when Zoe was born that the two would never meet. Zoe and I would be completely alone, something unfathomable to me back then. What would I do with no job, no education, no family, no friends? Nowhere to live, nothing to eat. I'd been to the worst sections of Bridgeport and Philly. I knew how the impoverished lived, and I wanted *more* for Zoe. So I stayed and stayed. Stayed when Teresa, always a horrific bitch, became infirm and insisted on living with us, just as I'd stayed after multiple trips to different ERs and urgent care facilities across the state. Just as I'd stayed after catching Jeremy red-handed with a redhead who worked in the "office" he kept downtown. I stayed even after he threatened to kill me.

Despite all those years of me "hanging in there," following his heart attack, Mac exhibited a newfound urgency to liberate me and my daughter from the Perotta home. His insistence alarmed me, only not in the way he'd hoped. I began to distance myself from him, which visibly worried him, concerning me even more, driving me to dissociate myself further. By the time I discovered Teresa at the bottom of the stairs, my friendship with Mac hung by a thread. I ran to him only because I had no one else in the world. I ran to him for Zoe.

"Let me explain," he says, studying my body language. "Once you vanished, detectives turned up the heat on Jeremy. The cops were convinced the two of you conspired to kill Teresa and had a falling-out. When you split, they figured Jeremy would flip on you. And he might have, only he didn't have the goods. Everything he said only further incriminated him. His attorney Ray Fitch finally gave him an ultimatum: shut the fuck up or he'd withdraw as counsel. Jeremy shut the fuck up. Then his focus turned to you. You running was as good as a confession. He was too stupid to catch on to the fact you were running from him. He hired some hotshot investigators out of Boston. Ordered them to look under every rock, first on the coast, then the entire country, then the globe. He was going to find you if it killed him."

Mac shakes his head, half-amused, half-disgusted. "The Boston investigators had no great luck. Those guys couldn't find their ass in a paper sack. So Jeremy went to Uncle Gun. Uncle Gun set up a fucking war room at your house. They turned their search for you into a manhunt. Gunther sent people to every major city, first in New England, then the entire Atlantic coast. When that failed, they started west. They thought they located you in a small town called Broken Arrow in Oklahoma. Jeremy went personally to pop the surprise on you. But the surprise was on him. Because the anonymous tip that led them to Broken Arrow was mine." He smiles at his own cleverness. It's not his usual *thank you for shopping at Wegmans* smile but a menacing split of the lips that dominates his face.

How does he know all this about Jeremy? He was watching him *this* closely? Practically running a private spy operation since I left?

"After that, your ex eased up on the gas. Until, that is, his lawyer Ray Fitch informed him they'd hit a roadblock in probate court. See, under the so-called Slayer Rule, one can't inherit from someone they murdered. Only in probate, the murder doesn't need to be proved beyond any reasonable doubt, just on a preponderance of the evidence. In other words, more likely than not. And Zoe's statements to Bridgeport PD were more than enough to do him in, at least as far as probate goes.

"Needing someone to pin the murder on, he recommitted himself to finding you. Meanwhile, the police were watching every move he made. I worried the idiot was going to lead them straight to you. Then something happened. Few weeks ago, Jeremy received a phone call. Not at home or on his mobile or at work but at Fitch's law office. Just about the only place in Bridgeport I didn't have ears. I only learned about the substance of the call hours later when Jeremy got sloppy."

Mac hacks into his elbow and apologizes. He'd picked up smoking his first time in the joint, he once told me, and hasn't been able to kick the habit since. Despite a severe case of emphysema, he still goes through a pack a day. "It's like my lungs starve for the poison," he says. "It's them, not me, that's got the death wish."

"After leaving Fitch's office," Mac continues, "he went straight to his pal Iggy. I don't know what was said, but next thing I knew Jeremy was making elaborate plans. Real ones *and* decoys. His paper trail placed him in Miami, but Iggy picked him up. From there they flew to Mexico in his private jet. In Cabo San Lucas, they hired a skeleton crew and met up with *Big Dottie*—the *Dorothy*—the yacht currently sitting outside your window. When they pointed her straight for the islands, I knew he'd found you. I just didn't know how. I didn't know who called him at Fitch's office. And I still don't."

He notices me staring at the bulge in his right jacket pocket. His eyes fall on it and linger as he debates what to say. Finally, he looks up at me. Slowly he reaches in. When he pulls his hand free, it's trembling and holding a handgun.

"Don't worry, doll," he says. "This isn't for you."

Zoe

The day Grandma died, Dmitri picked me up from school at the regular time and drove me home. We'd kicked around the idea of getting a burger, but I didn't have much of an appetite. Besides, he'd been getting a bit pushy and a bit personal on these fast-food runs. He always wanted just a little more than I was willing to give.

Besides, I wanted to get home to see Grandma.

Despite Mom's adamant disapproval, Grandma and I had been spending so much time together back then. We were sixty years apart, yet I swear I had more in common with her than I did kids my own age.

Just before we approached the driveway, Dmitri slammed on the brakes. My father's silver Lincoln entered the street like a shot and sped away.

"Where's he going in such a hurry?" Dmitri said.

Chances were he wasn't going anywhere in a hurry. He was leaving in a hurry as he often did following particularly bad fights with Mom and Grandma.

I tried to put him out of my head and replace his image with a much more pleasant scene: me eating rice pudding with cinnamon while Grams eats green Jell-O with whipped cream.

In the circular driveway, Dmitri rolled to a stop in front of our house. I was so anxious to get inside I was practically at my front door the moment I stepped out of the Rolls.

Oddly, the door was already open. I thought, Someone's going to get shit for that.

With my knuckles I shoved it in and went inside, curious but apprehensive.

What I found nearly knocked me over. Mom standing over Grandma, who lay on the floor at the bottom of our staircase like a broken mannequin.

I saw all the blood.

Then I heard myself scream.

19

Entering the local biker bar in Kihei, I half expect to step out of Hawaii and into another world entirely. But there are signs and symbols of aloha even in the dimness: a hula girl on a beer poster in the corner, a state license plate proudly displaying a rainbow, a plumeria lei wrapped around the old-fashioned cash register behind the bar. All the guests appear happy and friendly. It strikes me that maybe *Sons of Anarchy* wasn't the best way to acquaint myself with the ride-or-die lifestyle. *Go figure.*

While Mac orders us beers, I search for a quiet corner and quickly conclude one doesn't exist. The biker bar was Mac's idea. My level of fear dropped precipitously when he suddenly said, "Let's go." My eyes were still on the handgun when I asked him where. He replied, "Somewhere the cops ain't." The way he's speaking to the bartender, it's clear he's been here before. Probably to scope out the place. Although this is my first biker bar, I feel safe among these (mostly) men with long gray hair and beards and black leather vests. I feel hidden and protected under their strange heavy-metal umbrella.

Still, I may be the baddest outlaw in here. Almost certainly the most wanted.

But then, the way I feel about these bikers, I once felt about Jeremy. Despite how frightened I was of him, he made me feel safe from others. In hindsight I feared him much less than his money and what he could get away with because of it. Ironically, it was also the money, not Jeremy, that had made me feel safe and less concerned for my daughter's safety.

I *so* miss my missing daughter, and it's true: I can't bear to think what life will be like if (*when*) she leaves the islands for college. What will I have left but shadows of decades-old memories? Bringing her home from the hospital, seeing her for the first time standing on her own. Taking her to her first day of preschool, when I cried, and to her first day of kindergarten, when she cried and I gave serious consideration to homeschooling.

I never wanted to be one of those mothers who wish their children could stay forever five years old. But looking back, that year was the happiest of my life. It was the last year she ran into my room, frightened by nightmares, and crawled into bed beside me. The last year she insisted on removing the cheese from her pizza. The last year we were together more often than not.

At five, Zoe wanted to be an animal doctor who could help people, too, so she could fix mommy's sore neck and back. At five, she made easy friends. With children at school, with random boys and girls at the park. Best of all, at five, her eyes always lit like sparklers when she saw me, whether she was getting off the school bus wearing a paper crown made in art class or getting picked up from the "bestest bird-day party ever."

Was I too clingy? As she grew up and moved from grade to grade, my favorite nights were those spent working with her on creative school projects: the galaxy formed with painted Styrofoam balls; an American flag born of rolled-up papier mâché. Game nights, movie nights, pizza nights, nights laughing and splashing in the heated pool. All gone, all in the past, never to return again. How can that be right? How can that be *fair*?

Am I too greedy, wanting what's gone? Like the Christmases when I merrily spoiled my child rotten? The Halloweens spent guessing at what she would dress up as? One year a pirate, another a princess. A ghost, a goblin, a bunch of grapes, a scarecrow with a real beanstalk fastened to her back. Now all that'll be left is handing out candy to strangers—and even strangers are in short supply in Hana.

Oh, Syd, where have our summers gone? Our weeks "roughing it" in a cabin in Maine or being pampered at the Ritz in Grand Cayman. Our jaunts to Boston and Providence, our ski trips to Vermont. Our two months traveling around Canada, scooping up every type of shot glass we could find, from I 💜 NIAGARA FALLS to BLOW ME, I'M FRENCH CANADIAN.

All of it, gone. And though I made a concerted effort to always live in the moment, to live *for* the moment, I feel as though some of that time, even some of those memories, have been brazenly stolen from me, and I'd do anything to recover the entire package. Because while my teenage pregnancy may have been unplanned, unexpected, and even unwanted, giving birth to Zoe drained all doubt and resistance from my body. I fell in love with her even before I held her in my arms. Funny, I'd been so worried about Zoe's looks. Would she have Jeremy's sharp green eyes? Would she be the spitting image of Glenn? But she looked like no one, not even me, and certainly not my mother, thank God. She was gorgeous with powder-blue eyes and the sweetest tiny fingers and toes. She was perfect.

Sincerely willing to do *anything* for Zoe, at some point I convinced myself I had to do *everything* for Zoe, miraculously transforming my cowardly decision to stay with Jeremy into a sacrifice. I was his only victim, after all. I was his sole punching bag, the lone object of his wrath. I was Jesus on the cross.

Like my mother. Joanne used the term *single mother* like a cudgel to elicit sympathy, to gain an edge, even to seduce men. *Save me, I'm a damsel in distress.* It nauseated me even then. Although she worked hard, worked two jobs, she was always cold and overly critical, a religious zealot forever mad at the world.

To a beguiling extent, she sheltered me in my early years, so much so that what few relatives I had openly expressed concern that I'd always live in isolation. As a child, I was torn between forgiveness and resentment. Early on I knew (thanks to my crueler classmates) that my mother was a "head case." But wasn't that because of all the pressure she was under as a single mother? At the time, there weren't many single parents who sent their children to Catholic school, where divorce was strongly frowned upon. Mom had just gotten a raw deal, hadn't she? According to Joanne, my father had run off days after she gave birth to me "because the no-good bastard son of a bitch didn't want children." Especially not a girl. Especially not *this* girl, this snot-nosed wailing infant shitting herself in the crib. "You're just like your *goddamn father*" was her common line of attack against me, along with, "I wish you were *never born. I wish you were dead.*"

In the biker bar, distracted by my thoughts, I pick up the slim menu, which is simply a trifold black-and-white photocopy of a dirty old menu that has probably long since gone to that great big biker bar in the sky. My eyes fall on the remote control to the television behind the bar; buttons up, as usual. My eyes then move to the screen and I see Assistant US Attorney Charley Kay before a stand of microphones. To either side of her stand two federal agents identified as Arthur Delacroix and Dale Politz.

I expect to see another unflattering photo of me on the screen, but none materializes. Instead, a picture of the Honolulu mayor appears alongside a photo of a local businessman so nondescript, it could be a stock image. Relieved, rather than change the channel I reach across the bar, grab the remote, and pump up the volume.

"This morning," Charley Kay says, "federal agents arrested multiple men who were, for the past eighteen months, being investigated for corruption in connection with the pandemic. Those indicted include Honolulu's mayor and the wealthy and influential hotelier Tim Jedrick."

My jaw falls. The photo of Mr. Nondescripto is Jedrick. In my head, he'd been a mythical evil, older than time itself. He'd been seven feet tall with a gaze that could pierce through walls. The man on the screen looks vaguely like my FedEx delivery driver back east.

"As of now, there is one defendant still at large, and we ask the public to aid us in our search for him. A word of caution, however: this man should be considered armed and *extremely* dangerous. Do not approach him. If you see him, get somewhere safe and call the Maui Police Department or the FBI tip line right away."

All of my breath leaves me when I recognize the man in the picture that appears over Charley's shoulder. It's Graham Gephardt, identified here as Woody Graham. *Graham*, the Maui County Ocean Safety and Lifeguard Services guy. *Graham*, the suspicious name in Noah's phone last night at the motel.

A stern-looking anchor returns to the screen and says, "Incidentally, the United States Attorney for the District of Hawaii Aimee Yoshida is resigning from the office at the end of this year due to health issues. Many expect Charley Kay to be named as her successor."

I turn off the sound and hurriedly search the bar for Mac.

Twenty minutes later Mac helps me make some sense of all this. In the crowded back room of the biker bar he says, "There *is* no Graham Gephardt. *Woody* Graham, on the other hand, is a two-bit private investigator with an office down the street here in Kihei. According to today's unsealed indictments, he's also Tim Jedrick's bagman."

"Bagman?" I say absently. *Sounds retro.*

"The money guy. The fellow who physically hands over the bribe so the principals don't get their paws dirty."

My thoughts are circling *something*, like sharks so close, so hungry, yet unable to go in for the kill. Finally I surrender and go for the easier prey: what all this means for Zoe at the moment. "If Graham works for Jedrick, and he met me at the trail under false pretenses the day after Eddie went missing, Jedrick must be responsible for Eddie's murder. Which means Jedrick must have Zoe."

"Except Jedrick's tied up in federal detention just now."

169

"Which leaves her in the hands of the only bastard left at large."

Woody Graham.

Mac holds up a hand. "Let's not jump to conclusions here. We don't know whether Graham killed Eddie. One, being a bagman doesn't necessarily make you a murderer. Two, if the feds just indicted Graham, they may have had eyes on him the morning Eddie went missing."

For the first time ever I feel impatient with Mac, my irritability at a level fast approaching mania. "How can you think this is all a *coincidence?*"

"Because regardless of Zoe's whereabouts, a coincidence *does* exist here. If Graham kidnapped Zoe like you think, what the hell are Iggy and Jeremy doing anchored off the coast? Your ex didn't come here to make nice with you."

Charley's public statement and the photo of Graham made me forget about the *Dorothy* completely. *He's right.* With respect to Eddie's murder and Zoe's disappearance, we can't escape coincidence altogether. If I'm convinced whoever killed Eddie also has Zoe—and if it's Graham—then Jeremy's arrival on Maui just over a week ago *is* a coincidence. Unless . . .

Unless Jeremy and Jedrick are somehow connected.

Either that or . . .

"Could Eddie's killer and Zoe's captor be two different people?" I say.

"We're only going to know that once we find one or the other. But it's too hot out there right now."

"We're in *Hawaii*," I say. "We're practically *on* the equator."

"Not hot like that, doll. Your home has been searched. I'd bet my last buck your name's on a warrant by now. You've seen the heat out there. Trust me, once you're caught up in the system, it's no piece of cake getting out. And this Charley Kay—I've done my homework on her—she's a shark."

"She's good?"

"Worse. She's ambitious. There's nothing more dangerous than an ambitious prosecutor." He lowers his voice to a near grumble. "She's a political animal who's already expected to go far in statewide politics, maybe even nationally. She's hard on crime and fiscally responsible but progressive on social issues. She's young and attractive *and* served her country in Afghanistan. And she's got a smart, photogenic wife who's also a renowned local artist. Local pundits say Charley Kay looks a lot like the future."

"But we *can't* find Zoe sitting in this bar," I say.

Mac glances around. "No, but we can make it our base of operations. We meet anybody, we meet them here. And one of us sure as hell doesn't leave this place without the other. Understand? You don't walk out of here without my say-so?"

Is this how I sounded to Zoe the past two years?

"I need to get in touch with Kilo," I say. "He'll know something about Woody Graham, maybe even Graham's connection to Noah."

"Can we trust him?"

"Kilo's loyalty is to Eddie."

"Well, you can't say anything over the phone. Can we get him in here unnoticed?"

I consider the question. "We can't get him *anywhere* unnoticed. But there *is* a safe place to meet him."

"Safe how?"

"The outside world pretends this place doesn't exist."

20

"What else did you learn about Graham?" I ask Mac as we head toward a hidden homeless (*unhoused,* Zoe would rightfully correct me) encampment in Wailuku, where we plan to rendezvous with Kilo. Although Mac drives, he doesn't trust his failing eyesight, so I'm behind the wheel of his rented black Dodge Charger.

"He and Jedrick go back to their days in Vegas," Mac says. "Graham was Vegas PD until he got himself kicked off the force for putting some tourist in the hospital with a fractured eye socket."

"So he *is* violent," I say.

"Frankly, I don't know many bagmen who aren't." An uncomfortable silence hangs in the air before Mac turns to me and apologizes. "That was insensitive. We *are* going to get your daughter back, Kati, I promise you. Just keep an open mind. Graham might not be the cat we're looking for."

I'm worried Mac is just too focused on Jeremy. Jeremy is the threat he knows, the threat he's here to contain, the threat he's been obsessed with. As obsessed as I was, apparently. Maybe more. What did he once tell me? *I'm a hammer. To me everything looks like a nail.*

I tell him that in fewer words, leaving a question mark at the end.

"Look," he says, "I know everything I need to know about Eddie Akana as well. I knew he was a politician and a litigator. I knew he was a gambler. I even knew who bought up his debt. You don't think I was going to let you date another monster, do you?"

Let me?

I turn the wheel slightly onto a long, winding dirt road that leads to a sprawling yet hidden tent city that's probably existed for as long as there have been social classes in the Sandwich Isles.

These are the people *thrown* off the grid. They never asked to live off it. These are the forgotten masses I so feared joining if I left Jeremy after giving birth to Zoe. I was, after all, estranged from my mother, had never met my father, and my only friends were from my brief stint in college—and Jeremy had cut me off from them too. My daughter and I would have had no support system whatsoever. We'd have ended up in a place like this. We would've been invisible but not on purpose, willing to give anything just to be seen.

"There he is," I say.

Mac's eyes narrow. "Now I get it. The only place this boy's hiding is in plain sight."

The tent city is silent as we pass through it toward a small stand of trees. Yes, my heart *bleeds* when I see the condition in which the impoverished exist. Like everyone else, I tend to forget them when they're not directly in front of my eyes. Yet I can't help but think if I inherited the Perotta fortune, I'd actually have the power to help a number of unhoused people live indoors like human beings. Wouldn't that be the ultimate irony? Wouldn't that be the final thumb in Teresa's eye?

In the shade of some trees, I hug Kilo and kiss him on the cheek. I'm so grateful to see him just now. But he and Mac are all business.

According to Kilo, freelance private eye Woody Graham performed investigative services for the law firm of Walker & Akana for years, until the conclusion of the Lanyon shipping case. Although Kilo himself never had a beef with Graham, Eddie never truly trusted him—*He's one sketchy haole, eh?*—and finally put his foot down and refused to work with him following the big verdict. Kilo assumed it began with a billing issue. Sleazy investigators like Graham often double- and sometimes triple-bill for their time. They can stake out an apartment for one client while making calls for a second and writing a report for a third.

"His sketchiness didn't bother Noah?" I say. It doesn't escape me that Noah hasn't called to check in. Has he given up on me? Or worse, has he decided to turn me in after all?

Kilo shakes his head. "Noah actually kinda liked that in an investigator."

I understand how shadiness, even outright darkness, can be an attraction for some. Jeremy rooted for Jeffrey fucking Epstein and Bernie Madoff.

"Now that Eddie's gone," I say, "is it possible Noah and Woody are working together again?"

Kilo shrugs his meaty shoulders. "Could be."

That would explain the call. But then why did Noah pretend not to know him the day after Eddie went missing?

"What we know about Woody Graham," I say, "is that he's violent and desperate and he works for violent, desperate men. And I believe he has Zoe." My thoughts drift into blackness as I imagine a hostage situation with my little girl literally caught in the cross fire. I shudder.

Mac snaps me out of it. "I think you better get your lawyer on the horn. He might have more answers than we previously believed."

"When the lawyer gets here," Mac says in the parking lot behind the bar, "keep him here. Whatever you do, don't leave this bar, got it?"

Reluctant to trust Noah, Mac paid a biker to pick him up in Hana and bring him back to the bar, but only after frisking Noah and removing the battery from his phone.

Mac turns to Kilo. "Hey, small fry, Kati tells me you're one hell of a digital safecracker."

"I'm *awright*."

Mac brings me back into the conversation. "I'm taking Kilo to do some digital digging into Eddie's finances at a nearby storage facility." He points a finger at me. "You don't go anywhere with anyone until I get back, got it?"

"Got it."

With Mac and Kilo gone, I return to the bar and order a beer.

Twenty minutes later, in the cramped back room of the biker bar, Noah eyes me across the table. "Wanna tell me what's with the Hells Angels escort?"

"I needed to make sure you weren't followed. In case you missed the morning news, Kati Dawes is dead and Sara Perotta is wanted for questioning in two murders."

"I read the paper," he says, expressionless. "Does this mean your lawyer is finally gonna get the whole story?"

"No, your *client* is going to get the full story, starting with why the hell you pretended not to know Woody Graham at the trail the morning after Eddie went missing."

Noah sighs and drops his chin into a palm but otherwise appears unaffected. "Lemme guess. Did the big guy tell you?"

"I saw Graham's name come up on your phone while you were in the bathroom at the motel."

"Listen," he says with a mirthless grin, "I told him not to meet you that morning. Graham offered to talk to you to try to determine what really happened to Eddie. He thought pretending he worked for the Maui County Lifeguard Services would cause you to drop your guard." He raises his palms defensively. "This was *before* you asked me to stand in as your attorney. *After* you asked me, I'd already failed to acknowledge him, so it was too late."

"You *knew* he was associated with Tim Jedrick," I charge.

"I knew he was a scumbag—it's hard to avoid them in my line of work—but *no*, I had no idea he was working with the likes of Jedrick."

Suddenly, something I was searching for earlier surfaces and the sharks go into a frenzy. "The *agents' names* at Charley Kay's press conference this morning: Arthur Delacroix, Dale Politz." I pull out the Post-it notes. "They're the same names that were in Eddie's pandemic file, *remember?* Artie D., Dale P.? The third is Charlie K.—which Eddie must've misspelled hearing it over the phone."

Noah's eyes widen, nearly bulge, at the revelation. "Which probably means Eddie was tipped off about the investigation. He must have backed off when he learned the feds were getting intel from someone else, maybe from a whistleblower inside the mayor's office."

"Did Eddie push for this investigation? Is *that* why Jedrick had Graham kill Eddie?"

Noah sits back, shaking his head. "There's no *evidence* to support that. It's pure speculation. Look, Kati, coincidence alone doesn't cut it. In court, we're going to need a defense."

"Noah," I say, doing my best to moderate my voice, "the case against me means nothing at the moment. *Graham. Has. Zoe.*"

For a moment his face freezes. When his lips finally part, he says, "Even if I don't agree with it, I follow the logic that Graham could be responsible for Eddie given his association with Jedrick. But given this morning's presser, don't you think Charley Kay's already looked at him for this? He may have a rock-solid alibi. Besides, *why* would he take Zoe?"

"We've been over this, Noah."

"This isn't about the environment, though. This is about the pandemic."

"What about Jedrick's message?" I say. "His message to Eddie about buying up his gambling debt, remember? You said he was telling Eddie, *'Your debt to me doesn't die with you.'* That by making good on that threat, he'd be delivering a warning to anyone who might oppose his agenda of creating a gaming empire here in the islands."

Gritting his teeth, Noah sits up straight, the little blond hairs on his arms standing on end.

"Jedrick's in lockup," I say. "But Graham is still on the loose. You're the only link we have to him. You know more about Graham than anyone. You've been working together for years. *Where would he take Zoe?*"

Noah shakes his damn head again. "The Graham I know *wouldn't* take Zoe." He pauses. "But if he's wanted by the feds, I do have a good guess about where he'd go to lie low."

"Where's that?"

This time he hesitates. "You'll never find it. Either I go alone or I'm gonna need to take you there myself."

Following spare internal debate, I leave Mac a note with the bartender telling him where I'm heading and why. *Better to ask for forgiveness than permission, right?* Noah's reason for not acknowledging Graham on the first day of the search makes perfect sense, and though he's not convinced Graham is behind Zoe's disappearance, Noah's desire to keep me out of prison and find my daughter seems genuine. This is a chance I have to take.

"Now we just need a car," I say.

"Well, you picked a good place for a meeting," Noah says, "because I saw two of my favorite clients in the back room shooting pool."

"They'll loan you a car?"

"Or help us 'borrow' one."

As I drive upcountry in a gray Nissan Sentra loaned to us by a Kihei mechanic behind on his legal bills, Noah insists on making the prosecution's argument against me for Eddie's murder, claiming Charley

Kay is moving full speed ahead. For us, the corruption case is merely a distraction.

"I'm just playing devil's advocate," he says. "Because she has enough to indict if not convict. She has the probable murder weapon with your prints and Eddie's blood. She has Zoe's statement that you and Eddie had a heated argument the night before. She also has your admission that it was your idea to go hiking and that it was the first time Eddie slept over at your place, which is why he was wearing sandals instead of hiking boots."

"Why, though, Noah? Why *in the world* would I kill Eddie?"

"You *know* why," he says with a certainty I don't comprehend.

"What are you *talking* about?"

He remains silent until I repeat the question.

Slowly he says, "Are you seriously trying to tell me you didn't know about the changes Eddie made to his last will and testament a few months before he died?"

My expression should relay all he needs to know. "We *never* discussed our estates, Noah. We were young. We had plenty of time, or at least *thought* we did." I pause, suddenly choking back tears, consumed by a grief I've been holding back since Eddie vanished. Right now I'm the Big Island's Mauna Loa volcano finally waking after thirty-eight years. I'm rumbling, smoking, ready to explode.

"So what changes did Eddie make to his will that supply motive?" I finally ask between sobs.

"He left you everything," Noah says with a sigh of resignation. "*Everything.* His home, his Range Rover, his boat, his savings." He pauses as a sardonic half smile crosses his lips. "He even left you his financial interests in the multimillion-dollar Lanyon shipping case."

Zoe

The investigation following Grandma's death was frightening in ways I never expected, having watched all those shows, read all those books. There's no such thing as acting "calm and cool" when Detective Ratzinger stands over you, battering you with questions in a stifling interrogation room, his spittle repeatedly flying in your face.

"Tell the truth when you're innocent" sounds like a simple, straight-forward rule, but this was more complicated. To make matters worse, Dad demanded Ray Fitch sit with me during questioning.

With Big Ray at my side, I could hardly speak, let alone conjure convenient lies to protect my parents. So at times I remained silent, at times I was evasive. Evasive to the point where they became suspicious of me.

Between a rock and a hard place, I made the decision to dismiss Ray Fitch as counsel and tell the police everything, damn the consequences. I squawked about the jokes I'd overheard my parents tell, their arguments over money, and how much each of them jawed about Grandma's will when they thought no one was listening.

I told them how Dmitri and I had seen my father peeling away from the house just as we got home, how my mother, drenched in blood, insisted we call my father before 9-1-1.

The police looked at both of them even closer and, as the noose around their necks steadily tightened, it became obvious my parents blamed me for their plight.

21

Makawao is like no other place on Maui. Some call it a cowboy town, others a quaint upcountry hub. Lying on the rural northwest slope of Haleakala, it mainly consists of little farms and ranchland with alpacas, horses, cattle, and other livestock.

I drive us straight through the town and park in a gravelly lot in a clearing near the Kahakapao Loop, a six-mile trail in the Makawao Forest Reserve. Clear as bells, I hear the young park ranger's description of the surrounding wilderness when he drove me home that first day of the search. *Dense rainforest, steep ravines, falling lava rocks, and enough green that you can't see three feet ahead of you without a machete.* I'm suddenly hyperconscious of how alone we are out here.

Remembering the park ranger's words makes me wonder whether adrenaline alone could have restored my short-term memory. Whether hours—even days—lost could be recovered and accessed at will. Whether I really want to recover everything lost or only select parts that would help me find my daughter.

Overhead, hundreds of birds—doves, mockingbirds, cardinals, finches, sparrows—are squeaking and squawking, chittering and chirping, and I think of Billy Fires and crack an involuntary smile. See, roosters don't just crow at sunrise as I always thought. They crow all fucking day. So once, when a few hours went by without hearing Fires, I decided to investigate. Suffice it to say, I learned what he'd been up to with all the neighborhood hens. I turned red and almost felt the need to offer apologies at the next town meeting until I reminded myself that Fires isn't my pet. Truth is, I've never really had a pet in my life. My mother had no use for animals (or, to be fair, really any living thing).

Zoe has been fascinated with Fires since we first moved in. I suspect that the rooster is the only animal she ever truly loved. It's certainly her first pet, if we can call it a pet (and we do). Early in our marriage, I made the error of asking Jeremy for a puppy. "Why would you want a *dog*?" he barked. His tone surprised me, but I largely disregarded it. We'd just left his mother's house (this was long before she became "ill" and lived with us), and as usual, he was flustered and irritated by the brief visit. Still, I kept mum on the subject.

Later, as Zoe grew up, I realized she was lonely outside school, especially during the summer and winter breaks. Being an only child, I sympathized. She needed a companion, and Jeremy had already ruled out a sibling. (*I never really wanted the first one.*) Oh, he'd always smiled or chuckled when he said it so that when I stared at him aghast, he could retreat and claim he was only joking. (*Jeez, you're so damn sensitive, hon. Get a sense of humor.*)

We never did get a dog or any other pet, save for a single betta fish that went belly-up days after we got it home. When I offered Zoe a replacement fish, she looked at me as though I were an idiot. "*Why?* It's just going to die too," she said.

She was six or seven at the time.

A few years later, we won a hermit crab on the boardwalk at the Jersey Shore. Jeremy said, "We're not really going to take that thing home with us, are we?" Of course we are, I told him. But Zoe took his side. She handed the small cage to a younger child whose mother was trying like hell to win him one. It was such a kind and charitable gesture, I praised her. But I also feared Zoe had adopted Jeremy's distaste for animals. At that point I decided I needed to reduce the not-insignificant influence Zoe's father had on her development. Since he never *really* wanted children and took an interest in Zoe only at my urging, limiting her interactions with him would be as simple as remaining silent.

Or so I thought at the time.

According to Noah, Graham frequents a clearing a mile or so off the trail. It's a *long* mile, mostly uphill, but the confidence in his voice renews my hope that we'll find Zoe before the police find me. His conviction bites back at the pain that's been flowing like a current through my body since the accident.

"If Graham's still on Maui, he's near Fong Ridge," Noah says. "When you see this place, you'll understand why."

His words twist my nerves even further. This is where that hiker got lost for three weeks. Everyone was amazed she survived out here. As we ascend the mountain on foot and the surrounding mist thickens, it becomes clear why she was so hard to find.

Anyone could get turned around out here. This is the fucking fire swamp from *The Princess Bride.* That or the setting for any postapocalyptic movie. The word *wilderness* doesn't do it justice. The trees are gargantuan and look more like they belong in the Pacific Northwest than in Hawaii. Hell, I half expect one of them to open its eyes and start speaking à la *The Lord of the Rings.*

Ents. The trees in Lord of the Rings *are called ents.* My mind feels as if it's reaching out, trying to reconnect with me. *Definitely the adrenaline.* But while the fog in my head gradually lifts, the one outside is so thick I can taste it. Leaving Mac behind with Kilo may have been an error, but neither could have tackled this hike. So long as Mac reads my note, he'll know our destination. I do, however, wish I'd borrowed the handgun he offered me earlier. Because this is the scene of every horrifying forest-set folktale I've ever read. I mean, the *real* Old World versions where kids get hacked up and broiled and served to witches for breakfast. Right now I'm Gretel, unsure I can trust my own brother.

To escape the monsters of the forest my mind retreats to our former home, the haunted mansion in Bridgeport. When it finds no refuge there it attempts to move on but is stopped in its tracks on its way out of Connecticut. It fights but still only gets as far as New York.

On our tenth wedding anniversary Jeremy and I returned to the Carlyle for two weeks. While we were there I begged him to take me to this grand hibachi-style restaurant in the mountains roughly an hour north of the city. When he said yes, I immediately ran downstairs and caught a taxi to Saks Fifth Avenue to buy a new dress.

Later that night when we stepped outside, I expected there to be a limousine waiting—especially since Jeremy and Oz had just taken a limo to an all-you-can-eat buffalo wings buffet at a strip club in North Jersey earlier in the week. But Jeremy steered me toward the garage where he had a surprise waiting. The surprise being a rented mint-condition Ferrari Testarossa that *he* would drive to the restaurant. Woo-hoo.

When we arrived at the restaurant, Jeremy tipped the valet handsomely and warned him about joy-riding his "baby." Then he pointed at me. "Her, on the other hand, you can ride all night for what I just handed you." While he broke into hysterical laughter at his own one-liner, the young valet stared at me with a sad smile and I smiled back to let him know how fine I was with Jeremy's ribbing. He acknowledged the return smile with a subtle eye roll, then pocketed Jeremy's cash and pulled the Ferrari into the lot.

Inside Jeremy refused to wait for a table, explaining oh so politely to the maître d' that he simply *couldn't* wait for a table at this caliber of eatery. (Only four stars with rave reviews, most notably from Zagat, which Jeremy often quoted as his Bible.) The host eventually succumbed to Jeremy, declining the bribe but leading us to the next available hibachi with eight other diners who'd been waiting (*with* reservations) for over an hour. We were *not* a popular pair at our table from the get-go.

Little did they know, Jeremy was just getting started. Ordering three drinks at a time (*I don't give a shit about your policy*), he was drunk before the hibachi had time to heat up. (*Dare me to touch it? Double-dog dare me?*) Then, as the chef entertained us with his culinary acrobatics, Jeremy tried to steal the spotlight, shooting the garnish from his drinks into the chef's oversize pockets every chance he got. When the chef removed his hat to catch a flying piece of shrimp, Jeremy tossed in a handful of ice, then nearly fell off his chair with laughter.

I pleaded with the restaurant gods to call the manager and have us removed, but the staff was just too tolerant, presumably immune to drunk assholes and their constant disruptions. During the meal, Jeremy turned his attention to the guests themselves, calling out each in turn like some drunken Don Rickles who'd left his filter back in the seventies. Some responded, others ignored him. Neither approach slowed him down.

When we finally finished dessert I leapt from my chair and zipped toward the entrance, only for Jeremy to detour me to the dance floor to witness him bust some spastic MC Hammer moves punctuated by a few Kid Rock stomps and "Gangnam Style" pony rides. Had I any shame left by then, I'd have been embarrassed. As it was, I was happy just to get out of there an hour later with a single vodka tonic spilled down my dress.

Outside the wind roared through the mountains and chilled me to the bone. After searching his pockets for his claim ticket for ten frigid minutes, Jeremy finally found it in his wallet. Gallantly, he cut to the head of the line and tossed his keys at a valet, a gesture that did not sit well with the drunk bastard standing behind him. Before I knew it both were rolling on the blacktop, trying to pin one another to get in a volley of clean shots to the face.

No one tried to break it up. I shouted myself hoarse, but it was no use. Finally, I gave up, just thankful that this poor drunk received the beating probably reserved for me that evening. Neither came out unscathed but once the dust settled, it was Jeremy on top. Jeremy with blood not on his face but his knuckles. Jeremy with the smile. Jeremy the one who retained all his teeth.

I apologized to the man's girlfriend, who spat at me in response.

Needless to say, Jeremy should not have been driving. But when I tried to take the keys and get behind the wheel, he grabbed me so hard he ripped my new dress. "Nah, nah, you can't drive," he said. "I signed a thing with the rental company. No one drives but me."

"Does it say anything in that *thing* about driving *blind drunk*?"

"Get the fuck in," he replied, then he gunned the engine.

Stupidly, I got back into the car and we sped off down the mountain.

We hadn't been on the road long when Jeremy began nodding off behind the wheel. I pleaded with him to pull over, but he refused, and kept refusing for ten *terrifying* minutes, until I finally offered him a blow job. He pulled off at the next exit and followed the signs for food and lodging. For twenty more minutes I held my heart in my throat, knowing my life could end at any moment, and that my only consolation would be taking him with me. I kept my hand on his seat-belt buckle, ready to press the button, just in case.

The button wasn't necessary.

He eventually pulled into the parking lot of some shitty motel and parked as far as he could from the nearest streetlight. When I tried to exit the car, he grasped me hard by the wrist. "Where the fuck you going?"

"Into the motel."

"Nah, nah, nah, nah," he said, refusing to loosen his grip. "No motel."

I smiled, thinking that maybe in his drunken fog he'd forgotten why we turned off the highway. "For your blow job."

"What the fuck you think I pulled into the lot for?"

When I finished sucking his dick, while he still had his head back in drunk ecstasy, I snatched the keys from the dashboard, opened the door, and hurled them over a fence and into some trees.

"What the *fuck*?" he screamed.

"You're *not* driving tonight," I said. "I'll find them for you in the morning." I started toward the motel, expecting him to follow.

"Come back," he said almost calmly. "We need to get our shit from the trunk. I packed some stuff in case we stayed."

My stuff? Jeremy never packed anything for himself his entire life, let alone for me.

I turned to find him opening the hood, which on the Testarossa was the trunk. Or, as some people call it, the frunk. Slowly I started back toward the car, my arms folded tightly across my chest. I was tipsy, tired, tortured by how he acted in the restaurant. I was cold. Maybe he'd packed me a sweater.

When I reached him I peered in the trunk to find nothing. My face creased in confusion, then before I could ask the question, he grabbed me from behind, lifted me up like a basketball, and slam-dunked me into the trunk. He pounded and pushed on my legs until I stopped fighting. Then he slammed the door down on me, sealing the trunk shut with a booming thunk.

"See ya in the morning," he said, his voice fading away with each word.

Terror tied my insides. The darkness, the cold, the fucking cramps I'd already started to feel made me scream until my throat burned. To the extent I could move, I rapped on the metal overhead but finally realized it was futile. We were upstate in a remote town in the mountains, and we'd parked as far from the motel as possible even though there were only two other cars in the lot. He'd *planned* this. This was my tenth-anniversary present.

Is there enough air in here?

Just contemplating it caused me to become short of breath. Panic again wrapped its frozen hands around my windpipe and squeezed. I started to scream again but no longer had the voice. All I could do was wait and listen and hope. When I heard someone, *if* I heard someone, *then and only then* could they hear me.

So I waited, I wept.

Then I finally passed out.

The trunk opened at dawn, a hungover Jeremy staring down at me with revulsion as though I'd gotten *myself* locked in the trunk overnight.

"Get out," he said, as if I'd never thought of it. When it took me too long (*every part of me* was asleep, having spent the night twisted like a pretzel), he grabbed me under the arms and yanked as hard as he could. I cried out in pain, but he only got rougher. "I've got a fucking *headache*," he shouted, hurling me to the blacktop.

During the entire hour-plus that it took us to get back to the Carlyle, I counted the number of ways I could kill him if I really wanted to, if I *had* to. Electrocution, fire, drowning, gunshot, stabbing, poison, smothering, choking, blunt object to the head. All had their pluses and minuses. Some were harder to pull off, some made it too easy to get caught. Most were fairly messy. I pictured him dead in the bathtub, dead in the backyard, in the front yard, under the car. In the pool, in his bed, in his mother's room. Basement, attic, foyer, closet. Hotel, motel, ocean, bar.

I pictured him dead wherever I could picture him at all.

Deeper into the forest, Noah suddenly stops. "This is as far as you go, Kati. If he's here, he's off trail in a spot perfect for an ambush."

"I can take care of myself," I say, all too aware that I sound less like Wonder Woman and more like a Bond girl.

"If you're right and he does have Zoe, we don't want him to panic. Alone, he'll buy that I'm here to help him. If you're with me . . ."

He doesn't need to finish; I know what he means, but I'm already shaking my head. Then my phone vibrates urgently in my pocket. Instinctively turning my back to Noah, I pull it free, see a number I don't recognize, and answer. The reception is abysmal.

"Where . . . you?" Mac says uneasily. At least I think it's Mac.

"We just arrived at the forest reserve."

"Are you still . . . the car?"

"We're on the trail," I say, taking a few steps away.

"Can . . . hear me?"

"I can hear you but you're fading in and out."

"Not you, Kati. *Him.* Can . . ."

I lower my voice. "Not anymore."

"Kati, listen carefully." Mercifully, the reception improves the farther I rove. "Can you get away from him?"

"What?"

"He's lying to you. Kilo just hacked into the firm's financial records, then their email system. Noah's been skimming money from the firm trust account. *A client's* money. When Eddie found out, we think Noah had him iced."

I turn halfway. Noah's looking back at me. I do my best to remain expressionless, though I'm as frightened as I've ever been.

"What do I do?" I ask Mac, barely moving my lips.

"Can you make it back to the car?"

"Maybe," I say, moving away a little faster. "But Mac, if he's in on this, he may be leading me straight to Zoe."

"Kati, from the emails we read, he and Graham might no longer be calling shots out of the same playbook. It's unclear why, but at some point, their interests suddenly and severely diverged."

"All I care about is finding Zoe."

"That's not going to happen if you step straight into a trap." He curses himself. "This is my fault. I never should have left you alone with that damn lawyer."

As if the cell towers themselves mean to doom me, I suddenly lose the call but manage to keep the phone to my ear without giving anything away. I continue nodding and moving my lips, occasionally glancing back at Noah and flashing a single index finger. When he starts walking back in my direction, I instantly break into a sprint for the trailhead.

"Kati!"

Noah gives chase. He's considerably faster and not far behind me; he'll catch me before I can make it to the lot. I summon a burst of speed and lower my head, running as fast and as hard as I've ever run in my life, running until my sides collapse and my lungs catch fire.

"Kati!"

As horrifying a prospect as it is, my only shot now is a shortcut.

Without warning, I cut a sharp left and break from the trail, pushing forward, cold and alone, into the wild.

22

Hawaii is not all waterfalls and double rainbows, not all luaus and hula dancers, not all surfboards and suntans and sand. It's also *wilderness* in the purest, rawest sense of the word. Often a crowded wilderness. Yet here in the forest, where the towering trees shield the ground from the sun, little else grows. So unless I can find a freakishly large fern, my hopes of hiding are dashed. My only chance is to outrun Noah to the car.

Nearly as soon as I break from the trail, a sudden steady rain hits. A crack of thunder makes me gape in its direction, studying the skies for further signs—like *that*: a brilliant lightning strike that ignites the darkening overhead dome, soon accompanied by a second crack of thunder. Above me the clouds are now a raging shade of gray.

The wind picks up, chilling the air, smacking me in the face as if I offended it.

As I leap over a thorny raspberry bush, I come down hard on my right ankle and cry out but keep going. I can't be far from the gravelly lot where we'd parked our car. I'm sure I'm headed in the right direction, but that's all I'm sure of, because this shortcut appears on no map. I'm cutting a new trail by pure instinct, *my* instinct.

I hurdle a fallen log. On the other side, I unexpectedly slide down a steep muddy hill. My stomach drops and I bite my lip to keep from shouting out as rocks rip the back of my thigh raw. Once I'm back on my feet, the pain is intense but I can't afford to stop to check the wound.

Across a bed of stones, over a small stream, around some trees, and through more thorny bushes, I somehow stay on my feet. When there's a merciful break in the rain, the air swells with mosquitoes. As I swing my arms in a futile attempt to swat the pests away, they converge on me. Meanwhile, my boots are sinking ever deeper into the mud, slowing me more with each step.

Need to keep going.

The air's cold but I feel like I'm boiling, the sweat dripping down from my hairline, searing my eyes. My left knee feels like someone's taken a bat to it. My injuries from the accident are screaming for me to take a moment's break. But I don't have one to spare. I need to keep running. For myself. And for Zoe.

As I breathlessly cross a narrow mountain bike trail, I hold my tightening chest, reminding myself that we're four thousand feet above sea level. The mist may be thick, but the air up here is paper thin.

Somehow I keep going, snaking around coast redwoods, ducking under low-hanging branches, leaping over fallen logs. When I finally risk glancing over my shoulder again, all I see is the towering green wall of trees I just broke through. With every last breath in my lungs, I want to cry out but know it would be useless. All I'd do is confirm my location. My calves meanwhile remind me that I cannot run this hard for much longer.

Where the hell is the lot?

Mere moments later, the rain mercifully returns, scattering the mosquitoes, forcing them back into hiding. The greenery surrounding me is so lush, it feels more than alive, almost as though it's sentient and can reach out and kill me like those ancient vines in *The Ruins*. It's also breathtakingly beautiful, a genuine tropical rainforest that's somehow survived in spite of the greed and indifference of mankind.

I break into an unexpected clearing and immediately hear another crack of thunder, this one so close lightning may have hit one of the trees in my sight line. Then there's another. And another.

Not thunder.

Gunshots.

Shit, shit, he's shooting *at me?*

As I push on, the rain returns in full force, falling in sheets. The smell of wet earth envelopes and invigorates me, but this means I won't hear my pursuer until he's two feet behind me. Which means I need to keep ahead of him—*well* ahead of him since he has a fucking gun.

I summon the last of the breath in my lungs and dart past ancient trees, then through some brambles. My scraped and bloodied legs are about to give out from under me when I finally spot the roof of the Nissan Sentra in the lot.

Another shot. Then another.

I'm trying to gauge which direction they're coming from when it suddenly occurs to me that Noah was frisked by the biker who picked him up from Hana.

Which means he's not the only one hunting me.

Inside the car, panting to catch my breath.

As I smack on the wipers and turn the ignition, Noah bursts through the green monster into the teeming rain. In a single motion I kick the transmission into reverse and slam my foot on the gas. The tires spin for an instant, spitting up gravel, before jolting me backward at such high speed that I lose control of the wheel.

Next thing I know, I slam backward into something, *hard*, then plow over it. It's so large I hit my head on the roof on impact. Whatever it is—a rock, a fallen tree, a wild boar—it's stopped the car dead. I scream out as Noah races toward me, as he reaches for the driver's side door with a psychotic look on his face.

Rocking the transmission back and forth, practically *standing* on the accelerator, I'm going nowhere. The engine revs, the tires spin, but whatever is caught under the car gives no ground. The stench of burning rubber hits my nose. Finally, Noah flings open my door and snatches me by the forearm, reminding me of when Jeremy flung me to the ground in the motel parking lot.

Yanked out of the car, I land hard on the gravel, striking my funny bone, shooting pain through my entire body. I cry out. Then Noah vanishes.

Where is he?

From my spot on the ground, I consider rolling under the car when I see blood seeping forward from the rear. I twist my neck and find what looks like a carcass caught under the back left wheel. Noah is back there, too, presumably trying to save whatever animal I struck.

Now is my chance to run.

Only I can't gather my feet underneath me. Slipping and falling, cutting my palms on the wet gravel, I try to push myself up, only to land on my knees.

Noah comes for me.

Grabs me from behind.

I throw an elbow, connecting with his temple.

Reach for his hair and pull as much and as hard as I can.

I scratch at him, *claw* at him, try to bite him. Try to eat his fucking face off.

I want to murder him as much as I do Jeremy.

Caught in a great bear hug, though, I'm nothing against his strength, a kitten struggling against the jaws of a junkyard dog.

Gradually, almost gently, he wrestles me to the wet ground. All the while, he's shouting something in my ear, something I can't hear.

Something about Zoe.

23

I often wonder who I would have been, who I *could* have been, had I only had a different mother. Would I have been more prepared for the likes of Jeremy? Would I have received better guidance when I got pregnant? Would I have returned to school? Would I have left him had I not suffered such terrible abandonment issues? I lost the parent lottery as so many of us do. And the difference between winning and losing is often the difference between life and death, darkness and light, having to live in the past or being able to live for the future. As much as it sucks, when life's first slot machine delivers two lemons, it's typically game over regardless of what follows.

BAR BAR BAR

The words flash through my mind, and I can see Eddie's Polynesian casino as if it's right before my eyes. It's beautiful. It's busy. It's loud, it's rowdy. It's fun. And it's serving the purpose it was born to serve.

When I reopen my eyes, the man named Woody Graham lies on his back on the gravel half under the car, his eyes thin slits, his mouth a small fount of blood. Trying to smile or grimace, he reveals a mouthful of crimson teeth and a tongue half bitten through. It's so grotesque I dry heave, aggravating my sore knees, which seem to have melted into the gravel.

Noah stands over him, his nautical-themed aloha shirt saturated in blood. His eyes are wet, but I can't tell whether he's crying or merely drenched from the rain. He lowers himself to one knee and takes away Graham's gun. Then he leans in closer so that Graham can hear him without shouting.

"It's over," he tells him.

Graham says nothing, *can* say nothing, though he tries, grunting and spitting up blood.

Meanwhile, as I painfully rise from the ground, I'm fucking apoplectic. "It's *not* over," I shout, still thoroughly in shock and at risk of tipping over. "Where's *Zoe*? Where's my *daughter*?"

Looking up at me, Noah shakes his head. "I told you he doesn't have her."

"How do you *know*?" I shout over the rain.

Noah bows his head as if he's about to say the Act of Contrition before a priest. "Because I hired him to take care of Eddie. Kidnapping Zoe was never part of the deal."

Hearing him say the words, I rock on the soles of my feet, unsure whether to run, to lunge for the gun, or accept what seems to be his unconditional surrender. My face curls into one giant question mark.

"I dug myself into a hole," he says with marked resignation. "That big Lanyon case? The one that was supposed to make us both rich and fat? Well, I started spending as though the money was already in our pockets. I bought property in Honolulu, I purchased the *Reasonable Doubt*. Then Lanyon filed an appeal and everything came to a grinding halt. We weren't gonna see a dime for years. Lanyon might even be granted a new trial, or the award may be slashed by some parsimonious judge."

"I don't understand. How'd you have access to the money while the case is being appealed?"

"Smart cookie that he is, Eddie settled part of the claim with a third party—the company that manufactures the equipment that caused the accident—so that Lanyon couldn't use our client's financial situation as leverage in negotiations. But the attorneys' fees from the partial settlement barely covered our expenses. We *needed* that verdict. Once Lanyon appealed, I knew I was doomed. If the American tort system is one big Vegas casino, it's gonna be a long while before the Lanyon jackpot finally pays off. If it ever does at all."

Overhead, the sky remains angry but restrained.

Nonplussed, I say, "All *this* because you stole from a client?"

"It *wasn't* stealing, Kati. Listen, Eddie's ethics blinded him. This should've been a joint venture—Eddie needed the money too. He owed Jedrick *big*. He still does. The client never needed to know; he was happy with whatever he got. And he was still gonna receive a huge payoff in the end. He'd just wait in line with the folks who were doing all the work."

"So it's all true." I'm shaking, trying to keep myself warm with my arms across my chest. "Eddie caught you funneling money out of the firm's trust account. So you . . ." I can't say it. I can barely *think* it.

"He *threatened* me, Kati. Either I come up with the cash in ninety days or he goes to the disciplinary committee and pulls my ticket to practice law. That's how I justified doing what I did, all right? By blaming him, by telling myself he was acting more like a loan shark than a business partner and friend."

"But it's only a *job*."

"Not a job. My *livelihood*. Hawaii may *look* different," he says, gazing up at the skyscraping trees surrounding us, "but this is still America. You destroy a man's way of living, you destroy his *life*." Holding up his hands, he sighs. "Look, I don't expect sympathy. I don't want it—and I sure as hell don't deserve it."

I'm still trying to comprehend. "Why bring me here?"

He looks me in the eye as the rain pours down his face. "You were so damn convinced that Graham took Zoe, I almost started to believe it myself."

"But you *knew* it was you, not Jedrick, who hired him. Why in hell *would* Graham have had Zoe?"

With closed eyes, Noah tenderly touches his right temple. "I only found out when you did that Graham was Jedrick's bagman. I thought maybe he was double-dipping." He shakes his head. "But no, she's not here. He probably didn't even know she was missing. I assume that by killing you he hoped to tie off one more loose end."

I motion with my chin at Graham's corpse. "Am I going to jail for this?"

Noah shakes his head. "He had a gun. At best, this was an accident. At worst, it was self-defense."

My voice quivers. "And for Eddie's murder?"

"You're not going to prison for that either. When I heard Graham was indicted this morning, I mailed Charley Kay a long letter confessing to everything. This rat bastard would've given me up on the way to the station." He tilts his head and lifts a shoulder. "Of course, had I known when I mailed it that you were gonna silence him permanently, my calculations might have been a tad different."

"Is that a joke?" I say.

"Just a little gallows humor." He reaches into his pocket and retrieves a pack of Juicy Fruit. "Want one?"

I shake my head.

"I swear," he says as he unwraps the foil, "it was never my intention that you go down for this. That was all . . ." He pauses, considers. "That was all Graham's doing, and it's what turned him from an ally to a murderous adversary this past week. He was never supposed to use your trekking pole as the murder weapon. He was supposed to use one of the thousands of rocks you saw sitting on the edge of the spur trail."

My trekking pole. My prints, Eddie's blood, found at the top of the spur trail fifty yards back from the Infinity Pool that empties over the falls. Only he *couldn't* have used the pole I brought to the trail. I still had it with me when Eddie was murdered.

"The *second* pole," I say uneasily. "How the hell did he get his hands on it in the first place?"

Noah frowns as he folds the stick of gum and pops it into his mouth. "Does it matter?" Before I can respond he says, "Look, I can't run from this anymore, Kati. I snail-mailed Charley to give myself a day. To end things. To end all this uncertainty, to get it the hell over with. Because this has been the second most grueling, second most painful week of my entire life."

"The second?" I say.

The first, he says, is the week he lost Tammy. And, again, I feel like a fool for forgetting his trauma even after what he's done.

"Where does this leave Zoe?" I say.

Noah's gaze remains on the gun in his lap. "My instinct says she ran away, Kati."

"No," I tell him, shaking my head furiously like a wet dog. "You don't even *know* her."

Quietly, he says, "I know her better than you think."

I glare at him. "What does *that* mean?"

For what seems like forever, he remains perfectly silent.

Then: "Why do people commit murder, Kati?"

The question takes me by surprise. "For money," I say, my voice breaking. "For revenge. For love."

He smiles. "Ya know, Kati, I never would've dreamed this up in a million years."

"Dreamt *what* up?" My pulse is racing, my patience ending. "Noah, I need to get out of here. Give me the gun."

He rests his hand on it. "I've spent enough time visiting clients in prison to know I can't live in one, Kati." He smiles thinly. "A pretty face like mine, I wouldn't last a week."

"Noah, *please*. I don't have time for this. I still need to find Zoe. She's still in danger. May I *please* have the gun?"

When he looks up at me again, there are genuine tears in his eyes. "You may. But only once I'm done with it."

Zoe

She's not coming for me. I can feel it in my bones. I was wrong, so wrong.

She's lost, maybe she's been arrested. Maybe she thinks I've run away—I've been acting like such an asshole lately.

Once this ordeal ends, if I make it out alive, I'm going to learn how to better master my emotions. I'm no longer going to let my feelings affect my decisions. I'll rely on my reasoning, which is sharper and more consistent.

I can't sit and wait any longer.

I need to do something.

If only I could pick up the phone and call her.

But no. I'd need him to do it.

I'd need him to call her and tell her precisely where we are.

He could tell her to come alone.

No police.

Maybe, just maybe, I can talk him into calling her.

Or at least sending a text.

He does have a flair for the dramatic, after all. Maybe he wouldn't mind playing one last game for all the marbles in my mother's head.

24

Fewer than ninety minutes later, Mac and I are back on the road in the rented Dodge Charger. Behind the wheel again, I ponder whether the letter Noah sent to Charley Kay will satisfy Nani Akana that I'm innocent. More than anything, I want her to know I didn't harm her son.

Despite the empty white sky overhead, a black cloud falls over me whenever I think of Eddie's family. I so wanted to be a part of it. I so wanted *Zoe* to be a part of it. As ridiculous as it sounds, I'd hoped to cancel out seventeen years of Jeremy's fucked-up family with Eddie's close, loving clan. Zoe will leave for college next year, and though I had hoped she'd stay nearby and attend the University of Hawaii on Oahu, where she'd have the support—and yes, protection—of Eddie's sizable squad of Akanas, she has her heart firmly set on Oregon. She and Eddie had teamed up to get me to surrender my blessing, which is why it should have come as little surprise that Eddie and I argued over the issue the night before his disappearance.

I need Zoe to know I'm innocent too. Zoe more than anyone.

She needs to know I would never hurt someone I love, no matter the circumstances. To this day I suspect she harbors doubts about whether I was involved in her grandmother's death. Excluding her from the defense may have further widened the crevasse between us. It may have rendered it impassable. I witnessed the hatred on her face—the distrust and distaste—when we last spoke about Eddie.

"Slow down," Mac says. "Remember, Noah sent the letter snail mail. It won't arrive until at least tomorrow. If you get pulled over now, it's as if he never confessed. The cops will consider you a dangerous fugitive and draw their service weapons—and you can't always predict what will happen next."

After Charley Kay gets the letter, the moment I pop my head up, Maui PD will nab me and ship me back to Connecticut and the Fairfield County District Attorney's Office.

One murder at a time.

I ease off the accelerator. We're heading back to the biker bar to regroup. But why? If the men responsible for Eddie's death don't have Zoe, who else but Jeremy could? His arrival in the islands is no coincidence after all. Only his timing.

Jeremy has my daughter.

I'm suddenly so certain of it, I grip the wheel tightly enough to make my knuckles crack, nearly steering us off the road. My stomach lurches when I see him in my head—just how I last saw him—his fuming visage burned into my brain.

Pearl Jam's "Jeremy" lit up my mind every time I heard the bastard offer one of his nonapology apologies or backhanded compliments, or try to butter me up, to smooth things over. As if false flattery could turn back time, as if it could heal wounds and mend broken bones. As if it could give me back those days and weeks I spent mired in a muck of depression.

He's getting even. No matter what it's for, Jeremy *needs* to get even. That's how I know he has her. He relishes using my most intimate thoughts and feelings against me like a bludgeon. *He keeps score*, in constant competition with everyone, more obsessed with "winning" than Al Davis and Charlie Sheen combined. When we were together he constantly compared me to his friends' trophy wives. (*If I buy you that Tonal smart gym, will you show up to bed with an ass like hers every night?*)

On the road I allow a small pickup to cross in front of me and smirk. Jeremy would never allow such a thing. He'd lose his shit over the honk of a horn at a light. He'd park, exit the car, and march toward the offender with such violence in his eyes, the other guy usually reversed course and ran the light, preferring to risk getting T-boned rather than face Jeremy's psychopathic wrath.

Intimidating others with his infinite rage keeps the few friendships he has left intact. He prefers hangers-on, people who fawn over him. He wants storm troopers or henchmen, not genuine friends, not anyone who would consider themselves his equal.

There's only one Vader, he likes to say.

That's how I know he has her.

Does he even love her? Did he ever? Is he *capable* of love? The only evidence is the degree to which he loves himself. He loves himself with the kind of passion you see only in old movies. *And the attraction!* In our seventeen years, he spent more days with his hairstylist than his family and more hours admiring himself in the mirror than doing just about anything else. Yet his ego remains as fragile as plate glass.

"When this is over," Mac says, "I'll make an anonymous call from the mainland and tell the cops where to find them."

It takes me a moment to realize he's talking about Woody Graham and Noah Walker. The events in Makawao already feel like a lifetime ago. My mind, though much clearer, is still fogged. I don't know whether my memory will ever fully return.

But now's not the time to worry about it.

When Mac initially arrived at the forest reserve, he checked Graham for a pulse, then went into the woods to find Noah's body and recover his keys. I'd told him where I thought I heard the shot come from. Turns out, Noah didn't journey that deep into the woods before resting against a tree stump and turning the weapon on himself.

The mechanic's car, meanwhile, has been reported stolen. Mac wiped it down as best he could, but there's bound to be evidence of my presence all over the nature reserve.

When we reach a three-way intersection facing the ocean, I crawl to a stop, reminded of the old Yogi Berra saying: "If you come across a fork in the road, take it."

At the stop sign, I stand on the brake and look both ways.

One direction leads to the biker bar in Kihei.

The other leads to the *Dorothy* in Lahaina.

"Hang a Louie here," Mac says. "That'll get us back to the bar."

I shake my head and cut a defiant right. "Zoe's not at the bar," I say. "Jeremy's holding her at the harbor."

25

Heading west along the leeward coast toward Lahaina, I lower my visor. The sky here is neither empty nor white, and the trees have been replaced with ocean. Over the Pacific, the horizon is progressively turning from cotton candy blue to bubblegum pink, painting for us the quintessential Maui sunset amid all this terror.

Predictably, traffic increases the moment we touch down on Front Street. The fashionable boulevard bustles with tourists, and the streets are crammed with their rented Mustang convertibles, leaving nowhere to park. Despite the carnival atmosphere, despite the uplifting sights and sounds and smells, all I feel is a stretching emptiness in the pit of my stomach, a gaping hole I may never fill again. Unless I find Zoe.

While Mac remains silent by my side in the passenger seat, I can hear the wheels grinding in his head. He's already strenuously objected to my plan, but unless he delineates a new one, a better one, I'm moving forward. I need to rescue Zoe, no matter the risk, no matter the ultimate cost. There is no question in my mind: I would do *anything* for my daughter.

Finally, I turn left off Front Street and point the Charger toward Lahaina Harbor. Drive down Dickenson, past the old prison, to the end of the block. There I abruptly turn into a park-and-lock.

"This is a mistake," Mac says again.

"Are you coming or staying?" I ask bluntly after I pull into a space and kill the engine.

He opens the door and steps out of the car. "That's a hell of a thing for you to ask me."

After paying the attendant, we hurry toward the docks, moving as fast as we can without drawing attention to ourselves. Uniformed officers continue to monitor the streets. Patrol cars sit in traffic, their occupants eyeing the crowds with barely restrained disdain and an obvious eagerness for action.

I lower my head and lift my shoulders, trying to look larger than I am, a regular She-Hulk.

Meanwhile, Mac fishes Noah's keys out of his pocket. "If one of these doesn't start the boat," he says, "how the hell do we get over to the *Dorothy*?"

"The ferry to Lanai passes fairly close to where she's anchored."

"*Fairly close?*" He stops walking and looks at me. "You want us to jump off the ferry and *swim* for it?"

Now that he says it aloud, it sounds pretty stupid. "Let's just hope Noah's boat keys are on that key ring, all right?"

We continue walking. Slowly at first, but then we pick up the pace. Fortunately, Noah's coast guard friend is again on the phone in her booth and doesn't see us. Stepping lightly, we enter the main harbor without notice. Stride right past her, then make a ninety-degree turn, hastening our steps along the dock.

We don't slow until we reach the *Reasonable Doubt*.

Once on board, we scurry across the deck, through the cabin, and into the cockpit. Given my only boating experience is with Eddie aboard the much smaller *Pilialoha*, I'm not even sure we can get the motor running, but we need to try.

Staring at the control panel, I begin to panic when Mac assures me, "It's going to be fine."

But it's not. The first key he tries doesn't fit.

The second key fits but doesn't turn.

The third gets stuck in the keyhole and we waste costly minutes trying to extract it.

Once it's finally out, Mac draws a deep breath and wipes the sweat from his brow.

Carefully he selects another key. Inserts it. Turns it. Then glides his rough hands across the control panel.

Moments later the boat magically comes alive, its engine humming, its lights blinking on. My hands curl into fists at my sides, my nails digging deep into my skin, maybe enough to draw blood.

"Here we go," Mac says.

Fuck that, I think. *Jeremy, here I come.*

The boat ride is brief, a huge plus since it doesn't allow my adrenaline to wane, my nerves to beat their way back in. But it does permit the coming of darkness. I'm frightened but more determined than I've ever been about anything in my life. The certainty, after so much uncertainty, is electrifying.

Despite the adrenaline, as we pull alongside the *Dorothy*, I feel numb. Not *inside* numb as I'd expected—inside remains a monsoon—but *outside*, as if I'm being physically manipulated by strings, an analogy that may prove all too apt for the occasion.

This is suicide. This is a trap.

But Jeremy left us no choice, did he? Ozzie's yacht can outrun any ship in the harbor. It's also equipped with a frigging helipad.

We can't let him get away with her. I'd never see her again.

Finding no immediate presence on deck, Mac ties Noah's boat to Ozzie's megayacht, a massive three-hundred-foot Moondance (*ten times* the size of the *Reasonable Doubt*). It's dizzying just to look at it, never mind hitting the open ocean in it. "It's a behemoth," Mac grumbles. "Five decks, seven guest cabins, seventeen crew cabins, and an Olympic-size swimming pool."

I'm staring at Mac without seeing him.

He says, "You didn't think I'd follow these bastards across the largest body of water on the planet without knowing everything there is to know about their mode of transport, did ya?"

Once we've secured our boat to the *Dorothy*, we board the ginormous yacht, me armed only with a flashlight from Noah's boat (currently off to avoid detection) and Mac a small-caliber handgun.

Mac leads the way, first crossing the deck, then entering the darkened cabin, which smells of rich Italian leather. As my eyes adjust to the moonlight, I gaze around the enormous circular room, which is tastefully appointed with ivory leather sofas and love seats, a wet bar, and a twelve-foot dining table and chairs. Floor-to-ceiling windows overlook the black ocean, while a skylight frames the stars directly above our heads.

We stop. We listen for signs of life. Footfalls or coughs or voices. But we hear nothing except the heavy winds beating against the windows.

Silently, we cross through the cabin.

When Mac comes to a door, he motions for me to halt before raising his gun, turning the handle, and checking the room, clearing it like a cop. He does it again and again, each empty room deflating us both a little further while also prompting silent sighs of relief.

After several anxious minutes it's obvious no one's here, and I feel like a token on the Monopoly board just sent back to Start. My heart rate plummets and I instantly feel faint.

Mac, meanwhile, continues to search for clues. Rather than remain standing alone and crestfallen in the cabin, I follow him belowdecks to the yacht's galley, a sizable space equipped with enough state-of-the-art appliances to impress Gordon Ramsay. I'm still surveying the cookware and cutlery when my burner phone lights up in my hand. I stare at it as though I've never seen one before, as if it's alien technology. Sure enough, it's from an unknown number.

You won't know until you answer.

I swipe the green icon and hold the phone to my ear while hurrying back to the cabin.

This time the voice on the other end is like a cold knife slicing down my spine.

"I wondered when I was going to hear your voice again, Sara."

Even with countless thoughts spinning like tops in my head, one question comes to the fore. "How did you get this number?"

"How do *you* think?"

Zoe. He has Zoe. Of course he does. "Where is she?"

"She's here with me."

"Ma—" she cries out.

"Sydney, I'm here!" I shout. *"I'm coming for you."* The name feels strange on my tongue. I haven't uttered it once in two years.

"You're becoming an optimist in your old age," Jeremy says. His voice is cold, completely devoid of emotion.

"You son of a bitch, if you put one *scratch* on my little girl—"

He repeats me, mimicking my voice like the good old days. Then: "You'll *what*, Sara? Throw me down the stairs like you did my mother?"

I close my eyes and brace myself to ask a question to which I dread the answer. "What do you *want* from me, Jeremy?"

"I want you to come to me. If you want to see your daughter again, you'll come and you'll come alone."

I'd die for her, you bastard.

I suck up some oxygen. "Just say where."

Moments later, I dash belowdecks and storm into the kitchen, where Mac stands silently in front of the walk-in freezer with his head bowed, his arms folded across his chest.

When I say his name, he slowly turns around, and I immediately know by the look on his face.

"Who is it?" I say.

"It's the friend. Ozzie. He's been butchered."

Zoe

When he ended the call with Mom, he set the phone down and glowered at me. He asked if I thought she'd really come for me. It made the bile rise in my throat. I told him that, yes, she'll come for me.

And she will, I believe that. Despite the irrational arguments and unreasonable punishments, there is one thing that I've always been certain of: my mother would trade her life for mine.

Whether that's what my father would like to see happen, I don't know, but I can see the murder in his eyes.

It's a wonder he's blind to the violence in mine.

PART III

JEREMY

26

As Mac guides the *Reasonable Doubt* back to the pier, Jeremy's words drift through my head like a spare tire lazing on the river. While the words themselves were as chilling as his voice, what frightens me most is how he abruptly ended the call when I said, "Just say where." Suddenly, a number of his words take on new possible interpretations. Although I know Zoe is alive—I *heard* her—will she still be alive when I find her?

What were his exact words? *If you want to see your daughter again . . .* Why say *your* daughter when we both always referred to Zoe as *our* daughter? Does he know that Zoe isn't his? That she's Glenn's? Something in my stomach plummets. *If you want to see your daughter again . . .* Why not say, "If you want to see your daughter *alive* again . . . ?" What was he implying? What does he plan to do? Just kill me—or does he plan to kill her too?

As Mac pulls the *Reasonable Doubt* alongside the pier, my phone pings. I pull it out of my pocket and open a text from an unknown number with three lines from his favorite Stones song, "Under My Thumb."

I stare at the words as if they'll change, as if the letters will rearrange, as if more are coming, but somehow I know this is all we'll have to go on.

When I read the text aloud, Mac shakes his head and frowns. "I hate this cryptic shit."

He likes to play games, the son of a bitch. He loves theatrics.

"They're song lyrics," I say. "But I don't know what they mean. I mean, I know what the *lyrics* mean, but . . ." I silence myself, regain control of my panting so I don't hyperventilate.

"Let me see that," he says.

Once I hand it over, he squints at the words, mouthing something as he does.

Counting?

"Back at SCI Somerset," he says, "my cellie Deacon took to poetry. Burroughs, Ginsberg. The Beat poets. Within a year he started writing his own. Terrible, truly horrendous stuff. Half read like macabre Hallmark cards, the other half like Dr. Seuss on bath salts. So I turned to this Morgan Freeman-in-*Shawshank* type and, for the sake of my own sanity, ordered Deacon a book—*Poetry for Imbeciles.*" He pauses, turns his head, produces that loud, wet cough that's been worrying me since he arrived. "Anyway, one of the most basic poems you can write has a pattern of—"

"Five-seven-five," I say, cutting him off. "Three lines. It's a . . ." For a moment the word escapes me, but my brain isn't giving up as easily just now—my mind *reaches* for it. "It's a *haiku*, a short form of Japanese poetry."

"Give that gal a Kewpie doll."

Then it all clicks into place. *That's it!* Zoe's favorite restaurant—Nama. Of the few places we'd snuck into over the past two years, Zoe's favorite is Nama, a Japanese eatery tucked away deep in Maui's northern jungle.

In a sleepy remote town called Haiku.

From the lot across from Lahaina Harbor, we take HI 30 for twenty-odd miles back through Kahului, all the way to the airport access road off Kuihelani Highway. Since Mac's eyesight worsens with the darkness, I'm driving again.

Minutes later, a long, straight line followed by a single sharp left turn deposits us on Haiku Road, which appears all the more intimidating now, in the middle of the night.

Beneath us, the blacktop ends. Suddenly, I'm navigating a narrow, winding dirt path surrounded by dense, dark jungle, standing like iron gates on either side of us. This is an ancient road built for a single horse and carriage. The Charger barely slips through while jutting branches rake its sides, generating an interminable *tat-tat-tat-tat* that coincides with my rising level of panic.

Because the universe hates me, a light but steady rain begins to fall. Mac remains silent beside me as I flick on the wipers and high beams with a heavy sigh. While I'm sure Jeremy throttled this location out of Zoe, it was smart of him to make his stand here in Haiku. He can see us coming from miles away. If we try to send the police, he could escape by water.

But then, why kill Ozzie? Why leave the *Dorothy* anchored in the harbor with a dead body on board? It makes no sense. Unless . . .

Only this time there is no unless, is there.

"You're awfully quiet," I say, hoping to exit my own head.

In the rearview it looks as though those foliage fences are sealing shut behind us. As if we need reminding there's no turning back.

"Concentrate on the road," Mac growls.

Along the outer edges of this jungle, Haiku is a micro community of old-time locals and hippie farmers, with a few über-rich peppered in for spice. Two years ago, when settling on a final destination, Zoe and I had narrowed our choices down to these two remote Maui towns, Hana and Haiku, each on opposite ends of Hana Highway. Both isolated, both beautiful, both with significant off-grid populations. Haiku, like Hana, is a splendid place to lie low, to start over, to vanish.

The corners of my lips nearly pull up in a smile as I remember the first time we drove this way, when Zoe insisted on rocking the new soundtrack to our lives, Guns N' Roses' *Appetite for Destruction*, kicking us off with "Welcome to the Jungle," rolling neatly into "Paradise City," and finally—*This one's for you, Mom!*—"Sweet Child O' Mine." We sang together for the first time since . . . *Since when?* It must have been years; I can't remember singing with Zoe since she was in middle school, not a single note, other than, maybe, a few in my head. Zoe wasn't interested in singing with me, and in her defense, I'd been otherwise occupied, exploring altered states of consciousness like some unholy combination of Hunter S. Thompson and Ponce de León.

Although I'm ashamed to admit it, I still long for the numbness of Zoe's high school years, months spent wandering aimlessly in a pharmaceutical fog of barbiturates, muscle relaxers, tranquilizers, and opioids, really anything I could get my grubby moneyed hands on. It was just medicine, I told myself. Just medicine and alcohol and a few illicit narcotics when available. Just a little help forgetting who I'd been, who I was, who I'd always be: the Cowardly Lion to Teresa's Wicked Witch and her flying monkeys.

Just a little help from my friends.

Right now I long for the numbness I experienced back on the boat. Unfortunately, my outsides have caught up with my insides, the pain like nails driven deep into the muscle tissue and tendons in my neck and back, all the way to the bone. Like lightning strikes down my spine and into my legs. This is more than just the lingering effects of the accident. This is my body telling me it's about to break.

Zoe's high school years were the Cohabitation Years, the Teresa-fucking-*lives*-with-us years, when the best of Jeremy went on strike and the worst worked double overtime. Those were the days he stopped even pretending to love me. Though he still smacked me around like when we were newlyweds, there were no subsequent apologies, no flowers, no candies, no post-ER makeup fucks. He wanted nothing to do with me. Which was something I thought I so wanted at the time, and yet when he came to bed with the smell of someone else on him every night, I felt an odd stirring of jealousy I hadn't experienced since we married.

So I drank, I drugged. I disappeared.

While Zoe and I physically fled Bridgeport, Connecticut, two years ago, the truth is, I escaped that life (at least in my head) years before arriving in Hana.

Deplorably, indefensibly, that was the first time I left my daughter behind.

Driving deeper into the jungle.

Glancing sideways at Mac, it occurs to me how bizarre it feels to go into battle with the bouncer from my freshman year college pub. But then, what are friends before they're friends but acquaintances or strangers? Is my friendship with Mac any odder than my friendship with my accountant, who just happens to be a woman around my own age?

One question, though, continues to tug at my gut: *Why?* When I ask him, Mac says, "Who said I'm doing this for you? You think I'm going to pass up *any* opportunity to go after the bastard who got me fired from the Black Pepper?" His outsize laugh devolves into an uncontrollable cough. "I *loved* that job!" Shaking his head, he adds, "Besides, that guy also cost me three years inside. Three decidedly *unpleasant* years."

I don't know why I always question people's motives when they do something nice for me, yet I don't give a thought to their reasoning when they do me wrong. Having escaped Joanne only to run straight into the arms of Jeremy, my cynicism has increased with my age. Over the years, surely my brain sustained irreparable damage. I'm certain I switched on some genes that were better switched off.

I no longer pretend to know what reality is supposed to look like.

I do know, however, that I need Mac. That *Zoe* needs him. Only Jeremy *cannot* know that Mac's here. We need to maintain the element of surprise or he'll run and take Zoe away from me forever. Because at his core, Jeremy is the *true* coward. It's why he'd choose poison over a pillow, why he never bashed his mother's skull in with a hammer yet, regardless of whether he did it or not, didn't bat an eye at my suggestion to push her down the stairs.

27

Spotting a rare clearing, I carefully steer the Charger off the path, past some trees, behind some bushes, and park well before Nama comes into view. It's the only way we'll be afforded any cover other than darkness. As I'm about to open the door, Mac stops me and shuts off the dome light above us. He then reaches into his pocket and offers me his handgun. I push it away, insisting I'm just as likely to shoot Zoe as I am to hit Jeremy. I've never fired a gun in my life and I've no desire to start tonight. I'm no John Wick. I just want my goddamn daughter back.

"Jeremy won't be alone," I say. "*Someone* will be there to frisk me the moment I step inside that door."

"There was no one else aboard that yacht but Iggy and her crew."

"Yeah, but who is part of that crew?" Ozzie Bent didn't exactly run your average background checks. He and Jeremy looked for very, let's say, *peculiar* qualities in their people. The right felony conviction could be an asset rather than a disqualification.

Or someone could have traveled here separately.

As soon as I crack open the car door, the smell of wet earth gives me the sense that I'm about to step into a different world. As if we just landed on some alien planet.

Now more than ever, I need to stay grounded.

Mac ushers me a little farther into the forest, where we synchronize our watches. "This is where we part ways," he says. "But I'll be there. You just keep him calm and keep him talking."

If I can keep Jeremy calm, that will make one of us.

As I trudge through the wet wilderness, I can almost smell the bonfire from our Wednesday keg parties back in college. Such a brief yet vivid period of my life, such an impactful one. For just a few measly months my life felt so large and promising. As if *everything* was fucking possible.

Is that how Zoe feels now? Or is that what I've taken away from her?

I tell myself I don't want her to make the same mistakes, but is that really what I fear? Or am I terrified of my own loneliness, especially now that Eddie is gone? What conceivable reason will I have to get out of bed in the morning?

Why bother waking up at all? Now that so many of us toil from home, it's more onerous than ever to convince ourselves we're key to the success of our respective companies, that we're contributing to society at large as opposed to a handful of wealthy executives and stockholders. Most of us are what we were all along: automatons, as easily replaced as any kitchen appliance. Our primary purpose is to grow others' wealth. The difference is, now we know it. We see it. We *feel* it. Our unnecessariness.

And it hurts.

For some of us, families provide our hope for meaning. Children are the only reason some of us can find for living—the perpetuation of the fucking species. I mean, what's more important than that, right? Only, what happens when those children no longer need us either? What happens when they leave *us* behind?

For me, those first several weeks of college were the best life would ever offer: all that promise, all that hope. The world was practically *bursting* with opportunities. How could I fail? But I left all that in the rearview mirror the day I moved from the college dorms in Bumblefuck, Pennsylvania, to our starter mansion in Bridgeport, Connecticut. My future ended during that dull-as-dirt three-hour drive.

I stop short and gasp, wipe the rain from my face. *My God, have I been saying this aloud the past seventeen years?* Did Zoe hear these words leave my lips? Did I do to her just what my own mother did to me? Did I make her believe she was unwanted? *Unloved?*

When did I start saying this aloud? *And why?* Because I had no one else but Zoe, no one else to turn to, especially since Shannon had killed herself. I'd cursed Zoe by making her my only confidante, damned to listen to her mother's constant drug-fueled ramblings. All my adult anxieties laid carelessly on the shoulders of a little girl.

What did I do to her?

How could she listen to me go on and on about how wrong it was to marry Jeremy without considering whether I rue her own existence? I remember being seventeen like it was yesterday, better than I remember thirty. I remember how I *felt*. How my incredibly potent feelings motivated every move I made. I remember how it felt when my mother wished me dead, wished I'd never been born—*Christ, did I do the same, only with some sickening subtlety that convinced me I wasn't doing any damage?* Is Zoe as excited to put *me* in the rearview mirror as I was Joanne?

If so, what can I do now but let her go?

Stop thinking, stop, just stop.

As the rain tapers off, I gaze up at the black night sky, then steal a look over my shoulder. Eddie's tales of the Night Marchers, ancient Hawaiian warriors said to haunt these valleys at night, play on a loop in my head. Although this particular area is famous for its ubiquitous rainbows, right now visualizing them isn't quite as easy as conjuring visions of armies of wandering jungle ghosts.

Over the light rain, I hear the falls, which means I'm moving in the right direction. My left leg aches, my right still itches like hell from mosquito bites. Panic rises, but I refuse to stop to take an Ativan. I need to be clean and clearheaded when I finally confront Jeremy.

What else did I lie to myself about back in Connecticut?

The question tugs at my mind like an impatient toddler. I know there are no quick, easy answers or else I would have discovered them by now.

Was Jeremy ever a decent father to our daughter? Decent enough to justify staying all those years? Once Zoe hit seventh grade, he surprisingly started to take an interest in her education, attending parent-teacher conferences, helping her with her homework, even driving her to and from school on occasion. He also finally included her on his frequent trips to the lake house in Maryland, formerly a boys-only club where I assumed conversations were limited to fishing, football, and high finance. Zoe stayed as mum about the trips as she did about most stuff those days. But I felt she had her reasons; she clearly didn't want me to feel envious or excluded because Jeremy never extended me such an invitation. I, of course, selfishly used the time to take trips of my own, the kind produced by LSD and psilocybin. Along with my usual booze and pill regimen, this meant I spent those weekends submerged deep underwater, surfacing just in time for father and daughter to return home for a silent Sunday-night game of Scrabble.

When I finally reach the falls, I take a moment to gaze up in awe. One hundred and fifty feet straight up from where I'm standing, the falls empty into a small pool of water, in which swimming is *strongly* discouraged by signage due to frequent rockfalls and the risk of contracting leptospirosis from the water.

Paradise is safe only in designated places.

I'd read about these falls. Several years ago, a beautiful valedictorian from the local high school lost her life when she fell from the top while snapping pictures. The cause of death was blunt-force trauma to the head consistent with the fall. A few years before that, an inebriated Florida man died from a misstep and subsequent drop. A few years later, a twentysomething hiker lost his life when he, too, sustained a lethal head injury on impact.

Eddie. What did he go through in his final minutes? Did the initial strike knock him out? Did he turn and look into the face of his attacker? Did he know it was Woody Graham? Did he *know* who was paying him? In the end, did he know the extent of Noah's betrayal? Maybe it was even Noah who called him when we reached the overlook.

I remember his words back on the gravel lot at the reserve.

Ya know, Kati, I never would've dreamed this up in a million years.

What did Noah mean by that? Was he implying that someone else was involved? Someone *besides* himself and Graham?

I shake the thought off with the rain. That's for another time. What's important now is recovering my daughter.

So I press on, favoring my aching left leg.

Minutes later, in the darkness, in the returning downpour, I finally see the tree line. I hurry over more rocks, under more branches, through more bushes and brambles. Finally, just past the tree line, I see it— the long, dark single-story structure I'm searching for—the popular Japanese restaurant formerly known as Nama.

28

I take the stone path I followed the first night I came here with Zoe. We had arrived at dusk, and the restaurant's exterior lights were on. Although the darkened windows and shutters prevented us from seeing inside, the smells were enough to quicken our pace—despite our fierce apprehension about appearing in public.

"Remember," I told her, "no talk of fish other than what's on your plate."

It's the little things that will give you away, Mac had said before we left. *You mention a plant that only grows in the Northeast, a bird only ever seen in Connecticut. A fish that exists only in the lakes of upstate New York. This is how folks get found.*

As I inch toward the abandoned eatery, the image of Ozzie's corpse refuses to leave my head. Did Jeremy kill him? His best and maybe *only* true friend? *Oh God.* What if he had a good reason to kill him?

Did Ozzie drug our daughter?

Take advantage of her?

Rape her?

I shudder. If he did, Jeremy *would* have murdered him. It's the only scenario I can currently imagine, and it burns through every inch of me. I double over and dry heave, covering my mouth with the crook of my elbow to stifle the sound.

I check my watch.

Years ago, the last time I saw Ozzie alive aboard the *Dorothy*, he read my exasperated expression and said, "C'mon, it's *impossible* to have a bad night aboard a boat like this."

I hope tonight he experienced an epiphany.

When I reach the building, my heart speeds up at the familiar sight: *An Open Door.* Now streaming everywhere. Visions of what could potentially lie on the other side of this door flood my consciousness like a horror film montage.

Zoe tied up.

Zoe hurt.

Zoe dead, her blood pooling around her head like Teresa's at the bottom of the stairs.

I hesitate, try to slow my heart rate, my breathing. We're alone out here; there's no cell phone service. Either Jeremy texted me before entering the forest or he has another boat sitting just off the coast of Haiku. Part of me wants to bolt back to the car, speed out of the forest, and call Maui Police. But I have no fucking idea what's going on in this abandoned restaurant. *Could be Maui PD are the last people I'd want to call.* So I steel myself and shake my head to clear the cobwebs once again. When I finally push the door open, the jungle draws a deep, fetid breath.

In Japanese, Nama means *raw*, and that's just what this room smells like: rotting raw meat. I tamp down my gag reflex and silently cross the threshold.

The interior of the restaurant is just as dark, maybe even darker than the surrounding forest. The once-backlit aquariums that line each wall are now empty and fractured, the light fixtures and fans overhead filthy and off. The tables still stand, but most of the chairs lie in pieces on the faux-stone floor. Although it hasn't been abandoned all that long,

Nama has already fallen victim to vandals and neglect. Another casualty of the pandemic.

I spot a silhouette.

A lone figure sits at the head of the farthest table: Jeremy, cutting a much less imposing figure than he did the last time I saw him. *Is he ill?* In the dimness, he possesses a sallow complexion and appears to have lesions on his forehead and neck. He's as thin as a war prisoner, and his back is hunched as if he's been tortured. Struggling to keep his head raised, he looks to be on the brink of exhaustion, or worse.

"Where is she?" I say. In the darkness, I can't see his expression, but his body language is strange: hands curling into fists, his forearms bulging but remaining affixed to the arms of the chair.

This isn't how the Mad King sits the Iron Throne.

"Don't come any closer," he says, his voice hoarse.

"I was just aboard the *Dorothy*," I tell him, eager for all this to make sense. "Where *is* she?"

In the faint moonlight seeping through the tinted glass, he strains to look away, his cheek glistening with, what—*sweat? tears? blood?* He tries to lift his arms but can't.

He's not sick.

He's injured.

He's restrained.

But why? By whom? What the hell is going on here? Suddenly, I flash on Ozzie's bloodied body back aboard the *Dorothy*. Did someone *other than* Jeremy murder Ozzie? Someone who now holds Jeremy hostage and, like a siren, has lured me against the rocks? Someone who wants us *all* dead?

Instinctively, I spin and make for the door.

"Stop!"

And just like that, I'm nine again, having just committed the mortal sin of forgetting to lock the passenger door of our green Buick Skylark in the Bethlehem ShopRite parking lot. Someone entered the car as we shopped and stole my mother's *Favorites from the '50s* cassette tapes from the glove box. She's shouting at me. (*Wait till I get you home!*) There's murder in her voice, and I've no choice but to climb inside the stifling-hot car (*You should've stayed in there; you should have suffocated!*) and wait to get home and hope against hope that her rage subsides just a fraction, just enough that she'll spare my life. (*You should have never been born!*)

Though the tone is dead on, this time the voice isn't Joanne's.

When I turn back, a wispy figure exits the kitchen carrying something much too large for her hands. The first person I think of is Shannon, the only other woman in the world who could tolerate Jeremy for more than a few hours.

But Shannon's dead.

The figure steps out from the deepest shadows into the gloom. Now I make out a gun, a large-caliber handgun, and who it's aimed at. I look down at the red dot in the center of my chest, then up at the person who's training it on me.

Immediately, my heart leaps and it's all I can do not to run and take her into my arms. As best I can tell, she isn't hurt, no visible limp or reduced range of motion. But she isn't unaffected either. Tears run like rain down her face. Her hands, the ones holding the gun on me, are trembling.

Something's wrong.

"Mom," she sobs, "take a seat."

"Zoe, what's—"

"*Sit down!*" she shouts.

Fumbling, I pull out the nearest upright chair and sit at a table. Even seated I'm dizzy, feel like I've been turned upside down and spun around in the world's worst game of Pin the Tail on the Jackass. My confusion invites further panic; panic accepts. Are Jeremy's restraints just a ruse? Is Zoe here with him *willingly*? Are they working together? Did Zoe just help him lure me into a trap?

He's brainwashed her.

Just like Teresa did the summer before high school, the first year of Cohabitation, when she spurned the aid of her nurses and servers and beseeched only her granddaughter to care for her. They spent countless hours together upstairs in Teresa's locked bedroom, and every chance the old bitch got, she praised Zoe in front of me, reminding me how much *my* daughter loved *her*, implying that, while I'd have no place in her will, Zoe would always be taken care of. If *she* couldn't tear us apart, maybe her money would.

Suddenly, I'm forced to my feet from behind as a set of hands travels roughly up my torso. Startled, I squirm and swing my elbow back, only to have it caught by a rough, powerful hand. He squeezes until I cry out in pain.

"Easy, Mom, he's just frisking you."

Who is?

For trying to turn my head, I earn a hard slap across the ear, knocking me to the floor. The intense throbbing seems to go on forever, the ringing lasting even longer than the sting, finally leaving behind a dull pain and fullness that indicates a torn eardrum. *Like the matching set Jeremy once gave me for Valentine's Day.* Before I can recover I'm lifted roughly to my feet again, then dumped back into my chair like a sack of rice.

"Everything in turn, Mom," Zoe says, her voice warbly with emotion. "We're on *island* time tonight. Tonight the Perottas sit down and 'talk story' as a fucking family. Tonight everyone finally gets what's coming to them."

In Hawaii, "talk story" is Pidgin for chatting and reminiscing, rekindling old times. No firearms involved, no assaults, no restraints, no threats. Zoe seems to have something different in mind. Something, I suspect, I am neither physically nor mentally prepared for.

Minutes pass in complete silence as my daughter paces the length of Nama's modern but ramshackle dining room. During those minutes, my confusion only deepens, my disconcertment swells like a balloon until I'm ready to burst. I tear my eyes away from Zoe long enough to find Jeremy's and confirm they're not the eyes of a predator but of prey.

"Zoe," I finally shout, "I don't understand what's *happening.*"

"Well, *there's* a banner headline," she throws at me with a look of disgust.

Not just disgust but contempt.

"This isn't happening," I mutter. It can't be real, *can't be.* This is a dream, a nightmare, something I'll wake from, parched in a pool of my own drool and sweat.

"That's what you *tell* yourself, Mom," she says, choking back tears. "That's how you *sleep at night.*"

I'm shaking my head, bleating that I don't sleep at all, but it's only making her angrier.

"For *years*, you slept," she says. "Just *admit*, once and for all—it's easier to eat an Ambien and chase it with a bottle of pinot than to confront all of *this.*"

Suddenly, I'm hyperaware that Mac is somewhere out there with a weapon. What if he completely misreads the situation? What if he fires at Zoe unaware that it's *her* holding the gun on me? What if he inadvertently kills her?

No, I need to trust him.

"Confront all of what?" I say quietly, hoping she'll mirror my tone.

"You *know* what," she shrieks at me. "You were *there*. You were *always* there. *Sleepwalking.*"

Always where? What the hell's going on?

She raises her sleek black audio journal above her head just like the one Koa used to record me in my kitchen. "But I've created a record of everything," she says. "I may have left a few things out, but otherwise, every word of it is the truth, and people will believe it. No one looks past the surface anymore. Not in this world where only headlines matter."

An anomalous sound from outside turns both our heads toward the darkened wall-to-wall windows. With a flick of her eyes, Zoe passes a message to the man standing behind me. He leaves without ever uttering a word. Though I'm grateful he's gone and out of earshot, my daughter still has the gun leveled at my heart, dashing the last of my quixotic hope that she's only doing this under duress.

Would she kill me?

It's a question I never would have dreamed up but for the red dot centered between my breasts. Noah's words at the reserve echo in my head again, only this time they've taken on new meaning.

Ya know, Kati, I never would've dreamed this up in a million years.

She finally sits directly across from me, only not at the same table. I steal a glance at Jeremy, who looks on the verge of death.

What did she do to him? What did *they* do to him? And who are *they*? Who is the monster that frisked me, the violent bastard presently outside searching for Mac?

"Where's Noah?" Zoe says.

The completely unexpected question slams me in the chest, not only because I was thinking of him an instant ago but because I can barely believe the answer. "Noah's dead."

Something passes over Zoe's damp face. Her lips betray the slightest quiver. Then she turns it off like a faucet, blinking away tears and swallowing her feelings. Suddenly, she's all business again. "What happened to him?"

I'd forgotten she'd have no idea what occurred after she went "missing." She doesn't know about Noah's skimming or Graham's involvement or Jedrick's arrest. I start with that, with Charley Kay's press conference and Tim Jedrick's charges, but she quickly scowls and cuts me off. She only wants to hear about Noah.

I tell her everything from our accident on Hana Highway to our visit to Maui Memorial to our rummage through Eddie's case files. I tell her about our trip to Lahaina Marina to search for Jedrick's yacht and instead finding the *Dorothy*. About the motel, the call from Graham on Noah's phone, his storming out. I leave out the bit about Mac and the biker bar but mention Kilo and the homeless camp, his hacking into the law firm's accounts and learning about Noah's thieving. Without referring to the call I received from Mac, I sum up what happened at Makawao Forest Reserve: how I booked, how Noah came after me, how I accidentally crushed the man named Woody Graham while trying to escape by car.

I leave out how we watched Graham die and stall altogether when I get to Noah.

But my editing is for naught. She wants to know what happened to him, and I regret mentioning his death at all. But then, how could I have possibly known?

Noah's voice sounds off in my head again.

Ya know, Kati, I never would've dreamed this up in a million years.

Did I even ask him what he meant? Or did I convince myself it was irrelevant to finding Zoe? Did I not care?

Or did I not want to know?

Noah, I need to get out of here. Give me the gun.

There's a distinct downside to having a complete memory of certain events. We see our own faults, our own blind sides. We watch events repeatedly unfold like moviegoers helpless to stop the final girl from going down the stairs or into the attic from which she heard an ominous noise. Maybe that's why I forgot so much of what happened the morning Eddie vanished. Maybe I didn't want to remember. And the stress and the benzos and the hangover were all too much.

Across from me, Zoe bows her head in, what? *Sorrow? Maybe even remorse?* "I'm the one who told Eddie about the discrepancy in their trust account," she says without joy. "When he returned from his trial in Honolulu." She looks up. "I begged Eddie not to tell you. I told him I didn't want to be a narc, but really, it would've just fucked up my plans. Good thing he kept his promise."

What the hell is she talking about? "Wait, you found out *months* ago while you worked at the firm?"

She continues as though she didn't hear me, as if I'm no one, as if I'm nothing, as if I'm *air.* "There was no other way to get Noah on board," she says. "He didn't care about the big payday. The only thing he was willing to kill for was his ability to practice law. It was his reason for living. The only reason he'd found since Tammy died."

"Zoe, are you saying . . . ?" *Stop, you don't want the answer to that.*

"That it was my idea to kill Eddie? Yeah, it was." She says it with such nonchalance that for a moment I'm sure she's not my daughter but an imposter.

"Why?" I'm just able to croak out.

She swipes at a tear. "Because I caught him going through your handbag. Late one night, at his house, I went downstairs for a glass of water and found him looking through your wallet."

"For *what?* My change purse?"

"For your Social Security number."

"What are you saying—that he was trying to steal my identity? With *my* shitty credit?"

"No," she says. "He needed it for his will."

29

The night my relationship began with Eddie, Zoe's began with Noah. "You left me there," she says. "At the restaurant at Hana Hills, remember? You told me, 'Noah's not drinking, he'll drive you home.' Well, he did. He drove me to his house, where we smoked a bowl of Gorilla Glue, watched *The Simpsons en español,* and made out on the couch."

I do remember. I don't want to but I do.

"The more time Eddie spent with you," she says, "the less time he spent with Noah. Eddie was Noah's only true friend; every other relationship Noah had was transactional. Colleagues, acquaintances, fuck buddies—that's all Noah ever had. Until me."

"He's *twice* your age," I cry, regretfully using the present tense (I don't want to upset her while she has the pistol pointed at me), but she seems not to notice. Or maybe she's over it already. Teenage girls are fickle, right?

"Do you *really* not get it, Mom? My age was the reason he was initially attracted to me. It's the reason he ultimately *fell in love* with me. I was the same age Tammy was when she died. Noah believed he was getting a second chance at life—how many of us ever get *that*?" She grins. "I think you already know how many of us *want* it."

He was a pedophile, I think but don't say. *A cradle robber.* "What the hell could you have possibly had in common?"

"Are you *kidding*?" she cries. "He was a big teenager himself. Arrested development doesn't begin to describe him." She shakes her head and looks at me with pity. "Besides, by taking Eddie away from Noah and leaving me behind every night, you *handed* us a common foundation. *Loneliness.* We only built on it."

Once Zoe knew Eddie was changing his will, she waited for an opportunity to get into his office. Eddie kept *nothing* in his house, at least nothing she could find. When he mentioned his upcoming trial in Honolulu, she thought, *perfect*—but that trial got adjourned so many times, she feared she wouldn't learn the contents of the will until its reading. But the trial finally went forward. Eddie left for Honolulu and she became a temporary legal assistant at Walker & Akana.

"We fought over this, Mom. You may or may not remember. You were worried I'd be too exposed to 'the public' if I answered the phones and sat in on meetings with clients. But Eddie, as always, fought *for* me and somehow twisted your arm. So I got not only two weeks' access to the office but a couple thousand dollars. He paid me *super well*." With complete sincerity she adds, "Eddie was *so* generous."

When Zoe saw Eddie had left everything he owned to me and my issue, she knew that, as much as she liked him—as much as she liked him for *me*—she had to get rid of him. The question was how. By the time she saw the will, she still had a week at the office, so she made use of her time going through the firm's accounts. That's where she found it—her ticket to paradise. Her *own* paradise. Away from me.

She says, "As you know by now, Noah was naughty. Stealing clients' money, keeping two sets of books. I had to think long and hard about how to handle things from there. *Blackmail Noah?*" She shakes her head. "Too unpredictable. Instead, I went straight to Eddie, Mr. Ethics himself, and told him what I'd found."

Eddie did *exactly* what Zoe expected him to do. Confronted Noah and demanded an immediate return of the money Noah no longer had. The money he'd spent on luxuries like the property in Honolulu and his boat, the *Reasonable Doubt*. Knowing Noah would never respond to an empty threat, he gave the ultimatum serious teeth. Return the money within three months or Eddie would take the matter before the disciplinary committee himself.

"By then, Noah and I were, well . . . *really* close. He actually shared the bad news with me, which I *never* anticipated. Came right out and told me that Eddie caught him with his paw in the cookie jar. Once he'd spent a few sleepless nights, biting his cuticles till morning, I suggested how convenient it would be if Eddie were to have an accident. *Jokingly*, of course. Just in case he wasn't quite ready for it."

As the night wore on and they fantasized, it started to become more real for Noah. But he could never do it himself—he *loved* Eddie. He just loved himself more. So he went to Woody Graham, someone Zoe already knew plenty about thanks to Eddie. Although Eddie swore her to secrecy, during their fight for the environment they'd learned that Graham was working for Jedrick. That's why Eddie refused to give Graham any more of the firm's business. He and Noah even fought over it.

So much for Noah's truthfulness at the end.

Knowing what she knew about Graham, Zoe then approached him on her own. She waited till she was sure he trusted her, then told him about Eddie's new last will and testament, leaving everything to his new fiancée Kati Dawes—and her issue.

Then she told him about the Slayer Rule.

I can't hold back the tears anymore. "All that hostility between you and Noah this past week—it was all an act?"

"Hardly," she scoffs. "After Eddie went missing, we had a slight difference of opinion."

I feel so empty. Not just depleted but as though I were hollow all along and didn't know it, didn't *want* to know it. "You wanted me to go to prison?"

"Well, Mom," she deadpans, "Hawaii doesn't have the death penalty."

Who is this person who looks like my daughter?

"But *why*?" Did Zoe do this all just because we left Bridgeport? Because I pulled her out of school and took her into hiding with me?

She ignores my question. "I knew Noah wouldn't go for framing anyone, let alone Eddie's fiancée, so I kept that part from him. But Graham and I had already decided that Eddie wasn't going to die by accident after all. Instead, Mom," she says, briefly lowering the gun to point at me with an index finger, "*you* were going to do it for us."

She smiles, a faint light still shining behind those eyes, like hope. "I warned Graham you were smart. Smarter than him, anyway. So we'd need to set the stage; it would take weeks of preparation. Meanwhile, you were already on so much shit, you never had a clue."

She bided her time. The stars finally aligned the night Eddie slept over our house. I had telegraphed it, allowing her to arrange everything perfectly. Zoe started the argument about college. She didn't anticipate me not remembering it and was actually pissed when I didn't because the only other witness to the argument was dead. Anyway, in the middle of dinner Eddie took a call.

He had been paying off his debt to Jedrick little by little. When Graham called to set up the next payment, Eddie told him he'd be on Haleakala at sunrise.

"They decided the drop would be at the top of the spur trail at Makahiku Falls that morning. Eddie promised you'd know nothing about it." She chuckles. "He never received a call at the overlook, Mom. There was no service there. He faked it so you'd keep going, then he hiked to the top of the spur trail. I *loved* that decision because I knew you'd remember the call and probably lead with it when speaking with the police, so when they pulled his phone records, they'd see what a liar you are."

"Because if I were put away for murder," I say quietly, "I'd be barred from inheriting by the Slayer Rule, and the estate would pass to my issue."

She smiles. "Your darling daughter."

I glance over at Jeremy. Now that my eyes have fully adjusted, it's clear that he's restrained to the chair. Meanwhile, I might as well be. I'm glued to this chair because I have no idea what I'd do if I moved. Run for the door? Try to get the gun from Zoe? But I don't even know who I'm dealing with. I've never seen Zoe like this before.

"Zoe, what did I—"

From the rear of the restaurant comes the sound of heavy hacking and a momentary struggle. Then the kitchen doors swing open and Mac is shoved inside with a gun at his back. My eyes go wide. As I turn from the gunman to Zoe, I see the look that passes between them and feel ill.

"Dmitri?" I say, unable to hide the disgust in my voice.

Before he responds, Zoe instructs him to take the old man out back.

"There's more to this story," she tells me.

30

Once Dmitri and Mac are gone, Zoe tells me how it happened.

Dmitri started driving her when she was sixteen—a year before Teresa's death—after she switched schools because "some bitch teacher" accused her of cheating. She and Dmitri chatted during the rides, in the mornings on the way and every afternoon when he picked her up. He was so interesting, she says. More mature than anyone Zoe went to school with, yet "still young and hot with a god bod." It took her a few weeks, but she finally gathered the nerve to ask him if he wanted to hang out.

"His response wasn't what I'd hoped for," she concedes. "He laughed it off, saying, yeah, that would be one way to get his head placed on a pike in front of the family home for posterity."

But the fact that he implied her father was the problem and not Zoe, not their respective ages ("he was only twenty-two"), made her feel that not all hope was lost. It might take some time, but Dmitri would eventually come around.

The next time she asked him, she made it sound much less like a date. "Can we grab a few burgers at White Castle? Please, oh, pretty, *pretty* please, I'm starving."

"Don't your folks feed you?"

Zoe loved his Romanian accent, certainly not the most romantic but it made her feel lighter all day. "They're snobs. They'd never get me

White Castle. Please, Dmitri. There's one on the way. Anything you want, it's on me today."

"As you wish," he said like the farm boy in *The Princess Bride*, a movie she'd made him promise to watch when he first started driving her.

The windows of the Town Car were tinted, so they ate in the car instead of inside the restaurant. While they ate, they spoke. He'd briefly dated one of Zoe's older cousins, one of Uncle Gun's daughters whom she followed on Insta, so learning about his likes was easy.

"His likes themselves weren't all that complicated," she says. "Eminem, Guy Ritchie movies, nightclubs, tequila, molly. More molly was sold around my school than school spirit merch."

So Zoe bought them a few tabs. By then they'd made White Castle a daily after-school ritual. She was free last period, so it wasn't hard to skip out early.

"As the weeks wore on, I could tell he was falling for me, hard. Once he started joining me in the back seat for our White Castle feasts, I knew I had him."

And she wasn't wrong.

Zoe knew how to rile him up. "I talked constantly about the guys at school. Where Alex was going to college next semester. How Daryl just got a football scholarship to Texas. How hot Connor looked in his new Abercrombie shirt that day. That kind of stuff drove him crazy."

So one night when he was driving her to Kaitlin's sweet sixteen, she ordered him to slow down and make the next left.

"As you wish."

It took him a moment to realize what she had in mind. Instead of the party, Zoe wanted him to take her to his place.

"I don't, like, have much to do there," he said, red cheeked in the rearview mirror.

She told him, "Let's just Netflix and chill."

By then he was already so accustomed to saying "as you wish" to her, it came naturally.

"Once I was in his apartment, I snapped some quick selfies so that I'd always have something to hold over him. But I never needed them."

Going to his place soon became a regular thing. They'd share a couple of beers, play some *Mario Kart*, and binge something on streaming. And they'd talk.

"He loved me; I could tell even before he said it. I never let him know how I really felt about him, though. Hiding my feelings was something I'd mastered years ago."

He knew she dreamed of going off to college, which, though still years away, scared the hell out of him. He knew it would be the end of them. So he tried to avoid the subject.

Meanwhile, Zoe kept him off balance. "One moment I'd reassure him, the next I'd worry aloud who was going to ask me to prom."

After prom, most kids went to the cabins by Candlewood Lake. Zoe and her friends had other plans. A road trip to Foxwoods or Atlantic City. As long as they could get their fake IDs on time. Dmitri was obviously invited as the driver.

They wound up in a shit town on the Jersey Shore.

It was all the girls could afford without using their parents' credit cards, thereby alerting us to the charges. But that's when she and Dmitri spent their first full night together. That's when they started talking about money.

"Most of my fam's fortune belongs to Grandma," she told him. Zoe described the size of the estate. Said if it was all hers, she'd marry him in a heartbeat, they'd move to the Caribbean and live off investments the rest of their lives.

"It's a nice fantasy," he said, "even if it's impossible."

Zoe grinned at him and said, "Real men make the impossible possible."

He initially thought she was clowning or reciting some recruitment slogan for the armed forces. But when she turned over naked in bed and looked him in the eyes, he knew she was dead serious.

31

My face falls the moment Dmitri returns with his prisoner and tosses Mac's gun onto the table in front of him. The gun slides a couple of feet across the surface, then stops, and with it any hope that I could beat Dmitri to it if I lunged. A large gash bleeds near the top of Mac's bowed head. Tears prickle the corners of my eyes. Mac peers at me apologetically, but I shake my head. I'm the one who got him into this. I'm the one responsible for his imminent death.

Dmitri pushes Mac hard, nearly knocking him off his feet. Mac clutches the table and steadies his legs. When he sees Mac still standing, Dmitri lifts a massive black boot off the ground like a cop about to kick in a door. I scream as he shoots the boot forward into the middle of Mac's back, sending him hard to the faux-stone floor. The old man bellows in pain. When I try to reach him, Zoe raises her brows and trains the gun on me a little higher. In the dark reflection from the windows, I can see the red dot centered just above and between my eyes like a Hindu bindi. "Mom," she says. "Don't test me."

Fucking Dmitri. Shit, he was my hire. I'd met him through a neighbor who'd hired him as a driver after Dmitri lost his track scholarship to a nearby college. The poor kid was a hard-luck story, his secondary education cut short not due to his own failings but because he'd been stabbed in the dark parking lot of the New York restaurant where he worked weekends as a valet. My neighbor was moving overseas and no longer needed his services.

When she first asked me to take him on, I thought, *I can drive my own damn car, thank you very much.* Then she told me why she was so desperate to find him a new employer. Dmitri was undocumented; unless he secured employment he'd be deported to his impoverished hometown in Romania, a place he barely knew. I imagined myself having to move back to Joannesville, Pennsylvania, and pulled out my checkbook on the spot.

Jeremy looks up at Dmitri with an air of defiance and spits blood at him. "You better kill me, you fucking traitor. Because I will hunt you down like—"

"Like *what*, Jeremy?" Dmitri's thickly accented voice is light, almost playful. "Like you hunted down your wife and daughter?" Dmitri laughs, then smiles at me. "Mrs. P, you know how Jeremy finally found you, right? Your daughter called him at his lawyer's office and told him *exactly* where you were. This asshole wouldn't have found you if you'd hid behind some bushes on your own estate."

Yanking him up by the collar, Dmitri pulls Mac roughly to his feet. A trail of blood travels down Mac's chin from the left corner of his lip. And to think, one of my neighbor's greatest selling points for Dmitri was the safety he'd provide. *Dmitri was in the French Foreign Legion! He's a trained soldier. You're getting a driver and a bodyguard all in one. And he's not too hard on the eyes, wink, wink.*

For the first time, Jeremy can see Mac's face. His battered features scrunch like a used sponge. "Who the hell is this?" Everyone twists their neck to look at Jeremy, who wears a baffled expression. Then: "Wait, I've seen you before."

Give that fella a Kewpie doll, I think.

"Twenty years ago," Mac growls at him. "The Black Pepper Pub. The two of us weren't tight, yet you had a profound impact on my life."

Jeremy turns his head toward me. "*Pennsylvania?* The old *bouncer?* How the hell long has *this* been going on?"

I shout back, "Maybe if you'd shopped for the fucking groceries once in a—"

"*Really*, Mom?" Zoe cuts in. "*Now* you're going to domesticate him? When he has, like, ten minutes left to live?"

Zoe's words frost the windows while sucking every last bit of oxygen from the room. Everyone remains perfectly still, perfectly silent. Even Jeremy appears terrified, maybe more frightened than I've ever seen him, even at the police station following Teresa's murder. Zoe clearly relishes the effect of her words.

"You're gonna kill me," Jeremy states as fact, his voice skipping like a lightly scratched vinyl. "Like you killed my mother."

Zoe shoots him a look. "No, *you* killed your mother. You and Mom. Or have you forgotten that the night before she died the two of you joked about kicking Grandma down the stairs for your inheritance?"

A light bulb blinks on over Jeremy's head, but I was so certain he already knew this. "*That's* what you told Bridgeport PD, isn't it. *That's* why they've been up my ass the past two years."

Hadn't Jeremy and I spoken about Zoe's betrayal? Or did I just tell Zoe that enough times to make it real in my head, a manufactured memory?

"I still don't understand *why*," I cry. "What did we do? And why the hell are you lumping me in with this *sick, sadistic prick*?"

"Want to field that one, Dad?"

Jeremy says nothing.

"I wasn't even in Teresa's *will*," I say. "I couldn't have stopped you from inheriting, so why *me*?"

Zoe again ignores the question.

"Why *Eddie*?" I scream. "Why *him*? He was *good* to you."

I so wish Eddie were here. He made me feel safe, not just physically but in a way that ensured me *everything* was going to be all right. My whole life I've gone back and forth on whether I believe that to be true as a general rule. In Catholic school, I learned everything is in God's hands; in real life, though, not so much. What does *all right* even mean anyway? Having our health and enough money for bare necessities? Or is it more? Does it include the health and welfare of our loved ones? If they're just peachy keen but out of our life forever, is that *all right*?

Even if it feels all wrong?

Or did I have it right all along? Is the real balm for our broken hearts lying to ourselves? Is lying to yourself any worse than simple avoidance? Or is it just the way some of us *cope*? Whether we actually believe our lies, I don't know. Certainly at some level, I believed mine. Tell a lie for long enough and eventually your brain will fill in the blanks for you and make it real. At that point, does the truth even matter? If we believe something to be one way, isn't that enough? Do we need to know every word uttered behind our backs? Do we need to know every betrayal? I somehow doubt many of us would last long if we did.

Such a big deal, a real BFD, is made about being strong. What if we're not? What if we're made of glass? What if bravery can't be learned? What if we're born cowardly? Is that not a legitimate handicap? Something we should accept in others, something we need to accept in ourselves? Some of us fight, some of us run. Is running so morally wrong?

"You were going to inherit Teresa's entire estate," I say. "Why kill Eddie when what he had was a pittance compared to Teresa's fortune?"

"Back in Connecticut, Mom, things aren't going exactly as planned." She reminds me that Teresa's last will and testament is caught in probate hell because the decedent was murdered and police believe her son (and heir) to be the killer, or *one* of the killers. The other is . . . missing. Or at least was, until yesterday.

Jeremy's lawyer Ray Fitch continues to delay proceedings, confident that the more time that passes, the less likely his client is to be charged criminally or even hit civilly with a Slayer Rule suit. Which, if successful, would mean the money would flow to his issue—our darling daughter, *expressly* named in Teresa's will (i.e., not just as Jeremy's daughter).

Had she known, too, the old bitch?

"But then, I'm not *really* your issue, am I, Dad? Mom, what do you think?"

I tell the truth. "I don't know, I don't know." I hate the desperation in my voice, the guilt, the shame, even now, though there's no logical reason for it.

"Well, he does." She points at Jeremy. "He knows. He's known since I was nine. Ever since Uncle Gun so helpfully pointed out that blue eyes run in neither of your families. But he didn't even tell me for another two years. Only once I turned eleven. Only once I became . . . interesting."

I stare at Jeremy, perplexed. "What did you do?" I'm not sure if the words come out aloud. Something rises in my throat, too large to choke back down. For an instant I'm sure I'm going to puke.

"I did *nothing*," he insists in my general direction. "Do you not see that she's out of her fucking mind?"

"We made a deal, didn't we, Daddy? You keep mum on the fact that I'm not your daughter, and I keep mum on, well, everything else."

"What is she *talking* about?" I say. I direct the question at Jeremy. I don't dare look at my daughter, for fear my expression will give something away. That on some level, I'd known that something was far too wrong, that something was far too off.

"She's *lying*," Jeremy shouts at me. "She's a *liar*. Can you not see that?"

Mac speaks up for the first time since he reminded Jeremy of who he is. "She's not lying," he says quietly. "She's telling the truth."

The room is spinning around me, windows and tables and chairs and Zoe and Dmitri and Jeremy and Mac. I want to sink to the floor and curl up like a ball. "What are you saying, Mac?"

"I'm sorry, Kati," Mac says. "I'm so sorry I didn't tell you sooner. I found out just before the heart attack. Likely, that's what brought it on."

My mind pushes against Mac's words. He's the only one in this room I can trust, but trusting him, accepting his words, is unthinkable now.

"After my heart attack, you looked at me like *I* was the monster, not him. I was afraid you wouldn't believe me. I hadn't caught anything on tape. I had no evidence, only what I heard. Only my word. I was afraid you'd go straight to him and tell him what I said."

Is this new information? Or have I known this all along?

It was true. Following Mac's heart attack, I did view him differently. His newfound sense of urgency to get us out of Jeremy's home unnerved me in such a way that I felt I had to distance myself from him. The pressure he applied had the opposite effect of how he hoped I'd respond.

"I couldn't tell you," Mac says, eyeing me while tossing his thumb at Jeremy. "I was afraid if he knew that you knew, if he thought your daughter talked, that would be the end for both of you. I needed to get you both away from him as fast as humanly possible."

My eyes fall on Zoe, and I immediately know that all this is true. Mac, too, is in tears, digging into his pocket for a tissue. He balls one up in his fists as Dmitri watches him.

"How do you like that?" Dmitri says. "A deathbed confession made standing up. Let's go, old man. You're on the shelf way past your expiration date."

Suddenly, Mac's balled-up fist shoots forward, then back, striking Dmitri in the face hard enough that the ex-soldier stumbles backward with blood gushing from his left eye socket. Beyond the blood and gore I can see Mac's travel size toothbrush-turned-shank. Only the very edge of the crimson bristles are visible.

Without warning, Dmitri collapses to the floor. Before I understand what happened, Mac grabs Dmitri's gun, aiming it at Zoe.

"Put it down, little girl," he says.

"Mac, *no*," I cry.

Zoe continues to hold her gun on me, something I feel strangely grateful for.

32

Once he knew they weren't blood relatives and could extinguish the word *incest* from his mind, Jeremy became intrigued. It started with watching—simple voyeurism. Walking in on her dressing, catching her just out of the shower following a workout. Who was this developing young girl living under his roof? No longer his daughter, he saw her as a version of me before I'd been ruined.

My God, he came to our bed smelling of my daughter.

He'd held all the power, he had her trust. All he needed was her guarantee of secrecy. For once, he decided not to use the tried-and-true Perotta way, not to employ outright fear. Instead he observed her. Helped her with homework, watched television with her, even prepared some meals for her and her friends. His insidious strategy was to become a sympathetic ear. He encouraged her to share things no one else knew about.

He became her friend. He bought her a phone. He watched her interact on social media. He installed keystroke loggers on her computers to track everything she did online. Then he tried to mimic the way kids relate. He played games with her. Took her to the movies. Out to dinner. And finally to our lake house in Maryland.

"That's where it started," Zoe says with trembling lips. "At our lovely lake house in Maryland."

I don't say anything. I can't say anything. My throat's completely closed, my lungs starving for air.

"It's pretty clear he chose the lake house thinking that if anything went amiss, he'd have time to chill me out, calm me down, or something more."

My heart pounds against my chest like a condemned prisoner begging for freedom.

"On the first night of our first visit to the lake house, Dad joked that he was afraid to sleep alone in the woods. Then he climbed into bed and spooned me."

She pauses to catch her breath, and I can see in her eyes that it's as if she's actually reliving the event, undoubtedly not for the first time.

When I finally part my lips to speak, no words leave my mouth, giving her time to access the darkest, ugliest aspects of her experience.

She says, "I could feel the sick son of a bitch, hard, pressing against me through his pajama bottoms."

"I can't *listen* to any more of this," I cry out. "We got away from him. Why did you bring him back *into our lives?*"

She says nothing yet conveys everything with a single eye blink.

She thinks I knew.

Oh God, no.

Did I?

For teenage me, leaving Joanne provided a once-in-a-lifetime chance to expand my world. Getting pregnant shrunk it back down to bite size.

Meanwhile, I traded one sadist for another. Jeremy and Joanne weren't so different after all. Sure, Jeremy was better at hiding it in public; he had learned from the best.

And now my daughter has learned from him.

Of course, she isn't to blame for the problems in my marriage. In retrospect I can see that, yes, she enjoyed the battles and certainly stoked the flames whenever possible. But I can't blame my failed marriage on my child any more than I can fault my failed marriage for neglecting to protect my little girl.

I should have seen the signs. If not of the trauma itself, then of its consequences, such as her anger, her contempt, her acting out.

Ironically, like Teresa, I perhaps too often ran to my child's aid, was too quick to take her side and even back her lies. Whenever I began to think too deeply about her behavior and how I enabled her, I'd wash the thoughts away with an expensive bottle of wine or something stronger.

Then, when Teresa died . . .

I no longer know what I believed at the time. I don't know what I believed during the investigation. I just knew that even if my daughter was somehow involved, a third party must have roped her into it.

Someone like Jeremy.

Like Ozzie.

Like Dmitri.

It was Dmitri after all, Zoe tells us, who bashed Teresa in the skull, knocking her down that forever flight of stairs. But he did it for my daughter. Because Teresa knew what was going on between her granddaughter and her son.

And she did nothing about it.

As for my own complicity, I couldn't imagine leaving Jeremy. I remained convinced that I drove my own mother mad. What would happen to me if I had to be a single mother like she'd been? Working two jobs, living paycheck to paycheck, would I snap the way she did? Would I crack? Would the pressure turn me into a Hyde capable of doing violence to my own daughter?

I never believed I was stronger than Joanne, yet I did believe I had a better heart. But under the same circumstances, would mine turn just as black as hers? Would I begin criticizing the way my daughter dressed (*You look like a filthy whore!*), what she ate (*You'll blow up like a pig!*), the friends she hung out with (*They'll all be dead or in jail inside a year anyway!*)?

Would I begin hiding food? Tell her she needed to pay her own way at fifteen just because she'd gotten a minimum-wage gig at the mall? Would I yell and scream and curse and throw things when I suffered a bad day? Would I refuse to seek help despite my daughter's pleading? Would I humiliate her in public the way Joanne humiliated me?

I didn't know who I'd become if I left Jeremy. I only knew it would be hard, not just on me but on both of us. I wanted better for her than I alone would *ever* be able to give unless I won the fucking lottery. Being unable to give your child what she needs is the most painful feeling in the world. And though my mother's neglect was willful, I know damn well how a child feels about it, how a child feels about the person who was supposed to love and protect and care for her. To that child, any dereliction of those duties is an unforgivable sin worthy of an eternity in hell.

Zoe's tears for Dmitri last no longer than those for Noah. Part of me is grateful for that. I don't want to see her in any more pain. But dawn is quickly approaching and now decisions need to be made.

"What happens now?" I say.

When I look over at Zoe, she slowly lowers the gun.

"The first thing we do," Mac says, pointing his own weapon toward the ground ever so slightly, "is we get the two of you the hell out of here."

"Where to?" This time it's Zoe who speaks. "Together or separately?"

Mac sighs. "Look, here are the facts. Connecticut has enough on both of you, so we can't know which way it'll go. As for Eddie's death, we still don't know what Noah's letter says. Maybe it implicates Zoe. Are either of you prepared to chance it?"

Mac lifts his shoulders. "With the criminal investigation still up in the air, there's not much you can do about Eddie's will. My opinion is to let the Akanas divvy it as they see fit. Same in Connecticut. They might use the money to lure you back; don't take the bait. The Perotta fortune will go where it goes."

He holds up a finger. "That still leaves us access to one fat pile of cash. Kilo has tracked down every secret bank account Jeremy owns. He's cleaning them out as we speak; I'll have him split the money two ways, half for each of you, minus his fee of course. I trust you can stay away from each other's shares. Whether you go separately or together, that's up to the two of you. But you don't have a lot of time to talk it over."

"What about Jeremy?" I say.

Jeremy opens his eyes when he hears his name.

"It's the only thing I must insist on. This bastard lives not one more day. You ladies go. There's a boat down the hill on the coast. It's waiting for you with a small crew I hired. Can't miss it. A twenty-seven-footer called the *Reasonable Doubt*." Zoe flinches just a fraction at hearing the name of Noah's boat. "She'll take you to a bigger boat with a helipad. From the helipad you'll depart for a small airport on a neighboring island, where you'll each tell the pilot your destination."

I shake my head in stunned disbelief. "You've prepared for *every* contingency. Why?"

"Force of habit, doll."

"No," I say, "I mean *why*. Why are you doing all this for us?"

Wincing, he smiles his genuine welcome-to-Wegmans smile. "I suspect you both already know the answer to that."

Epilogue

My father John "Mac" McGuinness passed away while awaiting trial at the Halawa Correctional Facility shortly after Zoe and I fled the islands. Charged with the murder of Jeremy Perotta, he pleaded not guilty "just to keep things interesting until I go."

I followed the Jedrick bribery story online at the *Honolulu Star-Ad*'s website. Koa Pualani milked that case for all it was worth. In the end, newly minted US Attorney Charley Kay got her pound of flesh—from Honolulu's former mayor. Jedrick, meanwhile, testified against the mayor in exchange for a far more lenient sentence. The mayor is still behind bars at the Federal Detention Center on Oahu. Tim Jedrick has already been released from prison and returned to Las Vegas aboard his private jet.

Noah's confession, though incomplete and inaccurate, was enough for Charley Kay and the National Park Service to close the case on the Eddie Akana homicide. Authorities believe that Noah traveled to the Makawao Forest Reserve on his own to locate his accomplice, Woody Graham. They theorize that Graham attacked Noah (there were bullets lodged in several nearby trees) and that Noah ran over Graham in self-defense. He then committed suicide as he'd intended, as he'd declared he would in his confessional to Charley Kay.

Back in Connecticut, the situation is more complicated. The murder of Teresa Perotta remains unsolved with one of the prime suspects, Jeremy Perotta, dead, and the other, Sara Perotta (a.k.a. Kati Dawes), still at large. Meanwhile, the Perotta family continues to duke it out in Connecticut courthouses to determine who ultimately inherits the family fortune. Sydney Perotta, reported missing, will next year be presumed dead, allowing the case to finally move toward a conclusion. As if it matters which of the bastards ultimately gets the money.

As I suspected, my daughter and I went our separate ways, she to the South Pacific, me to Northern Europe. It's been six years and I haven't seen or heard from her since. I'm not sure I ever will. I'm not sure it's even possible anymore.

I miss her.

I miss Eddie.

I miss Mac.

Why did my dad hide from me all those years? My mother, for one. Once Mac was arrested for manslaughter, she petitioned for and was granted full custody. Although I was almost five, I have no memory of any of it. Why she did that when she never wanted me, I'll never comprehend. Spite is the only reason that comes to mind. She hated my father just that much. Once I left home for college, he wanted to meet me but feared rejection. He'd been building the courage to tell me who he was when PO Ives found the ounce of blow Jeremy planted in his apartment above the Black Pepper. He lost his job and went to prison for another three years. Three decidedly unpleasant years, as he said. By the time he found me again in Connecticut, he saw in my face that I feared him. After struggling with the issue, he decided that it was too late. That introducing himself as my dad with everything else going on in my life would be too much. He worried I'd finally fall to pieces.

As for Zoe—*Sydney*—wherever she is, whatever her new name is, I hope like hell she's happy. I hope she's been able to put some of our past behind her. I hope she's found family and friends. I hope she knows some inner peace. I hope she receives at least some satisfaction knowing that her absence in my life is indeed a living hell.

And me? Once I reached forty, I decided there was nothing more I wanted for myself. I was cold, I was lonely, I was bone-tired. And the only place I wished to be was in that year and a half I spent with Eddie and Zoe on Maui. Moving forward, I saw only pain around every corner. Pain for me, pain for the people whose lives I touched. So I touched as few lives as possible.

Initially, I contributed to society by writing and editing dull-as-shit content for pennies per word on the internet. Soon, however, I realized that AI threatened to render me and my existence completely unnecessary. And that just wouldn't do.

Kati Dawes died with Eddie Akana that morning six years ago at the falls.

But Ella Bachus was born.

Once again, I've reinvented myself. I finally got out of the house and, more importantly, let people in. I met and dated several men (and a few women), some decent, more less so. But I never settled down. These days my work keeps me too busy.

After my father passed away, I maintained contact with his official contractor, who introduced me to Famke Bogaard, the director of a battered women's shelter in Copenhagen. For one year I volunteered full-time and met dozens of women not so different from me, in situations not so different from mine. I fell in love with the work and wanted to do more. So, in partnership with Famke, we expanded our charitable organization to reach abused women in Oslo, Stockholm, Helsinki, and Reykjavík.

Eventually, with the help of my father's contractor, Famke and I established a secret nonprofit program, our own version of WitSec for battered women. In Northern Europe alone there are hundreds of thousands of women in dire situations with nowhere else to go. We provide them with new identities, housing, and help them find employment. To date, we've successfully hidden over three hundred women in towns and cities across Europe.

For the first time in my life, I love what I do and know I make a difference. Free of motherhood and the need to earn a living (thank you, Jeremy's secret Cayman Islands accounts), I've been able to change—and perhaps save—people's lives. *Women's* lives. And, yes, many of their children too.

I wonder if this is how Zoe felt when she teamed up with Eddie to take on the Hawaii Tourism Authority to preserve the environment.

I certainly hope so.

Because the feeling you get striving to change the world is wondrous.

Or as Zoe might say: Changing the world is wondrous as fuck.

AUTHOR'S NOTE

While I've lived in Hawaii for the past twenty years, the single year I spent on Maui will always remain closest to my heart. As beautiful as it is here in Honolulu, Maui offers a different kind of paradise. Although it's among the world's greatest tourist destinations, Maui is also filled with wilderness and natural wonder, from its abundant dramatic waterfalls to its lush and towering mountain ranges.

For those willing to risk life and limb to explore the natural world, the island can also be a place of grave danger. Accidents *do* happen in paradise—some minor, some fatal. Vigilance is required. But the reward for heeding such precautions as set out by federal, state, and local law enforcement is an experience incomparable to any other. Whether you drive the scenic, twisting Road to Hana or hike the trails of the Makawao Forest Reserve, you are bound to learn something new about the world and about yourself.

As you may have guessed from reading this novel, one of my favorite destinations on Maui is Lahaina. At the time of this writing, nearly one year has passed since the tragic series of wildfires that claimed more than one hundred lives and destroyed more than twenty-two hundred structures, including residential homes and local businesses. Governor Josh Green described the wildfires as "the worst natural disaster" in the history of Hawaii. Indeed, the fires constituted the fifth deadliest wildfire in the history of the United States and the most lethal in more than a century.

As noted by Thomas Fuller in the *New York Times*, "The death toll and wrecked landscape of the town reinforced the grim reality that even corners of the globe generally blessed with plentiful rainfall—and until recently unaccustomed to powerful wildfires—are now, partly because of climate change, much more vulnerable."

While this novel is a work of fiction written prior to the Lahaina fires, many of the environmental issues touched upon in its pages are quite real and increasingly dire. For information on Hawaii's climate change adaptation policy, please visit Hawaii.gov's Office of Planning and Sustainable Development. For a list of verified organizations that are making sure resources are reaching the hands of those who need it most, please visit the Pacific Disaster Center (PDC), an applied research center supporting NGOs worldwide to create a safer, more resilient planet.

Finally, this novel touches on another subject that cannot receive enough attention. Child abuse is a continuing epidemic, with more than six hundred thousand children abused and/or neglected in the United States each year. The vast majority of offenders (77 percent) are the victims' parents. Abused children, such as Kati and Zoe Dawes, often suffer lifelong effects, including mental illnesses, physical limitations, and even death. More than a quarter of victims are under the age of two years. Meanwhile, the problem of child sexual abuse likely runs far deeper than federal statistics show. For more information or to donate, please visit the National Children's Alliance online. The Alliance boasts nearly a thousand Children's Advocacy Centers nationwide.

Douglas Corleone
Honolulu, Hawaii
May 8, 2024

ACKNOWLEDGMENTS

Thank you to David Hale Smith, Naomi Eisenbeiss, and the entire team at InkWell Management for their extraordinary patience and guidance throughout the writing of this novel. To my new favorite person in the world, my editor Chantelle Aimée Osman, thank you for recognizing my vision and helping me to craft the best book possible. Thank you also to our developmental editor Jodi Warshaw, who aided us in raising this story to an entirely new level. To everyone at Thomas & Mercer who made me feel at home and welcome from day one, your warmth and generosity is much appreciated.

Special thanks to my longtime friend Todd Ritter, who writes as the world-renowned novelist Riley Sager, whose encouragement and career advice were crucial to the writing and publishing of my first psychological thriller. And, of course, to Dotty Baker Morefield, to whom this book is dedicated. Dotty has rooted for me like no other ever since the 2011 Shamus Awards ceremony in Saint Louis. Her belief in me, as a person and as a writer, is unwavering and has gotten me through some of the toughest times in my life. I could not and would not have persisted without her emboldening presence.

Special thanks also to my dear friend Aida Corvelli, whose incredible strength and courage remain a constant inspiration.

Thanks, too, to those friends who supported me throughout my career, especially Stu Goldstein and Kaelyn Deeter, Vincent Antoniello, Jason Quintero, Tricia Schmidt, Susan Pontoriero, Katrina

Blumenkrantz Carroll, Suzette Corrine Merritt, Vik Pawar, Heather Fierro Witte, Colleen Patterson, Brian Ketterer, and Carolyn Beth Polito Hand.

Mahalo to Sarah Baglin, Jim and Eileen Knowles, Keith Bloesh, Dave Corpora, Frankie Magee, Tania Wigoda, Tricia Wiseman-Donahue, Mike Garza, Jen Badgley, Jennifer Dubeck, Mike Mumola, Tim Kalavruzos, Dave and Mary Putnam, Tara Staup, Jeff Musall, Beth Rudetsky, Judi Roberts, Caroline Reiginer, Sorina Maxa, Nicole E. Raffa, and her beloved late mother Pat Alexander Raffa, who proved to be among my greatest supporters.

To other absent friends, including John Krusas, Kimberly A. Kopp, Pete Ryan, Laurie Hanan, and my dear friend Susan's daughter, Domenica Pontoriero, whose exceedingly brief life made such an impact on so many, you are not forgotten.

Thanks, as always, to my family, especially Jill, my son Jack, and my daughters Maya and Kyra, who love that Alexa knows their dad's name. *Mahalo* to my larger *ohana* here in the islands, especially Brad Coles, who read and critiqued multiple drafts of this novel on the road to publication.

Finally, I'd like to hurl a superpowerful fiery ball of gratitude at my forever friend Ray "Mad Cow" McManamon, whose favorite planet is the sun.

That's why they call him Whiskers.

About the Author

Photo © 2024 Jill Corleone

Douglas Corleone is the international bestselling author of *Gone Cold, Payoff,* and *Robert Ludlum's The Janson Equation,* as well as the acclaimed Kevin Corvelli novels, the Simon Fisk international thrillers, and the stand-alone courtroom drama *The Rough Cut.* Corleone's debut novel, *One Man's Paradise,* won the 2009 Minotaur Books/ Mystery Writers of America First Crime Novel Award and was a finalist for the 2011 Shamus Award for Best First Novel. A former New York City criminal defense attorney, Corleone now resides in Honolulu, where he is currently at work on his next novel. For more information, visit www.douglascorleone.com.